TOO MUCH

Ella Miles

TABLE OF CONTENTS

TEXT MESSAGE #15

quinn

HE'S NOT COMING.

He promised.

He swore.

He said he would always be here for me ...

Except this time, when I really need him to be here, he isn't.

He isn't fucking here.

I glance down at my watch, and he is only twenty minutes late. Something could have happened. His flight could have been delayed. Yeah ... that must be it. A delay in his flight.

I lean back in my chair and glance out the window of the bar in the Denver airport at the perfect day. It's sunny here with not a cloud in the sky. The weather here wouldn't cause a delay in his flight. But it is possible his flight was delayed from wherever he is. I know he lives in Dallas, but he could have been anywhere this week, depending on if he had a home or away game.

I wouldn't know, though, because he doesn't talk to me. And I don't look up where he plays each week. I know if I did, I would be on the next flight out to see him. And once I saw him, I'd never leave even though he chose a different life than I chose. He chose a life where he could be free—live for the moment—while I chose to live for someone else. A life he made clear he didn't want.

I take a sip of the red wine sitting in front of me, wishing I would have ordered something stronger as the liquid goes down my throat. I didn't want to be drunk when I saw him again, but now, I don't know. Now, I wish I was drunk because I'm afraid he isn't going to show up, and I'm going to need something to deal with the pain.

I glance out the window and watch another plane land, hoping it is his flight. But I know it's not. If he were coming, he would have been here on time or he would have texted and told me he was going to be late. He wouldn't leave me stranded and worried like this.

I down the rest of the expensive red wine that I ordered, and I glance at my watch. It's thirty minutes until three. He should have been here a half an hour ago, so I'm giving him until three and then I'm leaving.

I shift in my seat in the booth and glance over at the woman smiling at me from behind the bar across the room. Initially, I didn't want to sit close to the bar because I wanted some privacy to talk to him when he came. Now, I wish I had chosen a seat at the bar—at least until he came— so I could talk with the bartenders. That might have distracted me from the fact he isn't coming.

The woman walks over. "Another?"

"No, I need something stronger."

She smiles sadly like she knows what I'm going through. Except she has no idea. She has no idea what I'm hiding. No idea the pain I will feel if he doesn't come.

"What's your poison? Whiskey, vodka, tequila ...?" she says in a soothing tone.

"I'll have vodka." I choose the one drink that gives me no memories of him. I never drink vodka and neither does he.

She gives me one final sympathetic look and hesitates for a second like she's trying to decide if she is going to hug me before heading back to the bar.

I continue to stare out the window and count the planes as they land. Thinking every single one of them could be him flying in to see me. Each time one lands, my heart does a little flip, hoping and wishing.

My heart is stupid, though. It doesn't understand what my brain already understands—he isn't coming.

The bartender brings me my drink. It's a double even though I didn't ask for it, but she knows I need it. She must be able to tell my heart is about to break.

I take a sip of the unfamiliar liquid. It burns a little, but it's a good kind of burn.

I glance down at my watch again. It's 2:47. Only thirteen minutes left.

I pull out my phone and read the text I sent him.

Me: It's too much. I need you. Meet me at the Denver airport tomorrow at 2pm.

I scroll through our previous messages and count about fifteen. We have only had fifteen conversations by text message in five years. That doesn't seem like a lot, but it is when you only text each other after life-altering events, and usually happy life-altering events. We have texted things when life is too hard, painful, difficult. We say I need you. Followed by a time: now, later, ASAP, tomorrow, next week. It's always the same. And we always come. We are always there for each other. Even when we hate each other. Even when we are with other people. It's been our unspoken promise for the past five years. The one constant. That if life gets too hard—which it always does because life isn't fair to either of us—we will be there to help each other. Not really to save each other—although that has happened—but just to be on each other's sides. No matter what.

I texted him yesterday like I always do, expecting him to come. It's never something I have questioned before. He just comes whether he responds to the text or not. I can count on him.

A single tear rolls down my cheek. I don't wipe it away. I feel the pain. I embrace it. I'm used to pain, but I just never thought he would cause me this much pain. I never thought what we had would ever end.

We broke up, yes. I expected that. I expected to break up. We didn't want the same things in life. We didn't want to live in the same place. We weren't in the same place in our life. We fought, a lot. He wanted freedom, and I wanted to settle down. All reasons for our breakup, among other things.

But just because we broke up doesn't mean anything. He promised he would always be here for me no matter what. No matter if he married someone else or if I did. No matter if we hated each other; he promised he would still come.

He lied.

He didn't come.

He's not coming.

I just wish he'd had the balls to tell me why. I deserve an answer. I deserve to know the truth. I deserve to know why he is no longer in my life. I thought I knew the truth, but now, I'm not so sure.

Instead, what I get is silence.

Silence from a man who I have loved since the moment I met him. Not always romantically, but with his soul, we connected. We just always have. And I thought he felt the same way.

I guess not. I guess I was just like every other girl who has come in and out of his life. And there have been a lot of them. More than I want to count. More than I even know about or want to know.

He said he was done the last time we were together, but I didn't truly think he meant anything other than our romantic relationship. He said we couldn't keep doing this—that this was all too much—but I never believed him. I thought he was just angry and saying things he didn't mean.

Until now.

Now, I believe him. Because he knows if he doesn't show up today that I'm done too. I'm not a forgiving person especially when he fucks up like this. He knows I won't be able to forgive him for this.

I glance down at my watch and watch the minutes tick by until only seconds are left. Only fifteen seconds to be exact.

Tick ...

Tick ...

Tick ...

With each tick, my heart breaks a little more.

Tick ...

Tick ...

Tick ...

With each tick, the pain becomes worse.

Tick ...

Tick ...

Tick ...

With each tick, my heart breaks—not just for me but for him too—because he's wrong if he thinks he can face the world alone.

Tick ...

Tick ...

Tick ...

I hold by breath through the final ticks, wishing time would stop.

Tick ...

Tick ...

Tick ...

But they continue anyway. It's not what I expect when the final tick passes. It's not an explosion in my heart so much as a slow break. A tiny crack that has formed, and although it hasn't destroyed my heart yet, it makes it weaker. It makes everything painful. And I know it's a pain I will carry with me for the rest of my life.

I pick up the glass and drink the rest of the liquid. I pull out my purse, hoping I have cash to pay, but I have none. I sigh.

I can't stay here any longer, so I get up from my booth, running my hand through my long brown hair as I do. Hair that I hate to admit I spent some time curling before I came. Not because I want him back—I know that boat has sailed—but because I wanted him to see that I am happy and healthy. But he needed to hear the truth from me. He needed to hear what I had to say before it was too late.

Now, he will always think of me as the weak one for texting him. He will think of me as broken. And that is the furthest thing from what I am. Even though he has seen me most at my weakest, just as I've seen him at his weakest.

But worst yet, now he will never know the truth. And if he ever finds out, it will be too late.

I walk over to the bar.

"I'll take my check, please." I dig into my purse to grab my wallet.

"Don't worry about it. We got you covered," the bartender says.

I glance up in confusion and see her motion to the three other bartenders standing behind her with understanding nods and sadness in their eyes. They don't know what happened. They don't know why I'm sad, why my heart is breaking, but they can feel it. And I know better than to argue with them about paying my bill.

"Thank you," I say as sincerely as I can.

They all smile and nod in understanding as I glance back at the booth I was just sitting in like somehow he might have magically appeared. That his hard, cut body is sitting in the booth in his tight jeans, T-shirt, and ball cap trying to blend in, but he would do anything but blend in. He would look at me with his piercing blue eyes and run a hand through his blond hair and make every girl here swoon. I wish it were true. That he is sitting there. But he isn't.

I take a deep breath as I look back at the door. As soon as I leave, it's over. We are over. And it's too hard to face.

It takes everything I have to take a step toward the door followed by another step and then another. Each step is painful and scary. I haven't faced the world alone in a long time.

But that's not why it's scary; it's scary because if he ever finds out the truth, he is going to regret not coming to see me today. My guess is he thought this was for the best. That our relationship was no longer healthy. That we needed to stop relying on each other to survive and get through life when it's tough.

I understand. I've felt the same way. But he's wrong.

Because today isn't about needing him; at least, not in the same way as before. Today was about telling him something that would have changed everything.

I take another step, and I'm at the door. I don't hesitate now because it doesn't matter. It's over.

I walk through the door and begin the long walk to my car and then the long, lonely drive back to Boulder, sealing the fact we are over. That I have to forget about Hunter Metcalf. That he no longer exists in my world. I have too many other things to worry about now and too much life to live for.

Still, I can't escape the pain that will follow me forever. Because I never thought he would be the one who hurt me worse than life ever did.

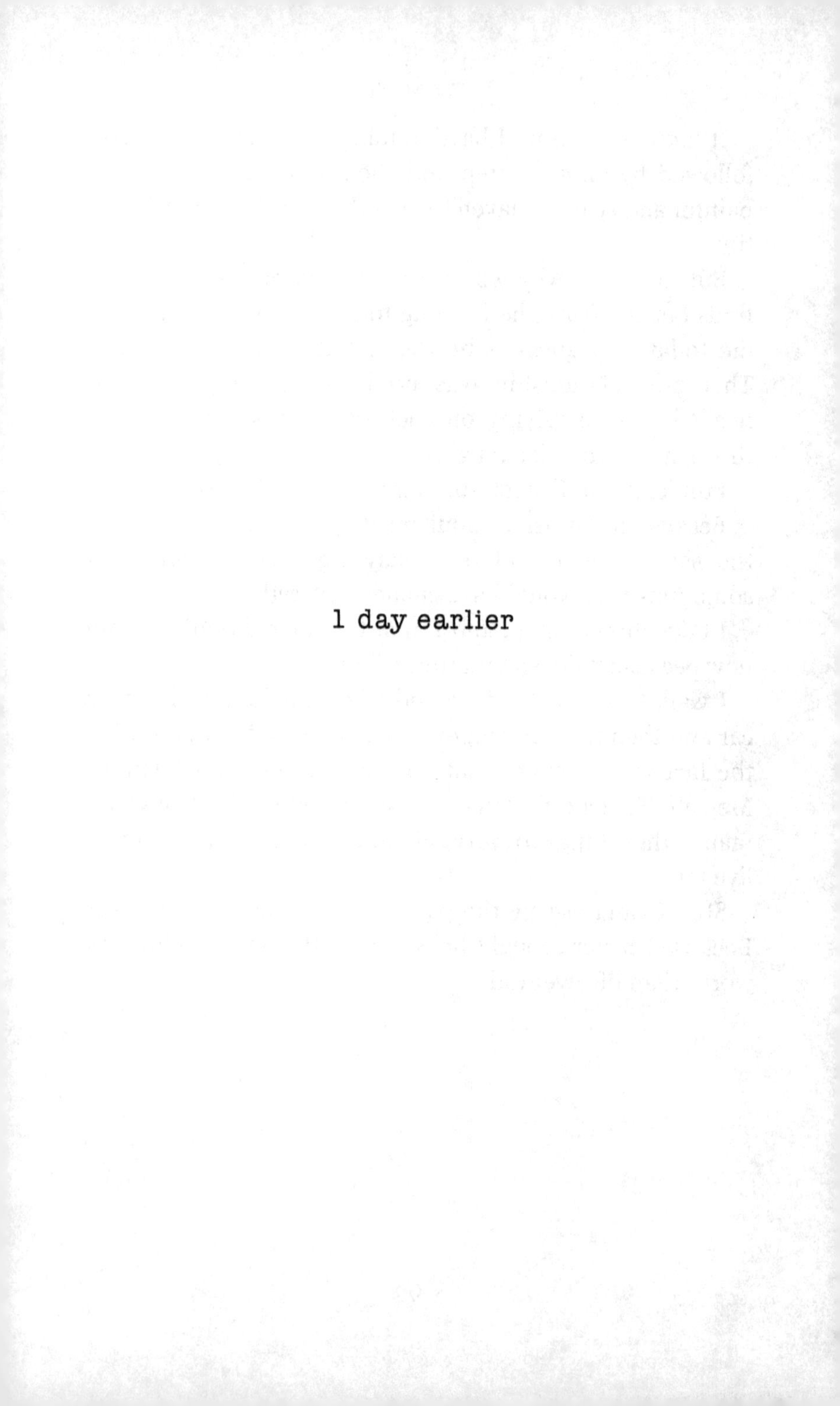
1 day earlier

hunter

I'M NOT GOING.

I press the heavy weights off my chest until my arms extend and then slowly bring the bar back to my chest.

I'm not going.

I exhale sharply and then press the weights again.

"I'm. Not. Going," I groan through clenched teeth as I barely get the weight up this time.

Marshall, my personal trainer and one of my closest friends since college, grabs the bar and helps me return it to the rack.

"What the hell was that? You didn't even finish your reps," Marshall says.

I get off the bench, ignoring him as I walk over to shelf of towels I keep in the corner of the large gym in the basement of my house. I love how expansive the room is. It allows me to keep every type of equipment I could ever need here. It allows me to just roll out of bed and come down here to work out. But I was an idiot when I had this house built. The one room I spend the most time in has no windows. It's dark and doesn't motivate me at all to work out. Instead, it's a depressing dungeon.

I take the towel and wipe the sweat from my forehead before I grab the bottle of water from the fridge next to it and begin to drink.

"What are you doing, man? We are only twenty minutes into your workout. You don't need a break already. We are just barely getting started," Marshall says with his eyebrows raised and arms gesturing around his body wildly as he talks.

I stare at him but don't really hear him or care what he is saying. All I can think about is I can't go. I *shouldn't* go. I have to stay here.

"Hunter!"

I blink a little before responding. "What?"

"Get your ass back on the bench and finish your reps!"

"No."

Marshall narrows his eyes. "What do you mean no? Are you sick? This is your workout time. You have over an hour left in your workout. Get your ass back on the machine."

"No. I'm done for today." I turn and begin walking back upstairs with Marshall yelling after me. I can't make out most of his words, but I do hear things like *you aren't going to remain the best if you don't stick to your workouts,* and *you aren't worth the millions they pay you if you can't even commit to working out every day.*

He's right. I'm not going to remain the best if I keep this up every day. Not even close. But I think I can take one break today and remain the best. I do two, sometimes three workouts a day. That's more than anyone else who plays for the Cowboys. It's more than most players in the entire

NFL. That's why I'm the best. I practice more, harder, and longer than anyone else. One day isn't going to change that.

I sigh. Except I know today isn't the only day I'm going to skip a workout this week. I'll also skip tomorrow. Because whether I go see her or not, I know I won't have enough focus to work out tomorrow.

Once upstairs, I head to the gigantic fridge that sits in our kitchen. Always fully stocked with the healthiest foods that money can buy, I grab an pre-made protein shake.

I watch as Marshall makes his way upstairs, glaring at me as he grabs his jacket from the coat closet. "I don't know what your problem is, but I'll see you tomorrow at six a.m. And you'd better be ready to work."

I ignore Marshall as he leaves my house without a goodbye. I pull my phone out of my pocket as I begin drinking my shake. I pull up her message and read it again.

Quinn: It's too much. I need you. Meet me at the Denver airport tomorrow at 2 p.m.

My heart aches to see that message. I want nothing more than to meet her tomorrow. She must be a in a lot of pain if she sent me this message because last time we were together, I made it very clear that I couldn't keep doing this. I can't keep helping her.

But it doesn't stop me from imagining what it would be like if I went. *If I just got on a plane, would she be standing there when I got off? Is her brown hair still long and wavy, or did she cut it short? Would her dark gray eyes still carry the weight of the world, or would they be happy? Would she hug me when she saw me? Maybe even kiss me? Or would she stay distant, thinking even an innocent hug would be too much. Would it make her feel too guilty when she went back to her husband?*

I can't go through with it as much as I want to. I can't go see her. Despite how much it will kill me not to go, it will hurt her worse if I do go. I can't help her anymore. I can't save her. I can't even just be a friend to her. I can't be someone she turns to anymore when life gets tough. When it becomes too much.

Even though I almost texted her myself just earlier today, I need her just as much as she needs me. But it doesn't change the fact I'm not going. I must leave her to deal with the pain by herself this time and every other time in the future. We can't save each other anymore. She knows that as much as I do. Even though she has hope that I will come and that we can still be a part of each other's lives, we just can't anymore.

Because this time it isn't about saving her or her saving me. This time, I don't have a choice. I can't go. Because it is too much, too painful if I go. And I wouldn't be able to say goodbye, and she wouldn't understand why.

"Honey, that was an awfully short workout. Marshall didn't push you too hard, did he? I can always yell at him for you if he did. He listens to me," Camille says as she walks into the kitchen with a teasing smile on her face.

"No, my heart just isn't in it today. I just need a break."

Her smile falters for a second and then she comes over and kisses me as she wraps one arm around my neck and presses her body close to mine. I try my best to kiss her back, but my thoughts are still on Quinn, not on Camille.

She pulls her lips away from mine for a second. I watch the lust form in her eyes as she grins at me. "Well, whatever the reason, I'm glad you didn't finish your workout because now we have time to do other things before you have to get ready for practice."

She kisses me again, and I kiss her back, but my heart is not into the kiss either. My body, on the other hand, is fully on board with a quickie with Camille before practice. She would be able to distract me, but it's not fair to Camille to fuck her while I'm thinking of another woman. Even a woman who I broke up with over a year ago. I'm not a cheater even though I'm not sure if thinking about Quinn while sleeping with Camille is considered cheating or not. I just can't do it.

Camille realizes something is wrong before I say anything, though. She stops kissing me and studies my eyes. Eyes I wish I could hide from her gaze to keep her from reading my thoughts because my eyes always reveal everything I'm feeling.

"What's wrong?" she asks.

I run my hand through her long jet black hair, trying to pull her lips back to mine for another kiss so that I don't have to discuss it.

But she pushes me away, not letting me get another kiss in.

"What's wrong?"

"Nothing. I'm going to go take a shower and get to practice early." I brush past Camille and head toward the stairs, taking them two at a time until I reach the top and then walk to the bedroom we share.

I shrug off my shirt and throw it on the floor as I walk to the bathroom.

"What's wrong?" I hear Camille say again from the bedroom. Her voice sounds worried and shaky, and I know I can't not say anything.

I turn the water on so that it warms, and then I walk to the bathroom door.

"Come shower with me."

Camille takes a seat on the edge of the bed. "I already showered."

I look more closely at her now and see she has already gotten ready for the day. She's wearing her normal attire; a solid dress and pumps. Her long black hair is curled, she's done her makeup, and she's ready to head into work at the Dallas Cowboys headquarters as a member of the marketing department.

"You sure?"

She narrows her eyes at me. "You won't fuck me, but you want me to shower with you instead? What's wrong with you?"

I sigh. "I'll fuck you if that's what you want." I take a step toward her.

"I want to know what the hell is wrong with you."

"No, you don't."

"Yes, I do."

Camille stands up and walks until her hands are around my waist. She looks up at me with her gorgeous green eyes filled with worry.

"Quinn," I say.

Camille takes a step back like I slapped her. And I did. It's why I didn't want to tell her. Because what I just said was worse than a slap or even a stab to the heart.

"Oh," she finally says.

I hold out my arms to give her a hug, but she jumps back like my hands are on fire and she doesn't want to get burned.

"I'm sorry."

She shakes her head. "I understand. You warned me before we started going out. I know I'll never be your number one. I know we are never going to get married. I know there isn't even a promise of tomorrow with you. I get it."

"Camille ..."

She wraps her arms around her body. "Are you seeing her? Sleeping with her? Are you cheating on me?"

My eyes widen like she just slapped me. I have been accused of a lot of things but never cheating. I thought she knew me better than that.

She takes my silence as a confirmation, though. "It's okay if you are. We never promised to be exclusive. We just need a code word so that I know you are seeing her. And we need to be tested regularly. But this could still work. I—"

I grab Camille's face with both my hands to get her to look at me and stop talking. "I. Did. Not. Cheat. On. You. I will not cheat on you."

"Oh ..." Her gaze drops, and I have no idea what is going on in her pretty head.

"Oh?"

She frowns. "If you aren't cheating on me with her, then why won't you sleep with me? And what about Quinn? What's going on?"

"Because it feels like I'm cheating on you if I sleep with you while I'm thinking about her. I don't think it's fair to you. For you not to know if I'm visualizing her face, her body, her voice when I'm fucking you. I want you to know that when I'm fucking you, it's you I'm with and not anyone else."

She's silent.

"Do you understand?"

She frowns but nods.

I sigh and slowly let her go.

"Why are you thinking about Quinn, though?"

I run my hand through my too long hair. I desperately need a haircut. "Because she texted me. She wants me to go see her, like old times."

"Like when you were dating?"

"No. Just to help her as friends like we used to."

She nods thinking and then finally looks at me sadly. "Are you going?"

I take a deep breath because as soon as I answer her, my answer is final. I can't change my mind. I can't go back. When I answer her, I've sealed our fates.

"No."

She smiles weakly as her arms wrap around her body. Her hands slowly move up and down her arms like she is cold and trying to warm herself up.

"I should shower. And you need to get to work. I don't want you rushing and getting into an accident." I walk over and kiss her firmly on forehead with my eyes closed. "I don't know what I would do if I lost you."

She's smiling when I stop kissing her, which makes me smile.

"I think I'm going to call in sick to work today," she says as she begins unbuttoning her blouse to reveal her lacy white bra underneath and cleavage that is poking out from beneath her bra.

"Oh, yeah?"

"Yeah. You should call in sick too."

I smile as she completely undoes all the buttons on her shirt, exposing her tight bare stomach.

"I can't do that. They would know we are playing hooky if we both called in sick."

"So let them think that. They aren't going to fire you or reprimand you. Let's just have fun today."

I grin as she walks toward me because what she is proposing sounds like heaven. It's exactly what I want.

But I reach out a hand to stop her from moving any closer to me until she understands what this means.

"I want to fuck you. I want to spend the day doing nothing but that, but you have to understand that nothing has changed in the past few minutes. I'm still thinking about—"

She puts a finger up to my lips to stop me from speaking.

With a sly smile, she says, "You might be now, but in a few minutes, I don't think you will be thinking about anything other than me. About how much you want my body. About how much you want me again and again and again. In your bed. In the shower. In the pool. On every inch of this house."

I grin and hope she is right. I hope Camille can make me forget about Quinn. It's something I've hoped every day since I started hooking up with Camille. And usually, she can make me forget—for a couple of hours, at least. But today is different. Today is the day I'm really breaking up with Quinn. I'm breaking up with Quinn, my best friend, the person who has seen me through more heartache than Camille ever could.

And I know nothing will be able to erase Quinn from my memory.

I take my phone out of my pocket and dial a number as Camille looks at me curiously. I wait for my coach to pick up.

"I'm sorry, but I won't be able to make it into practice today."

"And why the hell not?" Coach asks.

I look straight into Camille's eyes and say something that is going to embarrass her and take our relationship to the next level because that is what is needed. She isn't just the girl who I hook up with most nights. She has been more than that. And as much as I hate labels and will never get married, there is one label I can use to make her feel better. "Because I'm spending today fucking my girlfriend."

TEXT MESSAGE #14

5 days earlier

quinn

"HOLD STILL," Mandy says as she tries to apply my mascara for the millionth time.

"I am," I growl at her.

"No, you are not."

I blink; I can't help it.

"Dammit, Quinn!" Mandy pulls the mascara brush back, but it's too late. I turn to look at myself in the mirror, and I have a black smudge underneath my eye.

Mandy grabs a wipe to remove the makeup from my face while I stare at myself in the mirror. I can barely see myself behind the makeup she has already caked on my face. "This isn't me," I whisper.

"What?" Mandy asks as she wipes aggressively at my eye again, trying to get the black off.

"All this makeup isn't me. I shouldn't be wearing this much makeup. I don't even look like myself."

Mandy smiles and stops wiping at my eye. "You aren't supposed to look like yourself. You should look better than yourself. It's your wedding day."

I force myself to smile when she says wedding day because I'm supposed to smile. I'm supposed to be happy and cheerful. And I will be happy as soon as I see Callum. When I'm walking down the aisle with all our friends and family sitting in the pews, I'll be happy. But right now, letting Mandy play dress up and do my makeup is not how I wanted to spend my wedding day. It's not that I'm a tomboy. I like wearing makeup, wearing fancy clothes, and having my hair curled. I just didn't get the luxury of doing any of those things growing up, so it's not something I'm accustomed to. And working in a startup world with a bunch of nerdy guys has taught me that t-shirts and jeans do the job just fine.

"Don't you think I should look like myself, though, a little bit?"

"No." Mandy grabs my chin to hold me still. "Now, hold still this time so I can finish applying your makeup."

I hold still, trying to focus on my future instead of on the present. It doesn't matter that Mandy is torturing me with a makeup brush. It doesn't matter that my head hurts from how tightly she did my updo. None of that matters. What matters is that I am marrying a great man today.

Mandy sits back, smiling at my completed face. "There. You look beautiful. Now, we just need to get you into your dress and veil, and you'll be ready to go."

I smile, feeling more relaxed now that the hard part is over.

I watch as Mandy grabs my wedding dress off the hanger. I stand and remove the robe I've been wearing most of the day while I've been getting ready, and then I step into the crisp white dress that is fluffier than I remember. Mandy begins pulling the dress up until it goes over my breasts.

"Hold it up while I work on the buttons."

I hold the dress in position as Mandy begins the long process of buttoning the back of my dress. My mind wanders to Callum. Wonderful, loving, caring Callum. He's going to make a great husband. A great father. He's the type of guy every girl dreams of marrying when she is a child. He has a steady job, he doesn't drink or do drugs, and he actually enjoys spending time with me instead of just hanging out in front of the TV or playing video games. He's perfect. He's a great man.

Still, I don't understand the sinking in my heart. I don't have any doubts about Callum. I know I'm doing the right thing by marrying him. But something is just missing ...

I hear a knock on the door and then Camille pokes her head inside.

"Oh, my God! You look beautiful," Camille says, walking into the room in a beautiful gold dress that makes the green in her eyes pop and sparkle.

"Thanks," I say, looking at Camille with a large smile on my face. Looking at her makes me realize what is missing. Hunter.

He said he didn't want to come. That he knew Callum wouldn't want one of his future wife's exes at the wedding. But Callum is too good of a guy to care about silly things like that. Plus, Callum is smart; he knows he already won. I think Hunter just didn't want to watch me marry another man. But that's too bad. He made a promise to me years ago that he would always be here for me when I needed him. And I need him here today.

"Can you guys give me a couple of minutes?"

Mandy and Camille exchange glances, and then Mandy says, "Of course. Do you want me to get your mother or father? Or anyone else?"

I fake a smile as best as I can. "No, I just want a few minutes alone to calm any jitters before the wedding."

Mandy nods. "I'll be right next door getting into my dress if you need me."

I nod and watch as Mandy walks out the door of the small room we are using as a dressing room in the old church we picked out to go change into the dark red dress she picked out. She's my only bridesmaid, so she was allowed to pick any dress she wanted. Of course, she picked red so she would stand out. Camille begins to follow her but hesitates at the door. She opens her mouth to say something and then stops.

"You can tell me, Camille. Whatever it is."

She takes a deep breath. "He still loves you; if you're having second thoughts. If that's what this is."

My smile drops. "It isn't about him. I love Callum. Hunter is yours now. But ..." I stop talking because I don't know how to explain to the woman who Hunter chose to spend his life with instead of me that even though I'm marrying Callum, and she gets Hunter, that I still need Hunter in my life. Just not as a husband, or boyfriend, or lover. Not even as a friend. I just need him sometimes. I don't know what Hunter is to me anymore, or what he ever was.

"I know. Do you want me to call him for you?" Camille asks, her voice a little shaky as she asks.

"No." He won't come if she asks; he will only come if I do.

Camille's face goes white.

I hate hurting her, but she is going to have to get used to it if she wants to be with Hunter because this is our relationship. She will never have to worry about Hunter cheating on her; he's not that kind of man. But he won't abandon me either. Not when I need him.

"I'm sorry," I say, trying to make her feel better even though I'm not that sorry. Camille chose him, knowing I was part of the deal.

"I'm glad you found someone," she says.

I nod, knowing the real meaning of her words. *I'm glad you found someone who you should start turning to for help instead of Hunter.* She's wrong if she thinks marrying Callum is going to change my relationship with Hunter. Because it won't. Nothing will.

She studies me a moment longer and then walks through the door, shutting it quickly behind her.

I lift the many layers of my poofy dress as I walk over to my purse and dig out my phone. I begin to type in Hunter's name in the text messages app. A name I haven't texted in over a year. It pulls up the last time we texted. About six months ago when Hunter texted me.

I begin typing.

Me: I need you. Now. Meet me in the garden behind the church.

I press send, and then I wait a second, looking at myself in the mirror in my full wedding dress and makeup. I don't recognize myself. And I can't believe that today is finally here. Today, I finally get a family. I finally get real meaning in my life. I make everything official.

I pick up the veil hanging from the mirror and press the comb into the updo that Mandy created, finishing the look. I blink several times at myself. I'm a bride. I never thought that today would be possible. I never thought I would be getting married.

My phone buzzes on the table in front of me. I pick it up and read the text message from Hunter.

Hunter: Here.

My eyes widen. He knew I would need him today. That I would text him. He was somewhere close just waiting for my text. I don't know if that makes me happy or incredibly sad.

I don't care, though, because I'm just glad he is here. I glance around the room, trying to decide if I need to bring anything with me. But I don't need anything but myself. I'm just stalling. I shake my head. I beg him to come, and then when he does come, I'm too nervous to go see him.

"I'm a mess," I say, walking out of the dressing room.

I don't see Mandy or Camille or my parents or anyone in the hallway, so I make a beeline for the back door, hoping no one will decide to poke their head out of their dressing rooms or come looking for me for the next few minutes. I don't have to worry about Callum seeing me, thank goodness. He's very traditional and doesn't want to see me until I'm walking down the aisle, so he's hiding in a building across the street from the church until time.

I walk quickly toward the door that is about ten feet from me. I want to run, but I can't in the dress and heels Mandy insisted I wear. Each step causes my anxiety to creep higher because I just know someone is going to stop me from making it to Hunter, or they are going to see me and assume I am trying to have a quick fling with him before I get married, which is the furthest thing from the truth.

I make it another step and then another until my hand is on the door to the exit that leads to the back garden. I take a deep breath, pushing the anxiety away as best as I can as I push the door open and step into the cold air. My arms immediately wrap around my body in the cold air. That's what I forgot, a jacket. I chose the garden because I knew in this cold weather no one would want be outside; I just forgot to prepare better myself.

It's too late now. I'm not going back. I march forward with my hands rubbing up and down my shivering arms as I head deeper into the garden at the back of the church thanking God that at least no snow is on the ground.

I look up, and I see him standing under an old oak tree with his hands in the pockets of his suit. He doesn't grin at me like he usually does when he sees me. He just chews on that damn piece of gum, which is my only clue to how he is feeling. Anxious.

I keep walking toward him as my arms drop to my side, no longer caring about the cold. I stop about two feet in front of him.

"You came."

He nods. "Obviously."

I bite my lip, not sure where to go from here. I don't know what to say; I don't know what to do. I don't know why I needed him here, but I just did. Because just being close to him makes me whole. If I had gotten married today without seeing him or knowing he was in the crowd, I wouldn't have been whole. And I need to be whole today.

"Thank you. I just needed you here today. I can't explain it. I thought I would be fine when you sent the invitation back, saying that you weren't coming. But obviously, I'm not okay with you not being here. And obviously, you planned to come anyway since you are in a suit and were so close when I texted."

He frowns, which throws me off.

"I had a meeting close by, that yes, I arranged because I knew you would need me. Not because I wanted to be here."

"Oh."

The wind blows hard, and my veil and dress hangs in the wind. My hands go back around my arms, trying to stay warm now that the warmth he usually brings me is gone.

He begins removing his jacket to give to me, but I hold up my hand. I don't want his sympathy. I don't want him to comfort me if he doesn't want to be here.

"Then why did you come if you don't really want to be here?"

"Because I made a promise to you. A promise we need to discuss."

My anxiety returns deep in my chest. He can't be serious. He doesn't want to change his promise to me, not on my wedding day. Not when I need him the most. Not when another relies on him too.

"Not today," I say.

He looks away from me, and I can see then that he is in pain. Pain I am causing. I just don't understand why.

He stops chomping on his gum and looks back at me. He doesn't look calm or put together like usual. He looks terrified.

Hunter may not want to help me, but I can't help but help him. I close the distance between us and wrap my arms around him, hugging him. He lets me and immediately relaxes. This is what we do. We help each other. Whatever it is. We help each other.

But this time, his heart starts beating faster again in my ear against his chest. His body trembles a little. And when I glance up, I see the sadness and pain in his eyes that I haven't seen in a long time.

I squeeze him tighter, hoping it will help. That it will make the pain and sadness go away. It doesn't.

Instead, I start feeling the same sadness and pain because I understand why he came here. To say goodbye.

Why?

Why would he say goodbye?

Just because I'm getting married doesn't mean we are over. Just because we don't see each other for months—sometimes years—doesn't mean we are over. We help each other when we need each other.

"You are not telling me goodbye. Not today. Not ever."

"Quinn ..."

Dammit. The tears well, and I know Mandy is going to have to redo my makeup.

"We are not doing this!"

"Yes, we are. We can't keep doing this! *I* can't keep doing this!"

"Why not? What's changed?"

He paces back and forth, trying to decide what to tell me. "Everything."

I narrow my eyes, not understanding.

"Nothing has changed. We are still the same people we have always been. We are just older now. Getting married and living our lives further apart. So what if we see each other a little less often than we used to? That doesn't change anything."

He shakes his head. "I can't explain it to you. But everything has changed."

"You're wrong. Nothing has changed."

Hunter runs his hand through his slicked back gelled blond hair. "I'm about to watch you marry another man! How has everything not changed!"

My eyes widen. "You're with Camille. What am I supposed to do? Stay single forever and wait to see if you might want me back in the future. We both know we are too different to be together. We fight too much. We aren't good together. We tried that. I'm not going to just wait."

"I'm not asking you to."

"Exactly, so nothing has changed. We are still the same people. We still need each other. We have been there through dating other people before. This isn't any different."

"You're getting married. Before when we were just dating, there was always a chance we could get together in the future. Now, there never is."

I watch him as he speaks. Hunter doesn't believe in marriage. He doesn't believe in forever. What he is saying doesn't make sense. He's lying to me. He's not telling me the real reason he wants to end this. Just like he didn't tell me the real reason he wanted to break up in the first place over a year ago.

"I don't believe you."

"You don't have to. I just came to tell you I'm here. I'll be sitting in the crowd at your wedding because you need me to, but after that, I'm done. I won't respond to another text. Or call. I won't be a part of your life anymore."

I don't believe him. He can't stand not to protect me. Not to take care of me. Not to help me. When he gets over whatever the hell is going on with him and I text him, he'll come. He's threatened this before, but he always comes.

"Then leave, now."

He cocks his head to the side.

"If you are really done, then leave now. I don't want you at my wedding. I don't want you anywhere near me today. Today should to be the best day of my life, and you are ruining it by being here."

Hunter stands frozen, staring but not really looking at me. His eyes are distant.

"Leave!"

Hunter jumps but then begins to walk away.

The wind picks up again, making me shiver as I watch him leave until he's gone.

Gone.

I don't believe it.

I don't believe him.

He'll be back. He always is.

I walk back into the church and don't stop until I get to the small room I've been using as a dressing room. I think I notice people as I walk back, but I can't be sure. I don't care if they noticed my tear-stained face. Or my windblown hair already falling out of the updo Mandy created. I don't care if they notice the goose bumps on my arms.

Or if rumors start that I don't want to marry Callum. That I was with another man. None of it matters. Because all I can think about now, when I should be thinking about Callum, is Hunter.

I throw open the door to the dressing room and slam it shut before I walk over to the bench in front of the mirror. I don't want to look at myself, but I have to if I'm going to get married in less than an hour. The photographer should to be here soon to take fake pictures of me getting ready.

I glance at the oval-shaped mirror that has seen better days. My mouth drops.

It's worse than I thought. Mandy is going to have to start from scratch to salvage me. It took multiple hours the first time, and we only have an hour left until I walk down the aisle. I don't think she is going to have time to be as elaborate as before.

I take the makeup wipes out of the container and begin to wipe the mess from my face.

I hear a knock on the door.

"Come in," I say with a raised voice while I continue to wipe the makeup from my face.

"The groom wants to give the bride a present before you get married," Mandy says as she opens the door.

I turn to look at her, and she gasps. She tries to cover up her mouth with her hand to keep me from seeing the shock on her face, but it's too late. I saw her jaw drop, and I can see her eyes widening as she takes in my appearance.

I look past her and see Callum with his hand over his dark brown eyes. His dark brown hair buzzed on the sides and short on top is styled perfectly, and he's smiling goofily. He looks tall and fit in his perfectly tailored classic black tuxedo. And he's holding a small box in his hands.

Mandy glances from me to Callum, obviously thinking about something deeply. Probably if she should tell Callum that I'm a mess right now and he shouldn't marry me. She might be my maid of honor, but that doesn't mean that Mandy isn't a bitch to me when she wants to be. I guess that's why we have stayed friends all these years, if you can call us that. Because we are honest with each other. And she wouldn't let me marry Callum if she thought I didn't love him.

Mandy turns to Callum. "Open your eyes."

He laughs. "I can't see the bride before she walks down the aisle; it's bad luck."

"Open your eyes, Callum," Mandy says, sternly pushing him into the room until he is standing right in front of me.

I brace myself for when he finally opens his eyes by holding tightly to the edge of the bench I'm sitting on because I know Mandy is going to get her way. She always does, and when he sees me, the wedding is going to be over.

"Open. Your. Eyes," Mandy says sternly.

Callum still doesn't to my and Mandy's surprise. But Mandy is right; Callum needs to see me.

"Open your eyes," I say calmly, trying to put a smile on my face even though I know it is going to falter.

Callum opens his eyes, but his smile grows larger instead of weaker when he sees me. "Beautiful."

A tear wells in my eyes because he is crazy if he thinks I'm beautiful right now. I'm anything but.

"I'm going to be right outside. Call me when you are finished," Mandy says with a smile and wink. She knew Callum would respond this way. How am I the only one who doesn't realize Callum will always react like this? That he is too good to me?

Mandy shuts the door, and I turn my attention back to Callum. "I'm a mess. I went outside and ruined my hair and makeup."

Callum kneels so that we are eye to eye and then touches my cheek. "Good. I'm glad you did. You look better, more like yourself now."

I glance in the mirror at my smeared makeup and hair that is falling down. "If this is how I normally look, I'm sorry."

Callum grabs my cheek again and forces me to look at him. "You look beautiful. You always do. You're confident, and strong, and stubborn, and mine. And I love you for all those things."

"I don't deserve you."

He chuckles. "No, you deserve better. You deserve a man who can give you a lifetime of happiness, and I'm going to do my best to give you that if you'll still have me."

I smile. "Of course, I will. We just might be a little late getting to the wedding. Mandy is going to need time to fix this," I say, gesturing at my face.

He shakes his head. "No. She's not going to need much time." He begins pulling the bobby pins out of my hair, letting my hair fall to my shoulders in long curls.

When he's finished, he wipes the tears rolling down my cheek. "I'm sorry. You didn't want to see me before I walked down the aisle." I hesitate for a second, looking at him and trying to decide if I should tell him or not, but I want to be completely honest before we get married today. "I'm sorry; I shouldn't have gone to see him."

Callum leans back a little until he's sitting back on his heels instead of being only inches from my face. He seems devastated. There is a look of shock on his face, and a pain in his eyes that I hadn't seen before. Callum is always happy, always smiling. He has never had anything to be sad or unhappy about. He hasn't ever experienced real pain; although if he decides to marry me, he will. He'll experience pain that will change him forever.

"I thought you were better. I thought I helped you. I thought you didn't need him anymore?" Callum asks.

I take a deep breath. "I am better. I don't need him to help me anymore. I just still need him to part of my life. Or so I thought ..."

Callum frowns. "What does that mean?"

"It means that Hunter thinks it's a bad idea to remain in each other's life. Now that I'm getting married, he thinks we should end our friendship. He won't be there for me anymore or talk to me. He's done."

I try not to let it upset me, but it does. I'm upset that I lost Hunter today.

Callum inches back closer to me. "I'm not sorry that you talked to Hunter today. He has and always will be a big part of your life. I get that. I don't want that to end just because you are marrying me. I'm not a jealous man, and I know you would never cheat on me. I know I can trust you. I wish I could be the man who you rely on for everything, but—"

"You are."

Callum shakes his head. "It's okay if I'm not. I'll be your husband. That's enough."

I smile.

Callum kisses me softly on the lips. "I get to kiss you like this whenever I want; he doesn't."

I moan and close my eyes even after his lips leave mine.

Callum grabs me and lifts me up as he stands, pulling me tight against his body so he can grab my ass. "I get your body. I get to fuck you; he doesn't."

I grin.

"But most importantly, I get your unconditional love. Forever. Hunter is just a friend who has been there for you for a long time, but he doesn't get all of you like I do. He only gets one tiny part. I think I can live with that." Callum grins wickedly.

I frown. "You don't have to share even a tiny part with Hunter. As I said, Hunter doesn't want anything to do with me anymore."

Callum kisses me again. "You're wrong about that, Quinn. Anyone who meets you can't just walk out of your life again. It's not possible. He's not gone. Trust me."

I smile, feeling relaxed and happy for the first time today. *Maybe I've been looking for comfort in the wrong place all this time? Maybe Callum can give me everything and more that Hunter was giving me?*

He hands me the box. I open it and see a pearl necklace.

"It was my mother's and her mother's before that. It means a lot to me and my family, and I want you to wear it if you think it goes well with your dress."

"It's beautiful, and I'm honored to wear it today. I'm sorry I didn't get you anything."

"You're marrying me; that's enough."

I hear a knock on the door.

Callum gives me one last kiss and then locks eyes with me to ensure I'm better now. When he's satisfied that I am, he says, "Come in."

Mandy enters. "Can I make you look beautiful now?"

"No. She already is," Callum says.

Mandy giggles. "Of course. Can I reapply some makeup and redo her undo?"

"No. Her hair stays down, more natural. And minimal makeup. She needs to look like herself," Callum says, looking at me for confirmation that is what I really want.

I smile and nod. I can fight my own battles, but it's nice when Callum offers to fight them for me. We make a good team.

Callum heads toward the door. "I'll see you in a few, wifey."

I laugh. "Almost wifey."

Callum shrugs. "Just wanted to get a head start."

Mandy walks over and begins fussing with my hair. "Actually, Callum is right. Your hair looks better down like this."

I smile as I look at myself in the mirror.

"We just need to reapply your makeup."

"Soft and natural looking, please. I want to feel like a princess."

Mandy smiles. "You will. Callum will make sure of that even if I fuck up your makeup."

***

"Where's Ava? I want to kiss her and talk to her before I walk down the aisle," I ask Mandy.

The door opens, and Ava comes running over to me in her matching white dress. Her long blond ringlets bounce up and down underneath her flower crown as she runs toward me.

I grab her in my arms and lift as her lengthy five-year-old body arms and legs wrap themselves around me. I see my mother standing in the doorway. I'm shocked she was the one watching Ava today. She normally wants nothing to do with her. I'm shocked she even made it to my wedding. She walks in, and I stop spinning Ava.

"You look beautiful, Mommy," Ava says.

"Not as beautiful as you, my princess."

Ava giggles. "It's just because you don't have a flower crown like me. You need a crown, and then you can be a princess too."

I smile. "You're right. Once I put my veil on, we can both be princesses together."

"You both look beautiful," my mom says, looking at me with sadness.

"Thank you," I say. This moment should be a happy moment between a mother and daughter. It should be a moment when we connect and cry together. But I don't have that kind of relationship with my mother.

"I should get to my seat," she says instead and then leaves.

I should be happy. I didn't expect to even get a 'you look beautiful' from her. I should cherish that.

"Can you put my veil on, Mandy, so I look like a princess too?"

"Of course," Mandy says.

Mandy puts my veil on, and I watch as Ava's eyes light up when she sees me as a princess just like her.

She plays with the long veil for a second, and I spend my last moments as a single woman kissing her soft cheeks, making her giggle and begging me to stop.

"You ready to be the best flower girl ever and watch Mommy marry Callum?"

"Yep."

I put Ava down, and Mandy hands her the basket of flower petals.

Mandy looks at me quietly asking if I'm ready. I nod.

"All right, best flower girl ever, it's time to do your thing," Mandy says, leading Ava out of the dressing room and to the entrance of the chapel. I poke my head out of the dressing room and watch as Ava throws petals as she walks down the aisle with everyone's eyes on her ooing and awwing at how adorable she is. I get a glimpse of her smile before she walks too far down the aisle for me to see her. She's loving every second of the attention.

Mandy fluffs my veil and dress one last time. "You begin walking when the music changes. You look gorgeous, sweetie. I'm so happy for you. You deserve this," Mandy says, hugging me one last time.

She winks at me again, and I swear I can see a tear in her eye. She turns away from me, though, and composes herself before she grabs her bouquet from the table in the hallway and walks down the aisle.

I pick up the bouquet of white roses and wait until the music changes. When it does, I take one last breath, and then I turn the corner to walk down the aisle alone. I plaster a smile on my face when I see the rows and rows of people looking at me. Ava may love the attention, but I'm not so sure I enjoy it as much.

I see my father sitting in the first row. He should be walking me down the aisle, but I don't have that kind of relationship with him. I glance past him to the man I really care about. Callum. He's smiling brightly at me as I begin walking toward him.

I watch as his eyes dart over to the side at the back of the church. I follow his gaze in confusion, not sure what he is looking at. It takes me a second to see him, but when I do, my heart is full. Because sitting in the last row by himself is Hunter.

I smile because even though I'm marrying Callum today, Hunter is the only man I couldn't live without. I know that as soon as the hole fills. Callum didn't fill a hole in my heart. I love him, and I want to marry him, but I could live without him. I could be happy alone. Living without Hunter is different, though. I'm not sure I'm strong enough to do it. I tried fooling myself, thinking Callum could offer me the same feeling. That he could make me whole. He can't.

Only Hunter can.

TEXT MESSAGE #13

6 months earlier

hunter

I GET UP SLOWLY from the ground after another hard pounding knocked me on my ass. Every muscle hurts as I stand. My legs, my back, my arms, my head. Everything.

I crack my head side to side, trying to make the strain in my neck less painful, but it does nothing to soothe the pain. But what's worse than the pain shooting through my body is that the stadium seems to be spinning. I blink several times, trying to make it stop, but it just intensifies. I hear the crowd screaming loudly. Some happy that I got up on my own, and others upset that they didn't have to carry me out on a stretcher. Or they think I faked an injury to give my team time to get ready for one last Hail Mary of a play.

I blink again, and the stadium stops spinning; now, everyone in the crowd just looks blurry. One of the athletic trainers pesters me again, wanting to see if I have a concussion. I have no doubt that I do, but I didn't get to where I am today without playing through my injuries. It's one last play, and I plan to be on the field during it. Because win or lose, this game is going to be on me.

I begin to walk toward the huddle with everyone's eyes on me.

"You going to be all right, man? You took one hell of a hit," our quarterback asks.

I glare at him. I hate getting asked that question. "I'm here. What's the play?"

"Red wheelbarrow forty-two," Kelvin, our quarterback, says, looking at me cautiously like he's not sure I can do it.

I nod. I hate that my own teammates don't have any faith in me. I was a number one draft pick. I won a national championship for the University of Colorado. They should give me some credit.

"Just give me the ball."

We break from the huddle, and I line up slowly on the line of scrimmage. No one expects me to get the ball after a hit like that yet can't imagine the ball on the last play of the game going to anyone else. I've already scored two touchdowns and rushed and caught for two hundred and twenty-five yards. I'm the highest paid rookie on any NFL team. Now is my chance to prove I am worth every penny. This is the most important game of the season so far. If I win this, we go to the playoffs; if we lose, our season is over.

I'm getting the ball, goddammit.

I stare across at the guy supposed to cover me. I'm faster than he is, but he's stronger, bigger. I just have to get past him, and he won't be able to touch me.

I hear the count called. I freeze in place as I count it out in my head, in my heart, my entire body feeling every count. I know the second the ball is snapped without even hearing or seeing it happen, now that the crowd is roaring wildly.

I run my route easily, getting by my man trailing behind me. I look up, waiting for the ball. I see it coming toward me, but it's fuzzy. The ball seems to be shaking in mid-air. Either our quarterback threw the worst ball of his life, which is doubtful since he's the best QB there is, or I need to get my head checked after this play.

I squeeze my eyes shut one last time, trying to clear my head, but it does nothing when I open them. Instead of relying on my eyesight, I let my body feel the play. We have run this play a million times in practice. Kelvin throws accurately. So I trust my body to know when to put my hands up. And I catch the ball.

But my job isn't over yet. Ten more yards to score the touchdown we need to win the game. I run, feeling my cover behind me just feet or maybe only inches away. I don't turn to see exactly where he is. I just keep running. I run until I see my body crossing into the end zone.

And then I'm hit hard from behind. My body falls, but I don't expect the weight or the twisting in my back as I am crushed. I hear the cheering as I come face to face with the ground. I scored. I won the game.

I don't care. All I care about now is the incredible pain in my back I have never felt before. And I've had a lot of injuries. Torn muscles, broken bones, concussions. I've done it all. But this is different. This is life changing. This is career ending.

I feel the weight of the tackle getting off me. But I don't move to get up. I know without trying that I can't.

My teammates jump on top of me to celebrate, oblivious to the fact I can't move. That this might have been the last game I ever played.

No.

This isn't going to be the last game I ever play. I'm a fighter. I'm not going to let whatever this injury is stop me. Quinn wouldn't let me if she were here.

Quinn.

God, I need her.

Why did I break up with her? What the hell was I thinking?

Because I didn't have another choice.

I try to think of Camille in the box with the other girlfriends and wives. But my mind doesn't stay there.

I try to think of my parents and younger brother sitting on the fifty-yard line. *Are they oblivious to the fact that I might be paralyzed for life? Or do they know?* But that doesn't hold my mind for long.

Instead, all I care about is Quinn. I need to see her. I need her to be at the hospital when I learn the news because she will have words to make it better. Only she will tell me to get over feeling sorry for myself and get to work. Only she will give me the kick in the ass I need instead of just telling me everything is going to be okay. Only she knows that everything might not be okay. That it might be horrible. That life may end today so embrace where we are.

I need Quinn.

But I'm not sure I can even move my fingers to text her that I need her.

I open my eyes and immediately know where the fuck I am. The white everywhere tells me I'm in the hospital. It isn't the first time I've woken up in the hospital without remembering how I got here. But I do remember why. The game, the hit, and the eerie feeling I may never be able to walk again.

I look around the room, trying to see who is here. Hoping to God Quinn is here. I look to my right and don't see anyone. I take a deep breath and look to my left. A woman is half asleep in a chair with a blanket covering most of her face. Long brown hair that could use a good brushing covers the other half. But I know who the sleeping beauty is.

"Quinn."

She blinks when I say her name. I'm surprised because Quinn has always been a deep sleeper. She's a dreamer. Albeit a dreamer who dreams about practical things like having a steady job, a three-bedroom house, marrying the man of her dreams, and having 2.5 children with him. Not like what I dream about.

Quinn smiles when she sees I'm awake and then throws her arms around me. I cherish every second. It's been too long since I've touched her. Seen her. Smelled her hair. Heard her sweet yet commanding voice.

She releases me, and I immediately feel empty. I don't like not holding her. So as she begins to sit back down in the chair, I grab her hand, needing to still feel her skin against mine. She doesn't protest.

"You came," I say.

She smiles brightly. "Of course, I came."

"But I didn't text you. You had no reason to know to come."

She laughs like I'm ridiculous. "It was all over the news that the star tight end for the Dallas Cowboys was in the hospital with an untold injury. You're kind of a big deal. So

I assumed you would have texted me if you could. If I assumed wrong, I'll go."

She begins to get up, but I grab her hand tighter, keeping her here. I look at my hand that is moving. A hand I couldn't move the last time I remember. But I'm too scared to try to move my legs. *What if I still can't move them?* I look at Quinn. *What if I could never fuck this beautiful creature again?*

Quinn knows me too well. She can read my emotions better than anyone can. Better than I can even tell myself. I don't need to speak to her to tell her what I'm thinking, and she doesn't need to speak to me for me to know what she is thinking.

"Stop feeling sorry for yourself. You're still going to be the star tight end and probably get a nice raise when you lead your team to the championship," Quinn says with a twinkle in her eye.

I move my legs and relax at the fact I'm going to be okay. That I will recover from this injury. But right now, I don't care about football.

"You look good. It's weird seeing you in a dress and heels, though."

She looks down at her black pencil skirt and pink blouse. "You caught me on one of the rare days when I have to wear this to work. I didn't bother going home to change; I just came straight here when I found out."

"There is something different about you. You seem ..."

"Happy?"

I nod. She seems happy. Something that in the end I could never give her. I could bring her comfort, love, and hot sex. But I couldn't make her happy.

But looking at her now, she's happy. She's found happiness without me. I'm happy for her, but it still stings a little. It stings to know I can't give her that happiness. I would do anything to be able to do that. I just … can't.

But as happy as I am to see Quinn, I also wanted to see Quinn because I thought—

"Baby, you're awake!" Camille says, bursting through the door of the hospital.

She runs over to my bed and kisses me over and over again on the lips. I kiss Camille, but I don't take my eyes off Quinn. I hate that I'm kissing Camille in front of Quinn. Even though Quinn and I broke up months ago, I know it must hurt her. But I don't see the pain and hurt in her eyes. Instead, she seems content to see me with Camille. Like she's fucking happy I'm with someone else instead of spending my days alone.

Camille finally stops kissing me and says, "How are you feeling?"

"Sore, tired."

She kisses my cheek. "Well, we will just have to get them to up your pain medications then. But don't worry. You are going to be well taken care of and everything is going to fine soon enough. The doctors say you might even be healed enough to play in the next game."

I smile when I see Quinn chuckle a little silently to herself. She knows exactly what I'm thinking. That everything is not going to be fine.

"Thanks, but everything isn't fine. I'm in a hospital bed, for Christ's sake," I say.

Camille frowns and plops into a chair next to my bed. That's when she sees Quinn, or at least, when she decides to acknowledge Quinn. "What are you doing here?"

Quinn smiles sweetly, not the least bit hurt by Camille's harsh words. "Just came to see an old friend in the hospital. I had a meeting in Dallas, so it really wasn't a big deal for me to stop by and make sure he was okay. But I'll get out of your hair now that I know he is going to be *fine*."

I grin at how Quinn says the word fine like there is no such word. I also wonder about the truth in the rest of her statement. *Did she really have a meeting in Dallas? Is the only reason she came to see me because she was already here?*

Quinn stands up and turns to pick up her purse from the floor next to her chair. I grab her hand.

"I need a moment alone with you before you leave," I say.

Quinn doesn't look at me; she looks at Camille. I don't want Quinn to look at Camille. It's not Camille's decision whether I talk to Quinn or not. It's mine.

But I find myself turning to Camille as well. "I just need a minute. Quinn has to catch a flight soon, and I won't get a chance to talk to her again," I add to let Camille know that I'm not planning to have Quinn stay or have her become a bigger part of our lives. I just need a few more moments with her to get me through this.

Camille swallows and takes a deep breath and then walks out of the room, leaving us alone.

Quinn sits down while I continue to hold her left hand.

"Can I see ..." *God, why is this so hard to get out? Why is it so hard for me to admit I miss her? That I need her in my life and ...* "Can I see Ava?"

Quinn looks sad when I ask to see Ava. I thought she would be happy I want to see her. That she would want a father figure in Ava's life. Or an uncle figure, at least.

"I know when we broke up I said I didn't want to be in your or Ava's life, but I was wrong. I miss you. Both of you. And Ava deserves a father figure in her life. I could be that stability. I could fly to see her a couple of times a month. I could teach her how to play football. She could be the first girl to play in the NFL someday. She could…"

I stop talking because Quinn's face has turned white.

"What's wrong?"

Quinn takes a deep breath. "I don't think you can, Hunter. You're not that guy. That's not what you want. You want to do more than survive, remember? You didn't want to be tied down. You disappeared from Ava's life months ago; you can't just pop back in whenever you want. It's not fair to her."

"But I was wrong. I know that now, and I can make it up to her. I can promise to always be in her life from this moment on. The same way I promised you."

Quinn shakes her head. "I don't think a five-year-old can understand that. And she would be devastated if you ever broke that promise." She stands. "It's just not a good idea."

But I don't release her hand.

"Every little girl needs a father figure. Let me be that."

Her eyes drop from mine, and I glance down at where she is looking. That's when I see it. I don't know why I didn't notice it before.

Because I didn't want to see it.

A very tasteful, beautiful diamond ring on the ring finger of her left hand. It's very her. Classic beauty that doesn't change with the fads.

"She already has a father figure. She doesn't need me."

Quinn looks back at me. Her eyes say sorry, but I know she's not sorry. Not really. She's doing what she thinks is best for Ava. Like she should.

It's my own fault I fucked up months ago by letting them go. Even if I thought it was the right thing to do. Even if it still is the right thing to do despite my run-in with death, making me temporarily forget why it was necessary. Now, I have to learn to move on and live the life I always wanted. That I always dreamed about. Without them.

9 months earlier

quinn

I FLIP MY PHONE OVER and over in my hand. I want to text Hunter. Every second that passes makes me want to text him more and more. But I really, really shouldn't.

I stare at my alarm clock. The red lights illuminate each number, revealing the time is just after six in the morning.

I stare at Ava asleep in the bed next to me. She is going to be awake in a little over an hour. If I text him now, he could be here by breakfast. He could hug me and let me know he is going to do everything he can to help me get through this rough patch. Because that is all this is—a rough patch. It's not that bad, not really.

So I got fired and haven't found a new job yet. So I can't afford this apartment after this month without earning more money. So I'm going to eat ramen noodles and SpaghettiOs until I find another job. So Ava has had nightmares every night since Hunter decided he no longer wanted to be a part of our lives. So what if all I have thought about for the past three months is how much I miss Hunter. So what if I can't ever imagine being with another man again.

This is just a rough patch. I've been through a hell of a lot worse. This is nothing.

Still, I would have texted Hunter if this had happened in the past. I would have shared how awful I felt, and we would have wallowed in our shared misery. It would have made us both feel better. It would have reminded us both that we can survive this. That today isn't that hard to get through.

I stare at my phone and then at Ava. But that was before I had Ava to worry about. Before Hunter coming in and out of our lives started affecting her. It's too soon for Ava to see Hunter again. She needs someone steady who is going to be here day in and day out. Not someone who only shows up every couple of months when we text him.

And if I'm being honest, it's too soon for me too. We broke up three months ago. If I see him now, I'm going to want to see him tomorrow and the next day and the next. I don't want to put myself through that.

I set my phone on my nightstand and pull the covers back over me. I'm not going to text him. I'm going to wait. It's only a matter of time until another disaster strikes, and I'm going to really need to text him for help.

I close my eyes.

"Mommy ..." Ava's sweet voice rings in my ear.

My eyes fly open, and I roll over to see her gorgeous smile looking back at me.

"I'm hungry," she says.

I smile and wrap her in my arms, pulling her to me. "I'm sleepy. It's still sleep time," I say.

She giggles when I hold her tightly to me. "No, it's not, Mommy. It's breakfast time. The sun is out."

I cover our heads with the covers. "Nope. I don't see the sun yet. It's still nighttime. Sleep time."

Ava giggles again. "No, Mommy! It's morning time."

I hear her little stomach growl, confirming she is hungry.

I moan just a little, knowing I'm going to need a lot of coffee to get through today. Then I climb out of bed and watch Ava's face light up as she gets out of bed too.

"What do you want for breakfast, my sweet goldilocks?"

Ava bounces out of bed and walks to the kitchen. I follow her.

"Cereal!"

I smile and head to the fridge to pull out the milk and cereal. Thank God, she's easy and will eat almost anything.

I pour her cereal and milk into the bowl and then place the bowl in front of her at the kitchen counter. She immediately digs into the cereal, eating large spoonsful that are often too big for her little mouth. Somehow, she makes it all fit anyway.

I fix myself a bowl of cereal and take a seat next to her, eating and thinking about what we are going to do. I need a job and fast. We need money.

"Mommy?" Ava says, breaking me from my daydream.

"Yes, Ava?"

"Can I have some money?"

My heart beats rapidly when she says that. I want to give her everything. She deserves the best. She deserves to have everything I didn't growing up.

"What do you need money for?"

She pauses, thinking a moment. "I want to join the flag football team, and I need money to join. That's what Cory at school said."

My heart rate speeds up. She wants to play football. Of all the things in the world she could join and play, my almost five-year-old wants to play football. *Why does she have to play the one sport that will remind me of Hunter? And why does she have to choose today to want to do something that involves money?*

I absolutely want her to get to do everything a normal kid gets to do.

"Okay, when I drop you off at school today, I'll ask about signing you up. How does that sound?" I say even though I have no idea how I'm going to be able to afford it. But I'll think of something. I always do. I'll give up eating if I have to, to give her this. Or...

The ring that Hunter gave me is sitting in a box in my nightstand. If I sold it, we could live off the money for years. And if I invested the money right, forever.

No.

I'm done taking handouts. I'm done with his help. He broke up with me. I look at Ava. With us. We are going to find a way to do this on our own. Ava finishes her breakfast.

"Go brush your teeth and get dressed quickly so you aren't late for school."

Ava jumps down and runs off to her bedroom to do as I asked. I really think she is the smartest, most well behaved, and most adorable kid in the whole world. Other than the nightmares, she has never given me any trouble.

I carry my bowl of cereal to my room to dress while I finish eating. But I find myself stopping in front of my nightstand. I take a seat on the edge of the bed as I pull the bottom drawer open and find the box. I don't open it; I just stare at the black box that I bought to hold the ring. A beautiful ring I only wore one day. Actually, only hours. I've never opened the box, but God how I want to. I want to put the ring back on and live the fantasy again. I want to pretend Hunter loves me and wants to marry me.

I hate myself for even thinking that. That I need a man to make my life worthy. I don't. I have Ava. I'm fully capable of taking care of myself. I don't need a man.

But I still want to be normal. I want to get married. I want Ava to have a father figure in her life.

Right now, I can't focus on that. Now, I need to focus on how to make enough money to keep us in this apartment. The only problem is I haven't graduated yet, I have a crap ton of student debt, and I don't have any real work experience besides working as a waitress.

I hear Ava singing to herself in her bedroom next to mine. I smile because that little girl is happy no matter what is going on in our life. She has no clue we don't have a big house like most of her classmates. She doesn't care that I'm still in college while most of her classmates' parents are in their late twenties or early thirties. She doesn't care that I can't always buy her the latest toy. She doesn't care about any of it. She is just happy.

It's contagious. I begin to return the box to the drawer so Ava doesn't see me with it and ask questions when I see a folder I tucked in the drawer months ago. I pull it out and place the box inside the drawer. I open the folder and find a business plan I had to write for a class earlier this year.

I begin reading it. The business was simple really. An app that would allow people who needed something—extra money, to borrow a car, a place to sleep, etc.—to get those things by offering to do odd jobs. For example, if I needed to borrow a car for a day, I could offer a couple of hours of programming work in exchange for it. Things like that. I would have loved something like this that is all about helping others out over the years. Something like this would have been invaluable to me.

"Mommy, I'm ready," Ava says while standing in my doorway.

I glance over at her. I want a better life for her than I had. I want her to be proud of me. That's what I want.

I close the drawer and stand, holding the folder.

"You look beautiful," I say, looking at her mismatched socks that I know she picked out on purpose. She doesn't care what others think of her. She's going to change the world someday.

"Thanks!" she squeals and then frowns when she sees I'm not dressed. "We are going to be late."

I watch her lip turn into a pout and can't help but laugh a little at how adorable she is, which only makes her pout more. I bend down and give her an Eskimo kiss. She tries not to smile when I do it, but she can't contain it.

"I need help picking out an outfit for today. Will you pick something out for me?"

A full-on smile frames her tiny face as she runs to my closet. I stand and stare at the folder in my hands. I don't have any classes scheduled for today since I was supposed to work. *But maybe it's time I went after something that could change my world and better the world around me?*

Ava comes back holding a red skirt, a white shirt with a heart on it, and a brown jacket. I take the clothes from her.

"Thank you. This is perfect."

She beams, and I change into the outfit she picked out. She runs over to a box with my socks and undergarments in it that sits on the floor while I finish. She grabs two socks, one pink and the other yellow, and hands them to me. I smile and put them on followed by the boots she brought me. I run my fingers through my long light brown hair, but I don't have time to do much else.

"You look pretty."

"Thank you. Now time to get you to school."

"And to get me signed up for flag football."

I nod. "And to get you signed up to play flag football."

Five hundred dollars. That is how much it costs for a five-year-old to join a flag football team that only plays ten games. That's fifty dollars a game. Fifty dollars usually pays our grocery bill each week. It's a lot of money.

Still, I wrote the check and filled out the form. I just might literally have to give up eating for the next couple of months to pay for it.

Or I can get one of the men who I'm meeting with today—venture capitalists, they are called—to give me enough money to start my own business since no one wants to hire me in the startup world until I have finished college.

"Hi, are you Quinn?" a tall man says, standing over me as I sit in the small lobby.

"Yep. I'm Quinn," I say, extending my hand to him.

He shakes it. "I'm Callum." He grins, and it's infectious. It makes me smile too. He's a lot younger than I was expecting. Like only a couple of years older than I am. To be running his own company and have as much money at his disposal to invest in other companies at his age is impressive.

"Come on in."

He walks into a small room that seems too small to be an office but somehow fits a desk and two chairs. He takes a seat in one, and I take a seat in the other.

"So tell me about yourself?"

I swallow the lump in my throat, and while crossing my legs, I smile when I see the top of my yellow sock that Ava picked out.

"Well, I'm a computer science major at UC-Boulder. I'm also a single mother to the smartest five-year-old girl in the world. I'm a hard worker; I've been waiting tables and doing odd jobs to make ends meet since I was in high school. Which is one of the reasons I want to start my own company. I want to start a company focused on assisting people who need the occasional aid because life has dealt them an unfair hand.

"I know more than most about how difficult life can be. I didn't have parents who supported me or gave me money when I needed it. I've been paying my way through college by working two or three jobs. I bike everywhere because I can't afford a car. I've lived off ramen noodles so my daughter can eat and do the absolute best. I'm probably going to do it again so my daughter can play flag football this summer. Do you know how expensive it is to play flag football?"

He shakes his head.

"It's a lot. Like five hundred dollars. I don't know how families can afford to pay that ..." I pause when I realize I'm rambling and get back to my point.

"But regardless of how life sucks for some people worse than for others, every person deserves a helping hand when life just plain sucks. I needed a helping hand, and although I got one sometimes, I was completely on my own at other times. What I want to create is an app, a way to connect people who are going through a rough time with those who might be struggling less at the moment. I want to connect people to support one another. Sometimes just emotional support, and other times to help with money in exchange for odd jobs, borrowing of cars, help finding a more permanent job, just overall help. And I want to reduce the stigma that it's not okay to ask for help because it absolutely is. It took me a long time to realize I needed help and that it was okay to ask for it. Sometimes, I need help, and that's okay.

I've had a rough life, so that makes me the perfect person to understand those who need help, and I know I can provide that help. I haven't finished school yet, but I know how to program, and I believe in the project enough to know to hire and listen to other people who may be smarter than I am. I know how to manage money wisely and make money go a long way since I've never had much.

"I need someone to work with me who believes in this project as much as I do and can offer their support and experience when we run into hiccups. Because I know anything connected to me is going to run into hiccups. But I believe in this and will work harder than anyone else to make this company succeed. I need it. My daughter needs it."

Callum leans back in his chair with a blank expression on his face. I can't read him; all I know is that I have been blabbering for the past five minutes when all he asked me was to tell him about myself.

"And how much are you interested in having me invest?"

I swallow. He isn't taking me seriously. He just wants to hear the number so that he can say he's sorry it's too much and then send me on my way. But I'm not going to let one man crush my dreams. So I say as confidently as I can the number I know I need to survive a year working on this new company. It's a lot of money, I know, but I'm worth it. "I looking for an investment of about twenty thousand in total and would be happy with several investors to make up that number."

Callum leans forward, studying me. "And how did you come to that amount?"

"It's enough money live off about a third of it initially so I wouldn't have to work another job. I could just have my complete focus outside school be on this job. And if you think school would get in my way, don't worry; I'm used to working fifty to sixty hours a week outside school, so I could easily devote that much time to this business. And the rest of the money would be for contractors and initial advertising money to get the app off the ground."

Callum blinks a couple of times, staring at me, and then says, "No."

I freeze. I wasn't expecting such a blatant refusal. I was expecting him to think about it and get back to me and then I'd never hear from him again. In much the same way that guys do after you date them and sleep with them and they say they are going to call you but never do.

I really don't know how to respond. But I know I can't let this asshole who barely even gave me a chance dictate the rest of my day or stop me from going after this. I know this is a good thing, and it could be the best thing. I stand and extend my hand. "Thank you for meeting with me."

Callum raises an eyebrow. "Sit down, Quinn."

Even though I'm not sure I should, I do. He just told me no. I don't want to hear all the reasons he doesn't want to invest in my company.

"I said no because I don't think you are asking for enough money. I believe in your idea, and more importantly, I believe in you. I haven't had someone as young as you walk through my door and pitch an idea to me like that, ever. I believe you will work your ass off to make this company happen, and I want to be a part of it. But to really have a shot at this happening, you need more than twenty thousand dollars. That will barely pay yourself what you are worth. You will need more money, and I want to be a bigger part of your company than what twenty thousand would get me."

"So what are you interested in investing?"

He leans back in his chair and folds his hands. "I'm thinking more like fifty thousand to start with, with the option to invest more before anyone else in the very near future."

He grins.

I grin back. That is more money than I ever imagined having at my disposal. That money would go a long way toward building a business to be proud of. Money that would ensure Ava and I would more than survive this next year.

"I would be very interested in you investing that amount of money in my company."

"Good. Are you available tonight for dinner? I would love to discuss the details with you then. I would discuss it with you now, but I have another meeting. I wasn't expecting such a good proposal from someone with so little experience. But really, great job."

"Thank you. And yes, I'd love to have dinner with you to discuss this further."

2 months earlier

hunter

FUCK THIS.

I'm going to text her. I need to text her. Today has been shitty. The worst in a month, and I miss her like hell. I miss Ava. I need to see them, both of them.

I pull out my phone and begin to type that I need her. That I can be on a flight tomorrow to Denver, or I can get her tickets to come out here.

I stop ...

It's only been a month. It's too soon to text her. We need more time apart. If I saw her right now, I'd automatically kiss her without thinking. Even though I'm casually dating Camille, it doesn't matter. My heart is still with Quinn and always will be.

Dammit!

I throw my phone against the wall and watch it break. Now, I can't text her.

But I need an escape. Today has been horrible. This whole week has been shitty. No, every day since we broke up has been a living hell.

I walk to the garage, grabbing my keys as I go, and head straight to my motorcycle. One of the many vehicles I bought along with the house and other expensive furniture when I moved to Dallas after signing with the Cowboys. I'm living the dream. I'm just not sure the dream is worth it. And I'm not sure with the way I've been practicing lately if they will continue to pay me if I don't get my act together by game day next week.

I hop onto my motorcycle, drive it out of my garage, and just ride, trying to get everything straightened out it my head.

I've been sucking at football, mostly because I've been thinking about Quinn instead of focusing on the game. It's a problem I have dealt with before and can again. And it starts with letting football take over my brain even when I'm not at football.

Camille won't like it. At least not at first. She already thinks I spend too much time focusing on anything but her. But once she realizes it's for the best, she will let it go. If not, then we can stop sleeping together. She's not worth the trouble.

I turn onto a busy street as rain pours down. It's not exactly safe to ride a motorcycle in this kind of rain, but I don't care. The rain only makes this ride more perfect because danger is exactly the distraction I need from Quinn.

It would really help me concentrate if I could see her. If I knew she was okay. But I can't. It's too soon.

I shake my head. No. I shouldn't see her. Not now. Not ever. It would be too hard to say goodbye again.

I see the car pull out in front of me, and I hit the brakes, but I know I won't be able to stop in time. Not with the rain and the slick pavement. I turn the motorcycle to the right where the least number of obstacles are for me to hit. The motorcycle slows but not enough. Not in time. I crash into a tree off the side of the road, but I missed the car. That's all that matters.

I land on my side, with the crushed motorcycle on top of me as rain continues to fall. I lie on the muddy ground for a second and enjoy sulking; I'm not ready to move to figure out what part of my body I damaged. Not yet. I'm sure I tore a ligament or broke a bone. At the very least, I bruised something badly. That's my life. Shitty thing after shitty thing happens, and I have to find a way to fight. This time might be too hard to overcome. I was paid millions when I signed with the Cowboys, but if I don't play in a single game, my career might be over before it even starts.

I slowly crawl out from beneath the motorcycle and start checking for signs of injury. But everything seems to work fine. I'm not even sore. Other than the mud covering my clothes and a large tear on my jeans, I'm fine. My bike, on the other hand, is destroyed beyond repair. I make a quick call to have someone pick up the bike and then I start walking back to the house. It's only a half a mile walk, but it's still raining. I should call an Uber or Camille to come pick me up, but I don't. I walk and let the rain refocus me.

It takes me about twenty minutes to get home. Much longer than it should have but I was in no rush to get home. I open the door to the house.

"Oh, my God! What happened to you?" Camille says. She runs over to me and checks every inch of my soaked and muddy body with her hands and eyes, looking for an injury.

I pull my soaked shirt off, let it drop to the floor, and then slip my shoes off as I walk to the laundry room, trailing water and mud on the floor. "I got in an accident."

Camille runs in front of me, stopping me. I see the fear and concern in her eyes. "What happened? Are you okay?"

"I look okay, don't I?" I brush past Camille and keep walking to the laundry room that is upstairs.

Camille rushes past me again and stands at the base of the stairs, blocking me from going up. "No. You don't look okay. What the hell happened, Hunter?"

I narrow my eyes, not wanting to deal with this right now. "A car pulled out in front of me. It was raining, and I couldn't stop in time. So I turned and hit a tree instead. I'm fine. Not even a scratch."

Camille frowns. "What the hell were you doing riding your motorcycle in a rainstorm? It's not safe. I don't want to lose you or have anything happen to you. You can't keep doing shit like this. I lo ... I care deeply about you, and I don't want anything to happen to you."

I like that she is strong and defiant, standing up for what she needs in this relationship, but I can't deal with it right now. Right now, I just want to shower and then to climb into bed and forget about today. And I sure as hell don't want to deal with hearing that she loves me right now. We've only been dating a couple of weeks. Yes, I've known her my whole life, but it doesn't mean I'm ready to hear her say she loves me.

So instead of saying something nice, I say the one thing that I know will get her to shut up. "Quinn used to say things like that."

Camille bites her lip. I can see the pain I caused her with those words. She'll do anything to distance herself from Quinn. Anything to make me forget about Quinn.

"I'm sorry," she says.

"I like dangerous things. And I don't owe you anything. We are barely even dating. Don't tell me how to live my life."

"I'm sorry. Forget I said anything." Camille moves out of my way, and I begin climbing the stairs to the laundry room. But I can't get the words Camille almost said out of my head. She loves me.

She can't love me. And I can't love her.

I also can't love Quinn.

I can't love anyone.

But I'm afraid I still love Quinn. More than I should. And I know that is Camille's fear. That I still love Quinn and always will when she wants me to love her instead. She just doesn't realize that is my fear too. That despite what I told Quinn our last night together, I thought I could stop loving her. I thought a few weeks would ease the pain. But I'm afraid the love I feel for her is never going away. And not even Camille can help me erase that love.

I can't love. Love leads to pain. To death. I can't love. Never again.

TEXT MESSAGE #12

1 month earlier

quinn

"I WANT TO BREAK UP," Hunter says.

My heart stops.

I knew this was coming. It has been coming since the first day we met.

We were never meant to be together. Not as boyfriend and girlfriend. Definitely not as husband and wife. Not even as friends.

We are too different. We come from different worlds and want different things.

Most women would have thought tonight was about a proposal, and if our relationship were like most, it would be. Hunter is leaving college to join the NFL next week while I stay and finish my last year of college. Tonight should be a night to celebrate. Hunter even made sure to get us reservations in the nicest steakhouse in Denver.

He bought me a nice blue gray dress that brings out the blue in my otherwise boring gray eyes. Mandy helped me curl my hair and do my makeup. Hunter is wearing a suit, and a new haircut ensures his blond hair is short on the sides and forms a wave on the top.

I glance down at the table covered in rose petals; whether that was Hunter's doing or just what the restaurant does, it doesn't matter because, from an outsider's point of view, this is a proposal or, at the very least, a night of celebration. That's what it looked like to me too until Hunter opened his mouth. A mouth I might never get to kiss again.

Maybe at one point that was what tonight was about? Hunter may even have bought a ring, planning the perfect proposal before something reminded him that we can't be together. We would have a lifetime of fighting, of giving up dreams, of sacrificing to make us work, and that's not fair.

But I hate I got my hopes up when he bought me this dress last week and planned this date. Except it's not a date. It's a breakup.

"Why are we here then?" I ask as I look around the restaurant. "Is it so I won't make a scene? Because I knew this was coming. It makes sense to do it now with you moving and me staying here. We need a clean break for a while. I get it, but really?" I raise an eyebrow not understanding why we are here.

Hunter touches my hand, and I immediately pull back like his hand is on fire, too hot for me to touch even for a second.

"Don't do that." His eyes are sad, broken.

"Why not? You just said you wanted to break up with me. Why would I let you touch me after that?"

"Because you still love me. Still want me."

I frown. Of course, I still love him. Still want him. But that doesn't mean I get what I want. We never get what we want.

"Don't touch me."

He lets out a large exhale as he sits back in his chair, and I watch as some of the rose petals dance across the white tablecloth from his breath.

I stare back up at him. I do not intend to let him get away with not explaining why we are here because I know it's important. I know he has a reason. He always has a reason for everything he does.

"What are we doing here?" I ask again.

He takes a drink of the wine the waiter delivered just before he told me he wanted to break up with me. I watch the muscles in his throat move as he swallows. My eyes linger on his strong jawline and stubble and then rake over his body. He somehow managed to fit snuggly into a suit that only amplifies his hard muscles. He really defines masculinity.

But none of that tells me what I need to know. I look into his eyes. Eyes that always tell me exactly what he is thinking. And right now, they are telling me ...

"You still love me too," I say, without hesitation and without question because I know it's true.

He leans forward, never taking his eyes off me. "I will always love you."

A lump forms in my throat, and my mouth starts to go dry. It's what every girl dreams of hearing, but I don't want to hear it. We can't be together, *so why torture ourselves?* It would be easier if I hated him.

"I wish you hated me."

He nods and leans back. "I wish we could be together."

I smile weakly. "We shouldn't wish things like this. It's not going to do us any good."

He frowns. "For one night, can you just pretend? Pretend that our lives are different. That tonight, instead of telling you that I want to break up, I asked you to marry me. Because we both know that's what we want."

I shake my head slowly. "We don't get what we want. I do what I can to survive, and you fight like hell to get away from here. We both know pretending the situation is anything other than what it is won't help. And you know I can't do that anyway. You know I can't pretend the future is going to be better than it is; I'm a pessimist. All I can see is the bad. The reasons we shouldn't be together." I don't add it's one of the reasons we are breaking up. I see the bad coming and hunker down and do my best to just survive. Hunter sees the bad coming and fights it and then fights to get away from it.

"Try. For just one night."

I look away from him, staring out into the restaurant, because I know if I look in to his eyes and see how desperately he wants this, I will cave. He wants me to pretend for one night that we live in a fairy tale. He forgets we have been pretending that we live in a fairy tale for the past year because I always knew it would end.

His hand on my chin turns me to face him.

I swat his hand away, but I look at him anyway.

"I need this memory. And so do you. We need this."

His eyes plead with me, begging me to say yes. To give in to one last perfect night together.

It doesn't sound perfect to me. It sounds miserable, knowing the entire time that this isn't real. That tomorrow when we wake up, this will all be over. That we will break up and only see each other a couple of times a year when we really need each other. Maybe less. The only comfort breaking up brings is that I know we will never disappear from each other's lives. He made a promise to me that night when we first met. A promise he will never break. And our lives are so fucked up that there is bound to be some sort of catastrophe or horrible event every couple of months, ensuring that I will get to see him. I can count on that.

I don't want to say yes. There is a reason I never dream of the perfect future. There is a reason I don't pretend everything is going to be okay when it isn't. I can't handle the heartbreak afterward. I've pretended before, and it almost killed me.

The only reason we have lasted as long as we have is because I always knew we would break up. I thought we might have a few more months and that Hunter would finish school before he left and we decided it was time, but I always played the relationship out knowing that everything was going to end. I've never pretended otherwise.

But I'll go along with him. I'll play his game. I'll pretend. I'll just still know in the back of my head that it means nothing. That we are over. That this is just for him. To make *him* happy. Because I can't not make him happy, even when it hurts me.

Hunter recognizes the shift in my eyes. I'm about to open my mouth to tell him I'll go along with his ridiculous plan for tonight when he gets up from his chair. I narrow my eyes at him, trying to understand. *Did he change his mind? Does he just want to leave and forget about everything?*

I'm just about to stand when he kneels next to the table. My eyes pop open wide as I realize what is happening.

"Don't ..."

He grabs my hand off my lap, and this time, I'm too shocked to do anything to stop him.

"Quinn, I love you more than anything. You have saved me so many times from myself. I don't deserve such beauty. I don't deserve such love. But I can't imagine life without you. I can't imagine ever giving you up, and I don't want to." He stops when he says he doesn't want to give me up.

I already know that because it's how I feel too. But he decided when we first met that he couldn't be with me. I would be perfectly fine being with him forever, despite our differences. All he has to do is say he's changed his mind, and I would be his forever.

"Quinn, will you marry me?"

That's why it's so easy for me to answer honestly, like he is really asking.

"Yes."

My eyes widen farther when I see him pull a box out of his jacket pocket. He looks up at me, and I raise an eyebrow. I know an expensive ring isn't in that box. It must just be something cheap he got at some department store to help me play the part tonight. Nothing more.

He opens the box, though, and my jaw hits the floor.

I look back at Hunter and then the ring and then back at him.

"You can't be serious?"

He grins as he pulls the largest ring I have ever seen out of the box. I don't know how many carats the ring is as he slips it on my ring finger, but I would guess if I sold it, I would never have to work again. I could just live off the money I made from this ring. I don't expect to like this large of a ring, but the second it slides on my finger, I never want to take it off again.

Hunter grabs the base of my neck and kisses me firm on the lips just like I imagine he would if he was really proposing. Like he loves me more than anything and never wants to let me go. I hear people clapping and cheering when Hunter stops and heads back to his seat.

"Champagne on the house. Congrats you two!" the waiter says, pouring us each a glass of champagne.

I don't pay him any attention; instead, I'm too focused on the ring that feels so real. It makes no sense why Hunter would spend so much money on the ring if he was just pretending. When the waiter leaves, I say, "I'm not giving you the ring back."

Hunter grins and his shoulders relax. "I don't want you to give it back."

My heart stops again. "This is still pretend, right? I mean this ring ..." God, I don't know anything about diamonds. It must be from one of those machines that you put a quarter in and get out a large fake ring. Or maybe he got a fake one from a thrift shop.

"The ring is real."

I gasp. "It must have cost you thousands. I can't be wearing this." I begin taking the ring off. "I'll lose it, and I'll never be able to pay you back."

Hunter grabs my hand, preventing me from taking it off.

"The ring is yours." He speaks calmly like he has thought too much about this. "No matter what tomorrow brings, the ring will always be yours." When he says that, I know he isn't just talking about the ring. He's reminding me again that he will always love me. But I don't need him to tell me that; I need him to propose for real.

"I'm sorry; I can't do this." I get up, throwing my napkin on the table, and make my way out of the restaurant. Feeling every emotion I have ever felt welling up inside me as I make my way outside. Love. Pain. Happiness. Fear. All of it. Everything I have felt since the moment I met Hunter. He told me that first day he could never be with me. I knew that going in, but I never felt that way. I never felt that we couldn't be together. And as much as I tried to believe we couldn't be together, I let hope in.

Hope that something might change. That he might have a change of heart and want to be with me, forever.

I should have never let hope in because now I'm going to suffer for far too long because of it. This is why I don't dream. So I don't feel like this. Like someone just took a sledgehammer to my heart.

Hunter drove us here. It's at least a thirty-minute drive back to my apartment. I need to call an Uber to get home. I pull my phone out of my purse and begin to pull up the Uber app.

His strong hands are on my shoulder. He doesn't say anything or do anything; he just holds my shoulders as we both breathe in and out. He slowly turns me around to face him.

"The ring is yours. I want you to have it. I wish it was a real engagement ring. I wish it could be a symbol of my promise to marry you. But it can't."

He takes a deep breath as he holds my hand that has the ring still on it. "But it is a symbol that I will love you forever. That I will still protect you when you need it. That I'm still yours."

"But ..."

He puts a finger up to my lips, shushing me. "It didn't cost me too much. I made a lot of money when I signed to become a Cowboy. You deserve every penny I spent on the ring because without you, I wouldn't have made it to the NFL. I wouldn't have made it past that first night."

I shake my head. "That's not true. You're a fighter, remember? You fight. You would have been just fine without me."

He grips my shoulders tighter and pushes me back, ensuring that I look at him as he says in a deep voice, "No. I wouldn't have. You saved me. Don't ever let me or anyone else tell you otherwise. You saved me."

I'm speechless. I didn't save him. He saved me. And if he feels that way, I don't understand why we can't be together. Something else is going on. Something he isn't telling me. I see it now in his eyes. Something I haven't seen before.

Ava. It's because of Ava. That's the only reason I can come up with. And if that is how he feels, then I don't want to be with him either. In fact, it makes it easier on me to know that is why instead of a mistake I made years ago.

His eyes travel side to side as they watch me come to the realization. He doesn't deny it. He just slowly releases me and takes a step back, letting me feel the pain. Too much pain.

He glances down at the ring on my finger. "You can sell it. Use it to—"

I don't let him finish. Because he was right. We are going to break up, and today is the last chance I have to kiss him and pretend otherwise. And I want it to be a night I can carry with me when I'm missing him, when I'm hurting. To remember one great night.

I press my lips against his as my arms wrap around his neck. He doesn't question what I'm doing. He doesn't stop me; he embraces me. He kisses me more passionately than he ever has before, and I let myself forget I only have a handful of kisses left with this man.

I keep my eyes closed through the kiss, and when it stops, he says, "Do you want to go back inside and finish our dinner?"

"No, I'm only hungry for you."

hunter

HER EYES ARE WHAT I'm going to miss the most. They tell me so much about what she is feeling. She can't hide anything. Her gray eyes look different, depending on the light—either blue, gray, or green—and also depending on her mood. She does well to hide her moods with everyone else but not with me.

Right now, her eyes tell me she wants to devour me. They are filled with lust, need. For me.

I don't hesitate. Even though I should. I should think this through because I know despite how much I want her right now that having her one final time will destroy me. It will destroy both of us.

But I don't think about why we shouldn't.

Instead, I kiss her plump soft lips.

I tangle my hand in her light brown hair.

I press myself against every inch of her.

Every kiss, every touch makes me realize how perfect this woman is for me. She is the woman I'm supposed to marry if I believed in such things. She is the woman I'm supposed to love for the rest of my life. She is the woman I will love for the rest of my life.

I grab her hand and begin walking back to the car unable to release her for even a second. We get to the car, and I open the door for her and watch her every curve as she climbs into the front seat. I can't take my eyes off her, and I'm still holding her hand as I stand outside the door. She smiles up at me.

"If you don't release my hand, we are never going to get somewhere where you can fuck me. I suggest my place; it's the closest," Quinn says with a wink.

I grin like the horny idiot I am and reluctantly release her. I slam her door shut and run around to the driver's side and climb into the seat, immediately grabbing her hand again. I kiss it as I start the car and pull out of the parking lot.

I hear the tiniest of moans slip from her lips as I kiss the back of her hand. I love listening to her. She moans at the slightest touch. And I can't wait to hear those moans turn into screams. Screams I plan to hear all night long because tonight, I don't plan to sleep. Tonight, I plan to fuck her, loving her enough for a lifetime.

I can't wait to hear her moan louder. I can feel every second tick by faster and faster, counting down the time I have left. Such precious little time left.

Quinn seems eager to spend every second we have left making memories. She pulls my fingers to her mouth and then slowly moves her mouth over my index finger.

"God, Quinn. I can't wait to fuck you."

She grins as she moves to my middle finger running her warm, wet lips over my finger just like she does when she is sucking my dick. She begins to move to my ring finger, but

I stop her and slip the fingers she has just been sucking between her legs and under her dress that has moved up her thighs. I bite my lip and groan when I discover she isn't wearing any underwear.

"You're killing me, Quinn. You aren't even wearing any underwear."

And if she was wearing any underwear, it would be soaked. I circle her entrance with my fingers while driving faster, needing to get to the hotel quicker.

She throws her head back against the head rest and gasps when I flick my thumb across her clit. "I didn't want any panty lines showing through the dress."

I move my fingers back to her entrance, enjoying every second. Loving how wet she gets when I've barely touched her. Getting hard from every womanly sound that escapes her lips, her throat.

She moans so loudly that I get lost in her voice instead of focusing on driving ahead and have to slam on the brakes to keep from hitting a car in front of me.

I pull my hand away.

"Don't stop."

I close my eyes, trying to resist pulling over to the side of the road and taking her once right now. But there is no good place to do that and we are almost to the hotel.

I have to stop touching her to keep myself from doing that very thing. Instead, I lick her juices off my fingers as she watches me. She loves that I love how she tastes. Just like I love everything else about her.

I take a turn to the right instead of to the left toward her apartment.

"I thought we were going to my place? Yours is all the way across town. I can't wait that long."

I stop at a red light and grab the nape of her neck to pull her into a passionate kiss. One that I know will leave us both unable to control ourselves once the kiss is over, but I don't care. We are almost there.

"I can't wait that long either. But tonight, we aren't going to your place or mine. Tonight is special. We are engaged, after all. We need to celebrate," I say, reminding her that I need this fantasy. That tomorrow will hurt, but tonight is going to make all that pain so worthwhile.

"Then where are we going?"

"To a hotel."

She grins. "The St. Julien?"

I grin too, but I don't answer her. She'll see soon enough. But of course, I'm taking her there. It holds special memories for us. It's our favorite place. I wouldn't take her anywhere else in the world after proposing to her.

When I pull up in front of the hotel, I can feel the excitement from Quinn without even looking at her. I park the car and then get out quickly to open her door before anyone else gets a chance. I open her door then hold my hand out to help her out of the car. She looks up at me, and I can see the sparkle in her eyes.

She takes my hand and climbs out of the car. The valet comes over and asks for my keys and says something else that I don't hear. I flip him my keys and escort Quinn inside, not caring what anyone else says. I guide her to the front desk.

"Mr. Metcalf and the future Mrs. Metcalf checking in." I wrap my arm around Quinn's waist as I say it.

The lady behind the desk smiles sweetly at us as she looks us up in the computer. She grabs our keys and hands them to me.

"Congrats on your engagement."

I begin to pull Quinn away when the lady behind the desk spots Quinn's ring. "And might I add that the ring is gorgeous. I hope you have many wonderful years together."

I kiss Quinn on the cheek. "I'm lucky to have her."

I lead Quinn to the elevator. I wish we had years together; instead, we will only have hours to enjoy our engagement. And as much as I want to be upset that I don't get more time with her, I'm not upset. It's more than I deserve. It's more than a lot of people get. Most people never even find a love like Quinn and I share.

The doors close, but I wait to put my hands on her. I wait to kiss her even though it is the longest elevator ride in my life. I don't say anything to her. I just let the anticipation build as the elevator takes us to the top floor. The only thing I do is keep my hand wrapped around her waist.

The doors open, and we both walk in the direction of the room. I don't have to tell her which room it is because she already knows. I booked the same room we booked four years ago; even though there are better rooms, more expensive rooms, this room is what we both want. This room holds all the memories.

I open the door, and Quinn gasps when she walks into the room. I follow behind her and watch as her eyes go over every rose petal on the floor in the room, every candle that is lit and provides the only light in the dark room, and the handwritten notes that contain all the reasons why I love her and will never stop loving her.

She stops to pick one up and reads, "I love when you let me fuck you in the ass, you filthy, dirty girl." She raises an eyebrow at me. "Romantic."

I laugh and then shrug my shoulders guiltily. Of all the romantic notes spread throughout the room, she chose one of the handful of naughty ones I also included. I bend down to search for a more romantic one and hand it to her.

"I love that you don't bullshit me. You always tell me exactly what is on your mind even if the truth is painful. It's what I need to hear. Nobody else tells me the truth, only you," I read to her.

Her eyes scan the room, trying to take in as many of the notes as she can, but she will have time to read all them later, after we say our goodbyes.

"I need you, now."

She tucks her long brown hair behind her ear and looks at me with lust in her eyes.

"I want you to take me in every way possible," she says.

I take a deep breath, happy we are on the same page. Happy she doesn't plan to sleep one second tonight either.

"How do you want me to take you first?" I ask, already knowing her answer.

"The same way you took me that night."

She bites her lip, and for a moment, she looks just as sweet and innocent as she looked that night. The only difference between now and that night is that I know the truth. That she isn't so sweet and innocent. She's wild, strong, and stubborn. She's fearless; probably because she has already faced the worse of life, just like I have.

I walk toward her, slowly closing the space between us. I can see her in my head, standing there just like before; only this time, she doesn't flinch when I touch her. This time, when I reach out and tuck a strand of lose hair behind her ear, she melts into my hand.

"Kiss me," she says.

I do, thankful that tonight I don't have to save her. Tonight is just about us.

She grabs my suit jacket and throws it off me. I begin working to find the zipper on the back of her dress, but as I pull it down, it gets stuck on the dress, making me growl in frustration. I can't wait any longer.

I begin to pull away so I can get a better look at the zipper, but she grabs my tie to keep my lips on hers. I quickly forget about the dress. I can fuck her in the dress first. Then when I've had her once, I can figure out how to get her damn dress off. Or I can rip the dress off her body. That would be sexy, although I have no idea what she would wear home if I did that. I didn't think to bring any extra clothes for her. Stupid.

She senses my frustration and stops kissing me. I can see the hint of laughter cover her lips.

I yank the tie over my head so that she can no longer use it to control me. I shake my head as my eyes bore into hers. Like taking off a tie would prevent her from controlling me. She is one of two women in the world who have me wrapped around their finger and know exactly how to control me. Whether I have a tie on or not.

I begin to unbutton my shirt, but I freeze and watch her turn around to show me her bare back and how low cut the dress is. I suck in a breath, trying to keep myself from ripping the dress off.

She turns her head and looks back at me as she licks her lower lip. "Rip it," she purrs.

She doesn't have to tell me twice. I grab the fabric on either side of the zipper and pull the dress apart, watching the hem unravel. I'm never rough with her. I'm not one of those guys who need to tie a woman up or use toys or whips to get off. But seeing how good it felt just to rip her dress off her might make me change my mind. At least about some things.

The dress drops to the floor, and now, she is just in heels and her bra.

I rip my own shirt off and my pants.

She bites her lip. "You went commando too?"

"Yeah, didn't want there to be any panty lines in my suit."

She laughs at my joke even though it wasn't very good. She laughs because she gets me, loves me.

She unhooks her bra, and as I watch it fall to the floor, I really can't wait another second. She wants it like the first night I ever fucked her. She wants it slow and meaningful. She wants me to show her how loving I can be. I want that too, but I'm not sure I have the patience to give that to her first. I need to fuck her hard and fast. I need to make her come as fast as possible because I'm tired of waiting to make her feel good. I'm tired of the hint of pain in her eyes since I told her that we should break up. I need to make that go away. Now.

So I break my earlier promise and grab her and kiss her harder than I ever have before. She kisses me back with equal force, letting me know she no longer wants to take it slow. She's just as impatient as I am.

I grab her ass, and she wraps her legs around my body as she digs her heels into my back. I carry her to the bed just off the living room. As we fall on the bed, the rose petals fly in the air for just a second before landing all around us. Quinn looks beautiful, like an angel surrounded by all the rose petals.

"I love you," I say against her neck as I begin kissing every inch of her within reach. Her neck, lips, breasts. I should memorize how it feels to have my lips on her body, but I can't. I'll have to do that later when I have more time. Now, I just need to be inside her. Need to make her forget about everything but this moment.

"I love you too, but I need you to ..." She groans instead of finishing her sentence as I thrust inside her. I already know what she was going to say.

We move in unison together. Thrusting. Fucking. Loving.

"Fuck, Hunter," Quinn says right before we both come together for the first of what we both know is going to be many times.

But as I collapse back on the bed, I become scared shitless. Because telling Quinn goodbye tomorrow is going to be the hardest thing I've ever done, and I've done some horrible, painful things in my life. But Quinn is special, one of the loves of my life. I wish things could be different. I wish I could go back in time and change things, but I can't. I have to say goodbye, even though Quinn will never know the real reason. It's because I made a promise to someone else a long time ago, and I don't break my promises.

quinn

WE DON'T SLEEP.

We fuck.

We make love.

We snuggle.

We pretend.

We live a fantasy.

But we don't talk. We don't live in reality. And we don't spend our last hours together sleeping.

And as the alarm I set in case we did fall asleep goes off, I know our time for pretending is over. But despite the annoying alarm going off on my phone on the nightstand, I don't move out of Hunter's arms, and he doesn't encourage me to turn it off either. Instead, he just holds me, and I stay wrapped in his arms for the last time.

A lump forms in my throat as I think that. *For the last time.* That doesn't seem possible, but it is. This is the last time I'll lie on his bare chest, completely naked and knowing that everything is right in the world. Because even though I know we will stay in each other's lives, it won't be the same. He's moving, and I'm staying here. We broke up. There will be no reason to see each other. No reason to fly thousands of miles.

The alarm eventually stops, but we still don't move. We just hold each other—unable to say goodbye even though we both know we need to.

My phone starts ringing, and I glance at the number. It's the babysitter, and she's probably calling to find out what time I'm picking up Ava. I roll over, hating that Hunter lets me, and that I immediately feel cold as I reach for the phone. I tap answer. "Hello."

"Hey Quinn, just seeing when you will be picking Ava up? I have to get to work by ten today," my babysitter says.

I take a deep breath. "I'll be there in about half an hour."

"Perfect. See you then."

I end the call and then turn to find Hunter dressed. I glance around the room, looking for something to wear, but I know my dress is ripped and not wearable. I'm going to be the weirdo wearing a robe or something out of here. But somehow, I can't convince myself to even get out of this bed.

Hunter looks at me, but he doesn't seem to know what to say either.

Typical man, I think. I guess I'm going to have to be the strong one who says goodbye. "I fucking hate goodbyes, but I guess we need to say it."

He shakes his head. "No. We don't. We just need to remember last night, forever."

I frown. I need to say goodbye. I need closure. I can't just remember last night and pretend my life is a fairy tale that will never happen. I glance down at my ring. I shake my head for even thinking the word 'my.' The ring isn't mine.

The ring belongs to Hunter. I begin to take the ring off, but Hunter stops me.

"I want you to have the ring. To remember tonight."

"What if I don't want to?"

"Then you can leave it here or do whatever you want with it. Donate it to charity for all I care. I just won't take it back."

I frown and get up from the bed, immediately regretting it because now I'm naked and exposed while he is fully dressed. I cross my arms over my breasts. "Ava is going to laugh when she sees me in the robe in the closet. I'll have to make up some funny story about what happened to my clothes. That I went to the spa and they lost my clothes. She'll laugh at that."

Hunter frowns. "Let me pick her up."

I narrow my eyes. "Why?"

"Because I need to spend one last day with her. I need to tell her why I won't be around as much anymore. I need to tell her goodbye."

I nod. "She needs that. Just let me get dressed."

"No. I need to spend time with her *alone*."

I bite my lip, contemplating what he is saying, but eventually nod. It would be good for Ava to spend time with him alone. I just hope he can find better words to explain why he is breaking up with us than what he told me last night because otherwise a four-year-old won't understand.

Hunter walks back to me and kisses me softly on the lips and then he walks out of the hotel.

"Dammit!" I say as I walk over to put on the robe from the closet. I remember why I hate this hotel. Because Hunter sucks at goodbyes. Especially here. The tears come now that I'm alone, but I quickly shake them off. I'm not alone; we just broke up. I'll see him again. This might even be for the best. We can both live the lives we always wanted but still be in each other's lives when it matters.

TEXT MESSAGE #11

1 day earlier

quinn

"IS HUNTER COMING OVER for dinner tonight?" Ava asks as she climbs up on one of the barstools in the kitchen while I pore through the pantry looking for something actually considered food that I can make for dinner instead of just macaroni and cheese like we usually have.

"Nope, it's just the two of us tonight." I move a box of macaroni out of the way and find a box of instant mashed potatoes behind it. I sigh. I'm going to have to make a grocery run if I am going to have any chance at cooking a respectable meal.

I look up and watch her bottom lip pop out. I know I've upset her, but I don't really understand how or why. "I thought we could have a good night together, just the two of us. We can go to the store and pick up things to cook and then cook together and maybe watch a movie later with some popcorn since I don't have to work tomorrow and you don't have school."

Ava tucks her pouted lip back in as she thinks about what I just said. I stand poised, ready to handle whatever argument she is about to throw at me in her attempt to get her way. She's too smart, smarter than her own good. And I've learned I have to always be prepared for her to try to argue her way at any time because if I'm not on guard, then she will get me to say yes to something before I even realize what I'm agreeing to.

"I get to pick the movie out?"

I smile. "Of course, you get to pick the movie out."

I can see her little mind working as she looks up at me. "If I let Hunter pick the movie, do you think he will come?"

I walk over and lean against the counter, looking straight at Ava. "Why do you want Hunter to come over so badly? We just saw him a couple of days ago." I try not to let her see my concern because as happy as I am that Ava and Hunter have a good relationship, I'm afraid of what would happen if Hunter and I don't work out.

"I want to give him something," she says.

"Give him what?"

She shakes her head. "I can't tell you."

"Well, what am I supposed to say to get him to come then if you won't tell me what you are giving him?"

She thinks for a moment. "Tell him I have a gift I need to give him."

"And this gift can't wait?"

She shakes her head again. "Nope. I need to give it to him tonight because tomorrow I'm going over to the babysitters and I won't see him. It must be tonight."

I smile. "Okay. I'll call him and see if he can come over for a little bit tonight." I walk over to where my phone is sitting on the other end of the kitchen counter.

"No."

I stop and look at her. "Why not? I thought you wanted me to call him."

"No, text him. He always comes when you text him, but sometimes, he ignores your calls." Ava hops down off the stool and runs to her bedroom.

I can't help but laugh at her, but I do as she says. I text.

Quinn: Ava needs you to come over tonight. She has a gift to give you. And she specifically requested that I text instead of call because you always come when I text, but not when I call.

I press send and then wait. I'm sure Hunter has plans for tonight. I told him earlier this week that I needed some alone time with Ava. He understood, so I'm sure he has plans with the guys, but hopefully, he can stop by to get whatever Ava came up with to give him.

My phone buzzes on the counter. I pick it up and read the message.

Hunter: Does an hour from now work? And I need to get that girl her own phone so she can text me whenever she needs me just like you can.

Quinn: I wouldn't do that if I were you because then she would be texting you every day needing something. She has no problem asking for help, unlike me.

Hunter: Maybe I want one of you to text me every day.

I smile at his last text message. "Ava!"
Ava comes running back into the kitchen.

"Hunter is coming over in about an hour. So let's go grocery shopping while we wait."

She smiles and nods and gives me no clue to what her secret is. No clue to what gift she has for Hunter. And I don't care. Because I get to see Hunter and spend time with Ava. Tonight is going to be a good night.

There is a knock on the door, and before I even get a chance to get up off the couch, Ava is running to the door to open it. I really should teach her about strangers. People could come to the door who she doesn't know and she shouldn't answer it without me. But that lesson will have to wait for another day because she already has the door open and is in Hunter's arms.

"Thanks for inviting me, squirt. If we left it up to your mother, I would never get to come over," Hunter says, winking at me as he carries Ava into the living room.

Ava laughs. "I always want you here. You should move in again like before. That was fun."

Hunter stares at me as he says, "I would like that, but I'm not sure if that is going to work out."

"You should come over, though, every night you can," Ava says.

"Will do, squirt," Hunter says.

"I have a gift for you," Ava says.

"I heard. When do I get it? I can't wait to open it," Hunter says.

"Now!" Ava says.

Hunter puts Ava down, and we both watch as she runs to her bedroom to get whatever gift she has up her sleeve for

Hunter. He then walks over to me and gives me a quick kiss before Ava comes back into the room.

Ava carries a large paper bag colored with markers in shades of blue and silver. She has a large smile on her face as she hands the bag to Hunter.

"What is this for? It's not my birthday, and I feel bad I didn't get you a gift in exchange," Hunter says.

"It's because you won the game, and Mommy said you were going to try to go pro, and I wanted you to have a gift to help you decide what team you should choose," Ava says.

Hunter takes the bag and sits down on the couch. Ava sits next to him, and I sit on the far end, watching them.

Hunter looks at me but doesn't have the heart to tell Ava that it doesn't work that way. Hunter doesn't get to just pick the team he is going to play for since he is drafted. But instead of crushing her dreams, he opens the bag and pulls out the gift. It is clear Ava has spent a lot of time thinking about it.

Hunter stares at the male Barbie doll that he just pulled out of the bag. It is covered in Dallas Cowboys attire that she created out of paper and glued all over his body to make a makeshift jersey and pants. A slow grin forms over Hunter's face before he turns to Ava and pulls her onto his lap so that he can hug her.

"I think it's the perfect choice."

She beams. "I love the Cowboys, and I think they are the perfect choice for you. They have a lot of money to pay you well, and they are due for a Super Bowl win soon. That's what everyone says. And ..." I watch as her cheeks flush a shade of pink.

Hunter raises an eyebrow at her.

"And I think their colors are the best."

Hunter and I both laugh at her adorableness.

"Well, I think you made an awesome choice. We will know soon if it works out, but with this doll bringing me good luck, I think my chances have increased," Hunter says with a wink.

"Good. Are you staying for dinner and a movie?"

"Did you cook or did your mother?" Hunter asks.

Ava smiles. "I did."

"Then I'll stay and eat and watch some of the movie, but then I have to go. I promised to meet someone tonight."

"Good. I'll get dinner," Ava says, running to put the pizza we made onto plates.

"Pizza?" Hunter asks, knowing good and well that I told him earlier I was going to try to cook healthier.

"I tried, I really did, to get healthier food, but it's hard to resist a four-year-old who wants pizza. But at least it's filled with lots of veggies."

Hunter laughs as Ava brings him a slice of pizza filled with all her favorite vegetables: carrots, olives, and strawberries. Ava brings me a slice as well and then grabs a plate for herself.

Hunter gives me an evil look over Ava's head for making him eat what we both know is going to be awful pizza. I just shrug because if he was here when we went shopping, he would have ended up with the same things, the same pizza, because Ava has us both wrapped around her little finger.

We all take a bite of the pizza at the same time, chewing as quickly as possible to get the strange taste to go down.

"It's yummy!" Ava proclaims.

Hunter and I both nod and moan our agreement as neither of us have finished our first bites.

When Hunter finally swallows, he says, "So what movie are we watching?"

Ava jumps up and grabs the movie *Remember the Titans* and shows it to Hunter.

"Excellent choice. One of my favorites," Hunter says.

I place my plate on the ground next to the couch, not sure I can stomach another bite, while Ava puts the movie in the DVD player. Hunter, on the other hand, continues to eat his slice of pizza.

I cock my head to the side as I raise an eyebrow at him for still eating the pizza.

"What?" he asks.

"Really?" I ask nodding toward the pizza.

"It's not that bad, and I'm hungry," he whispers back so that Ava can't hear him.

I roll my eyes and move closer to him. I'm going to at least get to snuggle with him if I have to suffer through a football movie. Hopefully, Ava will get out of her football-loving phase soon and move onto something else once Hunter knows which pro team will draft him.

I lay my head on his chest as Ava climbs back on the couch and snuggles next to me. I wrap my arms around her as the movie starts. I yawn. I'm exhausted. I know I'm going to fall asleep during the movie.

Hunter leans down and kisses me on the forehead. "I think I'm going to text you that I need you tomorrow."

I smile. "Oh yeah?"

"Yeah."

"Is that allowed? Telling me you are going to text me before you actually do?"

He kisses my forehead again, and I wish he was kissing me on the lips.

"Oh, it's allowed."

I smile and close my eyes and know I'm going to be asleep in about five minutes, but in the meantime, I can dream about what Hunter has planned for tomorrow.

hunter

I CARRIED BOTH QUINN and Ava to bed before I left. It's barely ten o'clock on a Friday night, but they were both completely out of it. It's been a long week for them. I left Quinn a note beside her bed, letting her know I left so she doesn't freak out when she wakes up and I'm not there. I also tell her not to plan anything for tomorrow because I'm definitely going to need her.

I've had tomorrow planned for a couple of weeks now. Looking for the perfect day, the perfect moment to propose. I never thought I would want to propose. I never thought I would find someone and especially not when I was this young. But I can't imagine my life without Quinn, without either of them.

And I know that once I'm drafted, it is going to be hard for a while. We will most likely be living in different states while I play for the NFL and she finishes college. Unless I can convince Quinn to transfer. That would be good. But I'm not sure she would be willing to uproot Ava so soon, and I understand. But we could make it work. We always have. This will be no different.

I smile as I pull up to the bar where I promised to meet Camille and jump out of my car and walk into the bar. Maybe Camille won't want to stay long, and then I can go back over to Quinn's tonight.

I spot Camille sitting in a private booth with a martini in front of her. I beam as I walk over to her, but she doesn't have a smile on her face.

In fact, I think she's scowling as she stares intensely at her martini. I'm not going back over to Quinn's tonight, I realize. Whatever is up with Camille is bad. Very bad. And I'm going to have to be the one to fix it. Hopefully, it doesn't impede any of my plans for Quinn and me.

I take a seat in the booth across from her. "That bad, huh?"

She frowns and gives me that stare that tells me I fucked up but don't know how. And I immediately regret saying anything.

The waitress comes over and asks if I want anything to drink. I look at Camille, trying to get an idea of what kind of night this is going to be. How drunk I need to be. Camille continues to frown and then turns to her martini.

So I go with a safe bet. "Whiskey and Coke."

The waitress nods and leaves us alone. But Camille still doesn't say anything, and I know enough to keep my mouth shut until she is ready to talk. Instead, I try to relax because nothing she says today is going to make today bad. Nothing.

I got to spend a couple of hours with my favorite two girls. And tomorrow, I make them mine forever. Nothing is going to ruin that. I sling my arm over the back of the booth and glance around the crowded college bar. A couple of my teammates spot me from across the bar, and I smile and lift my hand at them. They do the same back but are preoccupied with the girls sitting next to them. So I know they won't come over and talk to us.

The waitress brings me my drink, and I have finally have something to do other than just wish I had stayed at Quinn's place tonight and blown off Camille. I begin drinking the whiskey when Camille finally decides to talk.

"I'm glad you came. I wasn't sure you would. I miss you."

I take another sip of my whiskey, waiting for her to continue, but she doesn't.

"What I want to know is why I'm here? I have no problem hanging out and catching up with an old friend. I miss hanging out with you too and am more than happy to have a relaxing night tonight. But that's obviously not what you want. So why am I here?"

Her eyes drop down.

"Camille?"

"You can't be with Quinn."

I search her eyes, trying to understand why the fuck she would say that. I know that Camille has always had a thing for me. We've dated before, but it never went further than a date. She knows I'm not interested in her that way. We are just friends.

"I'm tired of dealing with your games, Camille. I'm sorry I'm with Quinn instead of you. I thought you and I could remain friends, but I was wrong."

I pull out my wallet to throw some cash on the table to pay for my drink.

"Please, just hear me out and then you can go. You don't ever have to see me again after tonight. Just hear me out. It's important."

I throw my wallet onto the table. "Fine but make it quick."

She takes a deep breath. "You can't marry Quinn."

I lean forward and talk quietly like I'm afraid the whole bar will find out and tell Quinn of my plans to propose tomorrow. "How did you find out I was planning to propose?"

She shakes her head. "I just know you. You will propose because it's the right thing to do, not because you want to. You don't ever want to get married. You don't want to give anyone that kind of power to hurt you."

"You don't know a thing about me." I lean back in the booth and say in a normal voice.

I see the tiniest hint of a smile. "I know you better than she does. She doesn't have a clue that you are planning to propose tomorrow."

"Quinn knows me better than you think, and you have no idea if she thinks I'm planning to propose or not. Only Quinn knows that."

"You can't marry her."

"Why the hell not?"

She hesitates. She has nothing. Nothing that will make me change my mind about Quinn. Nothing that will stop me from proposing tomorrow.

But Camille looks straight at me and says, "Sabrina."

One word. That's all she has to say, and then I know. I know what she is implying. I know the truth. I know everything.

And the most painful part about it is that I know I can't marry Quinn. I can't be in Ava's life. I can't because I made a promise years ago. And now that I know the truth—a truth that, if I'm being honest, I think I knew about all along—I have to break up with Quinn.

TEXT MESSAGE #10

1 week earlier

hunter

SHE'S HERE. I know it the second Quinn and Ava walk into the stadium. I can feel it even though I don't know where they are. It's thirty minutes until game time, but the crowd is already bustling. I guess it should be. We are vying for the championship, after all, so the crowds should be large.

I catch another ball in warm-up, and this time, any anxiety is gone. She's here. I always play better when she's here.

I want to impress her. I want to be worthy of her. And I plan on playing the best fucking football I have ever played. Today.

Not because this game will determine if and what round I go in the NFL. Not because this is everything I have been working up to every day since I was born. But because of her.

I know my parents are in the crowd somewhere. Watching and beaming, they always knew I would amount to something someday. How proud they are of me today.

But it's all a lie. They haven't been the most supportive of parents. They thought multiple times in my life that I was throwing everything away. That I would never get here. They just don't understand that this isn't the proudest day of my life.

"Hey, you ready? I don't want to have to win this game on my own," Marshall, our quarterback, says.

I laugh. "You wouldn't have a chance at winning this game on your own. I'm the one who always has to do all the hard work."

Marshall laughs. "You're right. So make sure your head is in the game and not on that pretty girl of yours in the stands."

I grin. "Don't worry; thinking about her makes me play better."

Marshall rolls his eyes. "Whatever it takes, man."

He tosses me the ball and then begins running toward the locker room with the rest of our teammates. I stand in the middle of the field with the ball in my hands just like I do every Saturday. Tonight is going to be a great night. I glance up into the crowd, and to my surprise, I find Quinn and Ava. They are my future. Win or lose, I'll always have them.

quinn

"HUNTER'S GOING TO THE NFL, Mommy!" Ava screams at the top of her lungs.

I smile at her as she cheers for Hunter and the rest of the team on the field after they won. They won, thanks in a large part to Hunter. I already knew that Hunter was basically a shoe-in to go pro. He's the best tight end in the game. The absolute best.

I knew he was going. But now, it's official. Now, it's just a matter of where and when and for how much. He's going to be making millions in the NFL while I stay in Colorado and try to scrape by with my waitressing job as I finish college.

We are no longer going to be equals—not that we ever really were. We have never been equals. He's always strived for more than I have. He's always gone further. Worked harder. Made more money.

And his life hasn't been that much easier than mine has; in fact, his life may be harder than mine is. He's faced something that I never have, and he's come out better for it.

I love him. And I think he loves me. But I know that this game sealed our fate. I'm just not sure if it sealed us together or apart. We have never talked about a future together. We have only ever talked about the impossibility of us being together.

"Mommy, cheer! It's exciting!"

I cheer with Ava, clapping loudly.

"Can we go down on the field? Mommy, please!" Ava begs, pulling on my hand toward the field.

"We can go closer, but I ..."

Ava pulls harder, and I let her pull me down along with the masses who are trying to do the same thing. I grip her hand tightly to make sure we don't get separated.

It takes us a long time to get anywhere near the field. Before I have a chance to say we should just stay in the stands near the field, the crowd sweeps us onto the field. When our feet touch the turf, Ava pulls hard, trying to run to find Hunter or any of his teammates she knows to celebrate with. I pull her back and scoop her up in my arms afraid that the crowds might separate us or trample her tiny body.

Ava giggles when I pick her up. "We have to find Hunter."

I scan the crowd but don't spot him. I want to see him just as much as she does, but I'm also anxious because this chapter of our lives is changing. I know that everything is going to change again. I should be used to it. My life is a series of serious events that significantly change my life. But I will never get used to it.

"There!" Ava says, pointing toward the far end of the crowd.

I see Hunter talking with reporters.

"Climb on my back," I say and wait until Ava moves to my back, hanging onto me with her arms and legs. I grab her legs and make sure she is secure before I begin making my way through the crowd toward him.

"Faster!" Ava screams.

I do. I run, darting in and out of the crowd. I need to be near him, and Ava excitedly cheers me on as I carry her, occasionally high-fiving passersby as we head through the crowd.

I stop just short of reaching Hunter. I don't want to interrupt him speaking with the reporters.

"Don't stop. We are almost there," Ava says.

"We need to wait until his interview is over before we go see him. And even then, he is going to have a lot of people he needs to talk to, so we will only be able to talk to him for a second."

I don't have to look at Ava to know she is pouting. She uses two looks to try to get what she wants—her adorable smile and her pout. And she knows how to work them equally as well.

"Hunter!" Ava screams over the crowd, trying to get his attention. But the noise level in the stadium is loud. Too loud for a four-year-old's small voice to be heard over the crowd.

"He can't hear you. You're going to have to be patient."

"But I can try?"

I shake my head and laugh. "Yes, you can try."

"Hunter! Hunter! Hunter!"

To my surprise, Hunter turns his head toward us; whether that is pure luck or because of Ava's shouting. He runs toward us, and Ava kicks me like I'm a horse, trying to get me to run toward him.

"Hey, none of that," I say.

Ava immediately stops. "Sorry," she says in her sweet little voice.

I do, however, move faster until Hunter grabs us both, hugging us tightly as his lips hit mine. We try not to kiss much in front of Ava. I don't want her getting her hopes up that Hunter and I are going to get married, and she is going to have a father. But right now, neither of us cares. We kiss with Ava on my back while I hold on tightly to Hunter. He tastes like sweat, but I don't care. It just makes me want to kiss him more.

When he pulls away, I'm speechless. I don't know what to say even though there are a million things to say—congrats, you were awesome, I'm so proud of you. The list is endless.

He doesn't seem to care, though; instead, he reaches up and kisses Ava on the cheek who says all the things I should be saying. "You were awesome! You ran all over those guys. You broke so many tackles! You kicked some serious ass!"

"Ava!" Hunter and I both scowl Ava for her language.

She just smiles. "Sorry, but it's true."

Hunter raises an eyebrow at Ava, and she says in a more genuine voice, "Sorry."

Hunter looks at me with a knowing look that Ava is going to be trouble. He grabs my hand, though, and begins to pull me with him through the crowd with Ava still on my back. I'm not sure where we are going until I see the cameras, and then I freak out, trying to stop. Hunter doesn't let go of my hand, and I can't really stop him.

"Sorry about that. I had to say hi to my girlfriend and her daughter," Hunter says to the reporters.

"We completely understand. How proud are you to have been able to cheer your boyfriend on here today?" The reporter sticks the microphone in my face. I take a deep breath, hating that I am now on a camera in front of who knows how many people.

"We are super proud! He kicked some major ..."

Ava glances at Hunter. "Butt!"

The reporters laugh and give Ava a high-five and then turn their attention back to Hunter. I can't move because Hunter still has a firm grasp on my hand as he speaks.

"Thank you. We will let you get back to celebrating your win," the reporter says.

Hunter pulls hard on my hand and then his lips are on mine. I close my eyes and kiss him, not thinking about anything other than the kiss. When he pulls away, he's wearing a goofy grin on his face, and I look to my right and see all the cameras on me. I smile and Hunter kisses me on the cheek again.

"You're a lucky girl ...?" the reporter asks, trying to get my name.

"Quinn," Hunter answers. "And I'm the lucky one." He winks at them while he pulls my hand, and we walk away from the reporters.

"If you have to get back to your teammates or do more interviews, you can. We will be fine here and can catch up with you later."

Hunter freezes, looking at me a raised eyebrow. "Are you kidding me? I don't plan on spending time today with anyone else other than you and Ava. Everyone else can wait."

I smile, and Hunter leans into my ear as his hand goes to my ass. "Plus, your ass looks great in these jeans, and I can't leave you alone for someone else to steal."

Hunter kisses me on the cheek, and then he looks at Ava on my back.

"Why can Hunter say ass and not me?" Ava asks.

I glare at Hunter, who just laughs and then whispers something in Ava's ear before he looks back at me. I'm going to kill him later for teaching my four-year-old so many bad words. But I let it go for now. I look at him and ask him *what now*. He answers back with his eyes. *I don't know.*

TEXT MESSAGE #9

1 month earlier

hunter

MY PHONE BUZZES in my pocket while I'm eating a triple hamburger with Marshall after practice. I pull it out of my pocket and smile when I see Quinn's name on the screen.

"You aren't going to bail on me, man, are you?" Marshall asks with his mouth full.

"Nah. I know we want to go over some plays today. I would never pass up an opportunity to spend all afternoon watching film of how horrible you all played," I say, my voice dripping with sarcasm.

I open the text message and read.

Quinn: I need you. Tonight. :)

That's all she texts. I need you tonight followed by a smiley face. It's not often we get to text each other positive things. So whatever it is, I'm more than happy to go see her when things are positive.

I text back.

Me: Can't wait. ;)

"Earth to Hunter," Marshall says.

"What?" I say, not looking at Marshall; instead, I'm imagining what could make Quinn so happy that she would text me in this way instead of calling to see if I'm available. We only text when it's important. Otherwise, we call. It's the opposite of how most of the world uses their phone, but it works for us. Could she have found a new job? Gotten a better apartment?

My mind races, trying to figure out what good news she has to share with me tonight. Whatever it is, I'm going to make sure we celebrate it right.

"Are you done? We are supposed to meet the rest of the guys in ten minutes to go over the film."

"Yeah, I'm finished." I shove the rest of the burger into my mouth. "Let's go."

Quinn opens the door to her apartment with more tears streaming down her face than I think I've ever seen on her face. I was wrong. She's not happy. Something horrible happened.

I drop the flowers and bottle of champagne that I brought onto the floor, not caring if either of them break. I grab her and pull her to me. My hand tangles in her hair as my other arm wraps tightly around her body.

"Shh. I got you now. You're okay. You're going to be okay."

It doesn't stop her tears. She's crying so much that I'm not even sure she can speak right now if I asked her a question. I've never seen her like this. I've never seen her in this much pain. Usually, I would tell her to toughen up. That she needs to be strong to face and fight whatever happened. But the way her tears are streaming down her face, the way her body is trembling in my arms, the way her sobs scream out of her body, I know that's not how she needs to handle this. Whatever happened is bad, worse than anything we have ever experienced. I'm sure of it.

Her legs go weak, and I've never been more thankful to be holding her. Still, I'm not fully prepared to have the full weight of her body in my arms, so I decide it'd be best if we sit on the floor. I slowly lower her body to the floor as I sit down.

"Shh ... you're okay, Quinn. I've got you. You're going to be okay." I rock her back and forth in my arms. "I'm going to fix this. Whatever happened, we can fix it together." I don't know why I say that. Both of us have been through enough to know that things can't always be fixed. That sometimes things can't be fixed. Sometimes, things suck.

I say the words, though, meant to comfort her because right now, I have no idea what the fuck to say to her to make anything better. She needs me, so I'm here, but she would have been better off finding a stray dog to offer her comfort. The dog would do more to offer her comfort than I am.

Still, I keep trying. "Just get it all out. Just cry. I've got you. Nothin' is going to hurt you."

The rocking doesn't work, so I switch to holding her tightly in my arms.

Nothing works.

Quinn cries. Quinn sobs. Quinn trembles.

And I can't stop it.

I hate not being able to stop it for her. I'm supposed to be able to protect her. But I can't.

I'm out of ideas of how to help her. So instead, I do something selfish. I lift her chin and stare straight into her bloodshot eyes, ignoring the tears and snot covering her face from the sobbing, and I kiss her.

I don't know what I expect the kiss to do, but God, does it make me feel better. And now that I've tasted her sweet lips, I won't be able to stop. This may be the exact opposite of what she needs right now, but I need her. I need to kiss her. I need to fuck her.

My heart breaks to see her broken like this, and the only thing I can think about is fucking. God, something is wrong with me. It isn't the first time we have had sex shortly after a horrible event that left us broken. When we've done it before, it was exactly what we needed. A life-affirming moment connecting us and reminding us that life goes on. That there are still things to look forward to.

Maybe that's what we both need right now.

The only difference between those times and now is that I had a clue what was going on before. I knew what pain Quinn was dealing with. We had talked. We had stopped crying. We had faced what had happened.

But this time, I don't have a clue. And I'm too chicken to ask. Because I have a feeling I know what could have Quinn this upset. Only one thing could get Quinn this upset. And if I let my mind go there, I'm going to become a ghost of a man who won't be of any good to Quinn. So it's actually better that she isn't talking to me. That I don't know why she is this upset.

So instead of thinking, I kiss her, pushing my tongue deep inside her mouth. Begging her to kiss me back. To let me take the pain away, if only for a couple of minutes in the only way I know how.

I hear the faintest of moans coming from her, and it makes me stop for just a second. It must be my imagination. She didn't just moan. She doesn't want this. I should stop. I just can't. If I do, I'll let the pain come for me as well, and I just can't handle that.

Her hand grabs my hair rougher than she ever has and forces our lips together again. She wants this just as badly if not more than I do.

She's still crying, still in pain, as she kisses me, but I plan to make her forget everything.

I lift her body from the ground and carry her to the bedroom where I expect to find her bed. Instead, I find an empty room. I carry her back to the living room. Also empty.

Was she robbed?

Is that what this is all about?

If so, it's an easy fix. She has insurance that would replace all the stuff, or I would happily replace everything.

I shouldn't ask, but I do. "Were you robbed?"

"No."

She grabs my neck hard again and kisses me.

I know it won't take many more kisses for me to stop thinking with my mind and let another body part that is extremely hard right now take over, so I have to use what little brain power I have left wisely.

"Were you raped?"

She wipes some tears from her eyes.

"No."

I take a deep breath and then ask the one question I vowed I wouldn't ask until after, but I won't be able to focus if I don't know.

"Did something happen to Ava? Is she ... is she dead?"

Quinn sobs again, and my world slips away. She's dead. What the fuck is wrong with me? I almost fucked Quinn when she's in mourning over losing Ava.

"No," Quinn somehow squeaks out through her sobs.

No.

It's the most beautiful word I have ever heard fall from her lips. And I've heard a lot of amazing words. *Fuck. Hunter. Oh, God. I love you.* All amazing words. This word trumps them all.

I kiss her as I scan the room, looking for any place that is better than the carpet to fuck her on. There is a small ottoman, that I notice for the first time, pushed up against the counter that divides the kitchen and living room.

Fuck, this isn't going to be comfortable. My instinct is to throw her over the ottoman and take her from behind, but I need to see her eyes. I need to know she is okay. That she still wants this as I take her. So that's not an option.

I walk over to it and scoot it out into the living room with my foot while I hold Quinn. Her lips covering me in kisses show me how much she wants this too.

I sit down on the ottoman, and Quinn automatically moves to straddle my lap. She stops kissing me, and I look up at her tear-stained face, feeling guilty again for even suggesting this.

"Quinn?"

"I want this."

I take a deep breath, trying to decide what to do. Her words don't convince me to keep going. In fact, I swear I heard hesitation in her voice.

She kisses me again, putting everything she has into it, and when she pulls back, her tears seem to have slowed.

"I need this. I need you."

I kiss a tear that is falling down her cheek. "Then stop crying."

"I can't."

I search her eyes again, but I don't know what else to do other than give her this. Try it and hope she doesn't hate me afterward.

"Close your eyes," I say.

She does without hesitation.

I kiss each of her closed eyelids, trying to get rid of her tears.

"Now, stop thinking and just feel."

I watch as Quinn takes a deep breath.

"You're beautiful."

I kiss her neck and wait for the perfect little whimper she makes every time I kiss her there. When she does, I move my lips to the other side of her neck.

"You're a survivor. You will survive everything life throws at you."

I kiss the other side of her neck and wait for the same whimper again before I lift her shirt over her head and reveal her full breasts beneath a plain tan bra that has seen better days. But I don't care. She would look beautiful in anything.

"You're strong. One of the strongest women I know."

I kiss her breasts while I unhook her bra. I keep an eye on her, wanting her to keep her eyes closed. I want her to stay wherever her mind has taken her. I don't want her to open her eyes and be reminded of whatever is hurting her so much.

My hand goes to her jeans. I unbutton them and pull down the zipper and slip a finger beneath her jeans, hooking my finger beneath her panties. She sucks in a breath right on cue.

I smile as I stare at how beautiful she is. I need more. She needs to know that I think more of her than even she thinks I do.

"I love you."

"Mmmh," she moans.

It's not enough. I move my finger over her clit teasing her, taunting her.

"You're a fighter. The best fighter."

Her eyes fly open when I say that. She has been looking for me to say those words since the very first time I told her otherwise. That she wasn't a fighter.

Fuck. Tears are streaming down her face again. I shouldn't have said anything.

We don't say anything else, though. Instead, her mouth clashes with mine, and we both agree to let our bodies do any further talking.

She grabs at my jeans, and I lift her body off my lap so she can pull my cock free. Her body slides on top of me.

"Jesus Christ, Quinn."

She moves; I move with her.

I growl; she moans.

I kiss her; she claws at my back.

She slides up and down my cock; I grab her hips to help her move faster, harder.

She comes; I come.

We both breathe hard as we collapse on the rough carpeted floor. Quinn collapses next to me, but I pull her body on top of me and ready myself for the tears I'm sure will come back soon.

We both just lie like this as time passes. Both spent, happy, and content even though there is something horrible, darker that we have to deal with. The anxiety slowly creeps back inside me until I'm not sure I can take it any longer.

"Are you going to tell me?"

I stare at the ceiling and not at her as I ask her. She slowly gets off my chest until I have to look into her eyes. I watch them slowly fill again ready to burst at any second. Fuck, this is bad. Quinn never cries.

But then she smiles. A genuine, big Quinn smile, which leaves me even more confused.

"My application to adopt Ava has been approved. She's mine. I can pick her up tomorrow."

Quinn bursts into tears and the happiest smile I have ever seen.

I grab Quinn and roll her over, pinning her to the floor. "Fuck, Quinn." I run a hand through my hair, trying to keep from exploding with either frustration or happiness. "You should have told me that the second you opened the door instead of bursting into tears. I thought Ava had fucking died or something equally as horrible. I was imagining all these horrible things. How could you put me through that?"

She laughs. "I'm sorry. I was just so emotional. So happy that I couldn't speak. I couldn't even smile. The only way I could express my emotion was through tears."

I shake my head, beyond frustrated with her. But I'm not going to stay mad at Quinn. Today is a day to celebrate.

I kiss her on the lips. "I love you, but if you put me through anything like that again. I'm going to—"

"You're going to what?" she says, smiling at me.

I grin; I can't help it. "Kiss you and love you forever."

She crooks her finger at me, wanting me to kiss her again. "Good answer."

I sigh and kiss her. There is going to be a lot of kissing tonight.

"Why is there no furniture?" I ask.

"Because I sold it. I need the money to buy some things for Ava."

I frown. I don't want to fight with her again about money. My family has more money than we could ever spend, and I've tried to give her money to buy things before, and she has refused. But this is actually perfect. I can have the apartment filled with new furniture, and there is nothing she can do about it.

"Get dressed. I'm taking you out to dinner and then we can go over to my apartment tonight."

She smiles and kisses me and then jumps up and begins running toward her bedroom. My eyes stay on her naked ass as she runs. "Sounds perfect!" she shouts over her shoulder before disappearing into her bedroom.

It does sound perfect. It should be perfect. I just have to determine what the fuck I want anymore. Football, that's a given. Quinn, another given. Ava, I love her to death, but I'm not sure I can handle being a father. I'm only twenty-two. But Ava comes with Quinn now, and I'm not sure I could ever tell either of them goodbye; no matter how much we both thought this was just going to be a short-term thing. There is nothing short term about this. I'm in this for the long haul.

TEXT MESSAGE #8

2 weeks earlier

quinn

THE DOOR TO MY apartment bursts open, and Hunter comes in, running over to the living room where Ava and I are sitting on the couch putting together a puzzle I checked out from the library. I should have never given him a key.

"I'm taking you out on a date tonight. I've already got a babysitter for squirt here," Hunter says, picking Ava up and hugging her before he hugs me. It melts my heart to see him put her before me.

I frown, though, as I look at him. "I don't think that's a good idea."

"Why not?" He cocks his head to one side as he takes a seat on the couch, and Ava climbs up on his lap.

I dart my eyes from him to Ava and back, hoping he will get the hint that I don't know think it's a good idea for Ava to be watched by a babysitter. She's not officially mine yet. And I don't want to do anything that would impede my ability to get her. I don't trust anyone with her but myself and maybe Hunter.

He grins and then looks at Ava. "You want to hang out with my friend Marshall for a couple of hours tonight? He has an Xbox and a PlayStation and all sorts of video games."

Ava's face lights up. "Yes! I want to go."

Hunter looks at me and shrugs while I give him a glare. He knew that Ava would say yes to playing video games. She's a complete tomboy who loves anything that involves sports. Of course, she is going to want to go over to Marshall's and play video games.

"Hunter, I need to talk to you in my bedroom for a moment."

I get up from the couch and walk toward my bedroom. Ava gives Hunter an uh-oh face as Hunter gets up and follows me into my bedroom. I shut the door when he walks inside.

"What was that?" I say.

"What was what?"

"You can't undermine me in front of Ava. You knew I wouldn't be happy with Marshall, of all people, watching Ava. I'm not ready to leave her alone. You knew what I was saying, and you went ahead and got her excited about going to Marshall's. I don't want her to go to Marshall's."

"It's been six weeks, Quinn. We didn't even get to celebrate your birthday. We need to go out, just the two of us. Ava will be just fine with Marshall. He's actually really good with kids."

"I don't care if he is the best with kids, which I highly doubt anyway. I'm not ready."

Hunter steps closer to me, grabs me, and then dips me while he goes in for what should be a romantic kiss. I don't think it's that great until his lips hit mine. Then I remember what I've been missing these past few weeks. We've kissed, sure. But nothing with this much passion. We didn't want it to lead to more in front of Ava.

I've been too scared to leave Ava's sight. Not since that night six weeks ago when I got one of the worst calls of my life. I'm not letting her out of my sight. But this kiss does something to me I wasn't expecting. It makes me want Hunter more than I think I ever have. It makes me miss being loved by him.

"Don't be mad at me for missing you. If you really aren't ready, then we don't have to go. But I'm going to die if I don't have you soon. I'm desperate for you. So at least consider us all going over to Marshall's even if we just go into the next room for a little bit while Marshall and Ava play video games."

I nod, but I know I should let Ava go hang out with Marshall by herself. She and Marshall would actually get along great, and it would be good for her.

"Okay."

Hunter smiles. "Okay, what?"

"Okay, Marshall can watch Ava while we go to dinner and back to your place for a bit. But no more than three hours total."

"Deal."

***

"You know you could have just taken me to get a burger or pizza. You don't always have to take me to fancy restaurants," I say as I take a seat in the white tableclothed booth at the Italian restaurant where Hunter brought me.

He grins as he takes a seat across from me. "I know you're a cheap date."

"I am not cheap."

He raises an eyebrow.

"Fine, I'm cheap. But there is nothing wrong with being cheap."

"Nope. But you deserve better than cheap."

I shake my head as I begin to look over the menu, trying my best to avoid looking at the outrageous prices next to each menu item. I don't want to tell him, but I secretly love when he takes me to a nice restaurant like this.

"Can I get you anything to drink?" the waitress asks.

"Just water," Hunter says.

"Same," I say, cocking my head.

The waitress leaves and then I ask, "No wine?"

He grins. "Oh, so you do like it when I take you to nice restaurants and order nice bottles of wine."

I blush.

"I have an early morning practice tomorrow and don't need to be hung over. Plus, I want to get in and out of here as soon as possible. We are on a tight deadline." He winks at me.

I blush even redder. "Well, if that's the case, we'd better order and eat quickly." I move my foot forward and run it up and down the inside of his pants leg.

He narrows his eyes at me. "Or we could just skip dinner."

I grin.

He sighs. "But I think you are going to need your strength for what I have planned for you."

I glance down at the menu and then motion to the waitress.

"Are you two ready to order?"

We both nod, not taking our eyes off each other. Secretly undressing each other, I know neither of us will be able to wait until we get back to Hunter's place.

"We'll both have whatever your heartiest meal is. We both need our strength," I say, handing the waitress our menus.

The waitress staring at us is not sure what she should to do.

"Just bring us two pasta dishes," Hunter says, dismissing her.

The waitress leaves.

"Come sit next to me," Hunter says as he slides over on his side of the booth.

I get up and take a seat next to him, needing to be near him. Hunter tucks one arm around my back, pulling me as close to him as possible.

"Don't react," he says as he reaches down and touches my inner thigh underneath the skirt I'm wearing.

I react, though, because I wasn't expecting it. I gasp and then immediately bite my lip to stop myself from doing anything else. I glance around the room at all the other tables because I'm sure they know exactly what we are doing.

I try to wiggle away, but Hunter's hand holds me in place.

"No one can tell what we are doing, and even if they can, I don't care. I need you," Hunter whispers into my ear.

His hand moves higher up my thigh until his fingertips brush against my panties. I bite my lip harder, trying to keep from screaming because God have I missed his touch.

His fingers glide across my panties, but I need more. I need him inside me. I need …

I jump up.

"What are you doing?" Hunter asks, frowning.

I smile and then lean back down and kiss Hunter on the cheek. "I'll be right back; I'm going to go make access to certain places a little easier for you."

I wink and then head to the bathroom to remove the panties I'm wearing so that Hunter can give me what I really need.

I smile not really paying attention to where I'm walking because tonight is going to be perfect. I bump into someone. "Sorry, excuse me," I say trying to walk past again.

But I can't squeeze between the man and the row of booths. I frown and look up at the man, and that's when I recognize him. It's Hunter's father.

"Hi, Mr. Metcalf. We didn't realize you were eating at this restaurant tonight as well; otherwise, we would have invited you to join us." I try to smile even though I'm not really happy. I don't want to have dinner with Mr. Metcalf and Hunter. I want to go to the bathroom, remove my panties, and get fingered by my boyfriend. Not have a nice, polite dinner with Hunter and his parents.

"Quinn, you and I need to speak," Mr. Metcalf says, grabbing my arm.

I look down at where he is holding my arm and then back at up at him completely confused what about what the hell is going on.

"Okay?"

Mr. Metcalf begins pushing me toward the entrance of the restaurant. I let him for a few seconds because I don't want to make a scene in front of all these people, but the second we get to the empty hallway, I throw his hand off my arm. "You don't need to manhandle me. I'll go with you and talk to you if that's what you want."

He nods in the direction of the lobby, and I continue walking that way with him following behind me. He doesn't scowl. He doesn't frown or smile. He gives no emotion, no clue to how he feels as he walks behind me. But if the grip on my arm earlier was any indication, it's not good.

I stop when I get to the lobby and cross my arms as I turn to wait for him to tell me whatever is so important.

"Outside," he says.

"Tell me what you want to talk to me about first."

"No, outside."

I hesitate. I really wish Hunter were here to deal with his ridiculous father. But it's probably best that he isn't. They don't really get along, from the few times I've seen them together. So I decide to go along with his demand and walk outside. Hopefully, I can just deal with whatever he wants without Hunter ever having to find out that we spoke.

The sun is setting when I walk outside. Seeing all the different colors is beautiful. It must be a good sign.

I turn around and again cross my arms, waiting for Mr. Metcalf to tell me what he needs to say.

"Stay away from my son."

I frown. I was expecting an insult. I was expecting him to say something about how I need to support Hunter's football career. I expect him not to be upset that I'm consuming so much of Hunter's time, but I didn't expect him to tell me to stay away from Hunter.

"Excuse me?"

"You heard me. Stay away from my son."

"I'm sorry if you don't like me, Mr. Metcalf, but I love your son very much and whether I continue to see him is really a decision for me and Hunter to make."

"No, it's not. Hunter has worked too hard to have a gold digger like you come in and ruin everything."

I frown. "I'm not a gold digger. I have never taken a penny from Hunter!"

He shakes his head. "No, that's true because Hunter doesn't have his own money yet. It's my money. You need to stay away from him."

"I can't do that. I love him. I want him to succeed and make it to the NFL just like you do."

"If you love him, you will stay away from him."

I don't know what to say to that. But when I look at him, I don't see an evil man who hates me and just doesn't want his son dating someone who he feels is beneath his son. When I look at him, I see a man who loves his son and seems genuinely worried that I'm going to ruin everything for his son.

Mr. Metcalf motions to something behind me and a blacked-out sedan pulls up. He walks over to the back of the car and opens the door.

"Get in, Quinn."

I stare at the car. *How did tonight go so differently than what I expected? How did it all go so wrong?*

I walk toward the car and hesitate at the door. "I should talk to Hunter."

"No. I'll take care of Hunter. You just go. I'll even pay off your college loans and pay your rent until you finish college if that's what it takes to get you to leave. But trust me, you don't know what Hunter has been through. You don't know how you are jeopardizing everything by being with him.

You don't have one clue. So get in the car and don't look back."

I get in the car. I shouldn't. I absolutely shouldn't. But I do. For some stupid reason, I trust him at this moment. I trust he needs a moment with Hunter more than Hunter and I need time together. That for whatever reason he thinks we shouldn't be together, he is genuine in that thought. And he needs to share that with Hunter.

So I get in the damn car. I watch him shut the door, and the driver begins to drive me away. It only takes me a moment longer to realize that getting in the car was a mistake.

"Can you turn around?" I ask the driver.

"Sorry, can't do. I have strict instructions to take you to a hotel tonight a couple of hours from here."

Crap.

I pull out my phone and send a text.

hunter

MY PHONE BUZZES, and I pull it out of my pocket and smile when I see that it's from Quinn. Probably wants me to meet her in the bathroom or the car or something. I open the message and frown as I read.

Quinn: I need you. Your father is at the restaurant. He talked to me and convinced me to get in a car, but I realized it was a mistake. Talk to your father. Then come talk to me.

Shit. Fuck. Shit.

I run my hand through my hair, and then I'm up out of the booth to go after her. I don't know what I'm going to do or how I'm going to figure out where my father sent her, but I'm not going to wait for him to come talk to me about whatever fucking reason he is going to give me for trying to make decisions in my life.

I run out of the restaurant and then I see him standing just outside on his phone looking smugly at me.

141

"What the hell did you do?"

"I saved your life."

"You don't get to fucking make decisions about my life!"

"Then start making better decisions yourself!"

"What did you say to her?"

"The truth."

"Which is?"

"That if she loved you, she would let you go. That she's not the right girl for you."

I have never wished I didn't have a father more than I do right now. We've been through some shitty stuff, but this is ridiculous.

"You're wrong."

"I'm not. I'm not going to let you ruin your life by being with this girl. You don't get to do something so stupid."

"I'll bite because it's obvious you aren't going to leave me alone until I hear you out. Why shouldn't I be with Quinn?"

"Because as much as you have tried to move past your past, you know that you won't survive another heartache. And sooner or later, Quinn is going to be the cause of that heartache. She'll decide you two aren't right for each other. She'll fall in love with another man. She'll cheat."

"Watch yourself."

"Or something bad will happen. She'll get sick. Cancer or something. Get into a car accident. Or something will happen to that little girl who she is so in love with. Something will happen and soon. Love doesn't last, not when you are this age. And when whatever happens, it's going to tear you up in a way that nothing ever has before. You won't be able to recover this time. And I just don't want you to give up everything you have worked your whole life for, for this girl."

"Where is she?"

"Just think about it tonight. Tomorrow, you can talk to her."

He walks away, and I resist the urge to run him over with my car. Instead, I just walk to my car and text Quinn. She can give me enough directions that I'll be able to find her eventually. Even if it takes me all night.

It's three a.m. when Quinn finally opens the door to the hotel room my father sent her to. It took me most of the night to track her down and find this hotel in Colorado Springs. Mostly because Quinn couldn't make up her mind if she wanted me to come see her or not and inadvertently sent me on a wild goose chase instead of just telling me where my father sent her.

I want to yell at her. My plan was to yell when I got here because I've spent the night alone driving through a thunderstorm instead of with her. When I could have been here hours ago.

"I want to yell at you," I say as she holds the door open to let me inside.

"Then yell."

"I can't."

She ties the robe she is wearing around her waist. Her wet hair is dripping and making a small puddle on the ground. She must have just finished showering, or maybe she took a long bath.

"You should yell. It will make you feel better."

I grab her and pull her into my arms realizing I really need that. Not to yell, at least not at her.

"You're not the one I should yell at. I was just scared. And frustrated that you let my father come between us."

She pulls away and goes over to the small couch. She curls her legs up underneath her.

"Hunter, we need to talk."

"No. We need to fuck. We need to forget that the past few hours even happened; that whatever my father said to you doesn't matter. I want to fuck you then sleep all night with you in my arms before we order room service in bed in the morning and do it all again. That's what I want. That's what you want. So please just forget about my father. He doesn't matter."

She fidgets with the tie that wraps around her waist. She doesn't look at me.

I sigh and take a seat next to her on the couch. When I've resigned, she says, "I love you, but you're better off without me, right?"

I jump off the couch. "What the hell, Quinn? Really, that's what you really think? We've been through all this crap together, and you let one sentence from my father ruin everything."

"It's true, though. I don't want it to be true, but it is. We've both known that we shouldn't date from day one."

"But we are dating! And this is working." I grab the base of my neck to keep from screaming.

Quinn stands and grabs my hand, stroking my hand gently with her thumb. I know she intends to calm me down, but it's only turning me on.

"I want to throw you on the bed, tie you up, and fuck you until you realize how ridiculous you are right now."

She smiles. "As much as I would love to be tied up since we never have before, we both know the truth. That this won't last forever. You've said so yourself."

"Does this need to last forever to make it worthwhile right now?"

She walks away and sits down on the bed before running her hand through her still damp hair. "No, you're right. I don't need forever. Not when one night could last forever."

I look in her eyes and then I'm on top of her. Kissing her, demanding her to be mine for tonight.

"Tie me up, Hunter. I want to know what it's like to be completely under your control—completely yours—if I'm not going to get forever."

I grin, grabbing the tie that goes around her robe, and then grab her arms, lifting them high above her head.

"I'm going to make sure that tonight will be ingrained in both of our memories forever. So even if we can't be together forever, we will always have tonight."

TEXT MESSAGE #7

6 weeks earlier

hunter

MY PHONE BUZZES on my nightstand. I glance up. It's before five in the morning. Morning practice isn't until seven. I hit the alarm off. Marshall, my roommate, will make sure I'm up in time to get to practice. I don't even know why I need an alarm.

I close my eyes, hoping I can go back to sleep so I'm not dead at practice. I can't afford to be dead at practice. We have a couple of important games coming up that we have to win if we want a chance to go to the championships.

"Hunter! Get up!" Marshall yells.

I groan. There is no way it has been an hour since I closed my eyes.

"It's not time to get up yet."

"Hunter! You really need to get up."

"This really isn't cool, dude. I need sleep."

"Hunter, it's Quinn."

I pop up and grab my phone confused why she would call Marshall instead of texting me. That's when I see the message she sent about fifteen minutes ago.

I read the message.

Quinn: I need you. Now. Come to the hospital.

"Shit."

I jump out of bed and pull some pants and a shirt on that I'm not even sure are clean. I need keys, though, to get to the hospital. I begin shuffling through the pile of dirty clothes on the floor, looking for my keys in the pockets of one of the pants.

"Hunter, what are you doing? You need to get to the hospital now."

I freeze. "Is she? What happened?"

"She wouldn't tell me, but—"

"You mean you talked to Quinn? She's okay?"

"Quinn's okay, but Ava. She's not doing well. She mentioned a ventilator."

I start digging through my pile of clothes again, frantic to find my keys.

"Hunter, what are you doing?"

"Don't ask me fucking questions right now; I need to focus and find my damn keys so I can get out of here!"

I grab another pair of jeans, and after finding the pockets empty, I throw the jeans at Marshall in frustration. I don't know what is wrong with Ava. But I know Quinn must be scared to death. I'm scared to death.

Something hard hits me in the back. I turn and see Marshall's keys lying on the floor at my feet. I reach down and pick them up.

"Take my car and get your ass out of here."

I don't ask questions; I just grab his keys and start running through the apartment to the door.

"My car is parked out back! And I want an update as soon as you find out. Nothing can happen to Ava."

I don't stop to respond. I just turn on my heels and head toward the back of our apartment and run out the door. I run, and I already know this is bad. I hate hospitals. Nothing ever good happens in hospitals. I shake my head.

That's not true. One good thing has happened in a hospital, or maybe that was a bad thing. I don't really know. Either way, I know whatever waits for me when I get to the hospital is bad. Possibly the worse thing I have ever faced. And I know there is nothing I can do to fix it. Nothing I can do to take the pain away for any of us.

quinn

I SEE HIM RUNNING down the hallway toward me, and he looks as scared as I feel. His face is whiter than a ghost, his hair is disheveled, and his clothes are mismatched and dirty.

But he's here.

His arms go around me, and for a second, the world doesn't seem so bad. For a second, I think I can get through today.

"How is she?" he asks.

And then my world shatters.

"I don't know. They won't tell me since I'm not family. But it's bad, Hunter. I got a glimpse of her when they wheeled her into the operating room. There were tubes everywhere. It was bad."

He holds me tighter.

"I know we don't say things without already knowing the outcome. That we tell each other to suck it up; things could be worse. We tell each other the truth. But I really need you to tell me that everything is going to be okay. That Ava is going to be just fine."

Hunter exhales deeply. "Ava is going to be fine."

The tears come, but I refuse to let them out. I need to be strong for Ava.

"Thanks for lying to me."

"I didn't lie. Ava is one of the strongest people I know."

"Who is the other?"

"The girl I'm holding in my arms."

I melt in his arms.

He scoops me up, and we sit on the small couch in the waiting room.

"Tell me what you do know," Hunter says.

"Ava's foster sister found Ava not breathing and called 911."

"I didn't know Ava had a foster sister?"

"It was a recent change. Ava's foster parents needed more money, so they got another foster child. She's twelve."

"It's a good thing she was there."

I nod. "I wish I could have been there. I wish I could go see her in the hospital room. I've been trying to find her foster parents to see if they will let me see Ava, but I haven't seen them."

"They are probably with Ava," Hunter says.

"Maybe ... I just have a bad feeling about this. About everything."

Hunter squeezes me close, and I rest my head on his chest.

"I just wish I could adopt her now or become her foster parent now. I know I don't have a lot of money, and I wouldn't be able to provide for her in ways that others could, but I love her. More than her foster parents do."

"Why can't you adopt her now?"

I sigh. "Because you have to be twenty-one in the state of Colorado to adopt. I still have another five weeks to go."

"Ava is going to be fine. I'm sure this is just something small, and they brought her here just as a precautionary measure. She's going to be just fine, and in five weeks, she is going to be yours."

I nod slowly against his chest but don't really believe him. Something is wrong. Five weeks is way too long. And there is no guarantee that I will be able to adopt her in five weeks anyway; even though I submitted the papers months ago, it doesn't mean anything.

Anything could happen.

Hunter rubs his hand through my long hair as I do my best to relax.

"Just try to sleep. I'm sure we will learn how Ava is doing soon. There is nothing we can do right now but be here for Ava and try to relax."

"Don't you have practice today, though? You don't need to stay. I'm okay now; I just needed reassurance. I can text you any updates."

Hunter's eyes are wide as he lifts my chin just a little to look at him. "I'm not going anywhere. I promised I would always be here for you. And I want to be here for Ava."

I don't question him again. I just lie in his lap and let him stroke my hair and pretend everything is going to be okay. Even if I've never believed that before, I have to believe it now. I need to believe it now.

"Hey, wake up," Hunter says into my ear before he kisses me on the ear.

I open my eyes immediately, terrified that something happened while I was asleep. I never expected to actually fall asleep, but Hunter made it so easy in his arms. So comfortable that I couldn't resist.

"Is she okay?"

He nods. "We can go in to see her now."

I sit up completely awake now. "What? Really? How?"

"I'll tell you later. Right now, Ava needs you."

That's all I need to hear. I get up and begin running down the hallway even though I have no idea which room she is in.

"Left," Hunter shouts behind me.

I turn left, scanning each room as I run by, desperately looking for her room and assuming I'm going to get stopped by a nurse or security or someone telling me that I'm not supposed to be here.

I see a nurse walking toward me, and I know I'm going to lose it if she tells me I'm not supposed to be here.

"Are you Hunter Metcalf?" the nurse asks, stopping us both.

"Yes," Hunter says.

"I'm going to need to see some ID."

Hunter pulls out his wallet and hands her his ID.

She turns to me. "And you are?"

"I'm Quinn Ashby."

"She's my girlfriend and roommate. I put her on the application, and she was approved."

The nurse nods.

"Okay, Ava is in the room here to your left. She's been through a lot but has been asking for you, Quinn. She has a lot of tubes and things connected to her but don't let that shock you. She's doing well. I think she will make a full recovery."

"Can I see her now?" I ask.

She smiles and leads me into the room, and it takes all my strength not to lose it when I see her lying in the bed.

Ava looks at me, though, and her face brightens, and I see the tiniest of smiles.

I run over to her and take her sweet little hand in mine and kiss it over and over.

"You came," Ava says.

I frown. "Of course, I came, Ava. I've been here all night waiting for them to let me see you. I love you. I would do anything for you."

"I love you too, Mommy," Ava says and then realizes what she said.

I shake my head. "Call me whatever you want, my little goldilocks."

Ava smiles and then coughs. "I don't feel good."

I stroke her hair, trying to comfort her the best I can.

"I know. But I'm here now, and I'm not leaving your side until you feel a lot better."

She smiles again. "Good. Will you get me ice cream? Ice cream always makes me feel better."

I smile. "I'll see what I can do."

"Is Hunter here?"

I look over my shoulder at Hunter, who is hiding in the corner of the room watching us. I extend my hand to him and wave him over so that Ava can see him.

She squeals a little when she sees him. He leans down and kisses her on the forehead. "I missed you, squirt."

"I missed you too, Hunter."

"I'm going to go see about that ice cream for you," Hunter says, and I can see the tears in his eyes. Hospitals are hard for him, and seeing her like this is tearing him up.

"No, stay. I want us to all be together." She doesn't have to add forever. It's implied in her little voice. She pushes a button, and a nurse runs in. "See that's what the nurses are here for to get me ice cream. That's what Miss Lori said."

"That's right. I'll go get you some ice cream, Miss Ava," Miss Lori, the nurse, says before winking at us and then leaving.

I watch as Ava's eyes get tired again. She's hooked up to a lot of tubes and wires, and I'm sure she's on a lot of medications. I don't even really know what's wrong with her. But I'm sure everything her little body is going through is making her exhausted even though her eyes try to fight it.

"It's okay, Ava; you can sleep. I'll be right here when you wake up, and I'll make sure to wake you when your ice cream comes."

"Both of you will be here?"

"Of course," Hunter says. "And in a few days when you feel all better, you are going home with us."

She smiles. "Really?"

"Yep. You're ours now."

She closes her eyes. "Good. I've always known you were my real parents."

It takes her two heavy breaths, and then she is asleep. I keep holding her hand as I turn to look at Hunter.

"You can't promise her things you can't give her. I already told you I'm not old enough to adopt her or foster her. The state won't let me until I turn twenty-one."

"Yeah, but I am old enough," Hunter says.

A tear I've been holding in all day rolls down my cheek. "What? What do you mean?"

"When you were asleep, I talked to Ava's caseworker. Her foster parents abused her, and that's why she is in the hospital. Her father beat her so hard that it knocked her unconscious. A rib went through one of her lungs."

I'm crying now. I can't help it, thinking about what she went through, and I wasn't there for her.

"Her caseworker was saying it was too bad you weren't old enough to foster or adopt her, or they would give her to you immediately. But since you weren't, they would have to put her in a new home for at least six months before you would be able to adopt her to ease the transition. I asked if I could foster her. I put in an application, and they approved it immediately."

I bawl into Hunter's chest.

"I put down your address as my home address. I wrote that you were my roommate. She's going to be able to live with you. She's yours even if the papers don't officially say it yet. She's always been yours."

I cry and laugh and say, "Is this your sly plan to convince me that we should move in together?"

He kisses me on the forehead. "It's definitely a bonus."

hunter

"WE SHOULD HAVE moved into Hunter's place. His is nicer. But I like it here too," Ava says as she walks into Quinn's apartment for the first time.

"Hey, nothing's wrong with my apartment," Quinn says.

"I know. I just like Hunter's better. He has a bigger TV, and he has an Xbox," Ava says.

I laugh. "I can bring those all over here."

She smiles. "Good."

Ava looks down at the one teddy bear she brought with her. One that Quinn bought her for her birthday last year.

"What's wrong?" I ask, kneeling in front of Ava.

"This isn't going to last forever, is it?" she says in her tiny, weak voice.

I stand back up because I honestly have no idea how to answer her. I have no idea if I should be honest with her or lie to her. *What are you supposed to tell a four-year-old? How are you supposed to explain complicated things?*

Quinn steps in and scoops Ava up and takes a seat on the couch with Ava in her arms. "Bad things happen, Ava.

I'm not going to lie. I can't promise that you will never end up in the hospital again. I can't promise that you will always get to live here with us. I can't promise that something might happen to me that will make it impossible for me to be in your life."

Ava frowns.

"But I can promise you that as long as I'm alive, I will love you. You will always be loved. And you can always come to me with anything. Whether I get to be your real mother or not, I will always think of you as my daughter. And I promise you that the only thing that matters is that you will always be loved."

Ava hugs Quinn.

"I wish I could promise you more. I wish I could tell you that life is always good and easy and right. Because if it were up to me, you would be mine right now, and I would never let you go again."

Quinn strokes Ava's hair. "You don't need to worry about any of that stuff right now, though. You're safe here. And I love you."

Ava yawns. "I love you too."

Quinn smiles sadly, her eyes drooping down as she looks at Ava.

I walk over and lift Ava out of Quinn's arms and carry her to the bed I bought for her. Although I told Quinn that the adoption agency donated one of their unused ones to us. Ava's bed is next to Quinn's bed in her bedroom, and I tuck her in. Quinn couldn't handle Ava being alone, and I don't think Ava could handle being alone. So that is why they will share a room for a little while at least.

I kiss Ava on the forehead and then walk back to the living room where Quinn is still sitting on the couch looking completely broken. I take a seat next to her.

"If it's possible, I think I love you even more," I say.

She narrows her eyes at me and then shakes her head softly. "I think you are crazy. I'm a mess. I don't know what I'm going to do if someone else adopts Ava, if I don't get to keep her. She's my everything. I've always told you that you were the one who saved me, but while you played a huge role, you weren't the one who saved me. Ava was."

I nod. "I think I always knew that."

"My neighbors, her foster parents, adopted her the day after we met. She saved me. She became everything I focused my life on. She became the love of my life. But I won't survive if they take her away again."

"You're not going to have to live without her again. She's here until the adoption papers go through and can be finalized."

"But what if—"

I kiss her on the lips and then hold her tight. "Then you will do what you told her. You'll love her no matter what. You'll love her forever."

TEXT MESSAGE #6

1 month earlier

quinn

"YOU'D BETTER TIP better this time," I say with a wink as I hand Hunter the bill he owes for the pizza and beer.

"Oh, you know I will. I just have to get you back to my place later," he says.

I laugh. "I can't. I have to work late tonight. Besides, I'm not your girlfriend, and I've already spent every night with you this week. I thought you would have a hot date with someone else tonight."

He frowns. He knows it's the truth. We promised we wouldn't start dating because we knew it would never last. *So why even start?* That what we have between us is just sex and friendship. Nothing more. But so far, neither of us has dated other people, so we basically are dating without the title. Which isn't going to work.

Mandy brushes past me. "You have another table."

I sigh. "I'll be right back." I turn but realize the table is only one away, and it's Chaz. The only guy other than Hunter who has been trying to get me to go out with him. A guy I have absolute no interest in. I was just his tutor for all of five minutes, and I don't want to have to wait on him.

I glance around for Mandy to see if she'll swap a table with me, but she has disappeared.

I'll just get his drink order, I decide. I walk over to his table.

"Hi Chaz, what can I get you to drink?"

He smiles at me and checks out my legs and boobs, which makes me uncomfortable.

"Whatever you recommend."

I resist the urge to roll my eyes. "It depends on what you want. But beer is always a good choice. We have several local choices."

"Then bring me your favorite beer."

I nod and head to the bar to put the order in. I still don't see Mandy when his beer is ready, so I walk it back to his table, and when I do, I see Camille sitting at Hunter's table. They are both talking and smiling. I know there is history between Camille and Hunter, but he has never told me what their connection is. But it always makes me uncomfortable anytime they are together. The way they look at each other is *different*. It's different from even the way Hunter looks at me.

"Here's your beer. I'll be back in a minute to take your order," I say to Chaz, moving to Hunter's table before Chaz has a chance to flirt again or ask me out again.

"Hey Camille, it's good to see you again. Can I get you anything?"

"No, I'm good thanks. I just spotted Hunter through the window and wanted to say hi, but I'm sure the two of you have plans tonight. I should go."

Hunter opens his mouth to say something, but instead, I say, "Nope, we don't have plans tonight. We aren't dating, despite the rumors going around campus. But you two. You two would make quite a good pair. You two should go out tonight."

I grab the cash that Hunter laid down on the table as his angry gaze lands on me. I look up and give him a smile and wink, and then I leave them alone. I have no idea why I just did that. I know we need to date other people. That I can't get too attached to Hunter. He's not mine. Not really. And even if we were dating, he wouldn't really be mine. *But why did I have to set him up with Camille?* Of all the women, I chose Camille. The one woman who I would actually be jealous of. I can't imagine them kissing, or him having his hands on her. They might even fuck tonight.

Dammit. What the hell was I thinking?

I walk back over to Chaz's table. "Are you ready to order?"

"I am, but I want to take my time. Order an appetizer, then a salad, then my meal, then dessert."

"You must be really hungry?"

Chaz smiles. "No, I just want to spend as much time with you as possible since you won't go out on a date with me. I guess I'll be spending a lot more time here until I get you to go out with me."

"And what makes you think I will ever go out with you?"

"I don't. But I'm persistent, and persistence usually works. Eventually."

"Well, what appetizer do you want?"

"What appetizer takes the longest to make?" he asks, cocking his head to the side in a similar way to what Hunter does.

"The pizza rolls usually take the longest."

"I'll have that then."

I begin to write it down on the small pad of paper I use to keep track of everyone's orders on when someone brushes past me. I look up and see Camille smiling as she leads Hunter out of the bar. Hunter stops and says into my ear, "This only works if you date someone too. Tell Chaz yes now, or I won't go out with Camille."

He takes a step away, but he's still watching me.

I hate him. I send him a glare that makes my feelings known. Hunter just raises one eyebrow, though, waiting for me to tell Chaz yes before he leaves.

"Chaz, I changed my mind. I'll go out with you tonight after I get off work."

Chaz glances from me to Hunter and then back again to me, clearly realizing something is going on. He slowly smiles. "Excellent."

hunter

WHY THE FUCK did I tell Quinn we needed to see other people to make this work? I never thought she would actually want to see other people. I just wanted to make it clear that we aren't serious. That we *can't* be serious. But now, I'm holding Camille's hand as we walk toward a late-night club, something I never thought I would be doing, ever.

Camille shivers a little in the cold night air as we walk hand in hand although it's really not that cold out. She's just cold because she's wearing a skimpy dress, and she wants me to give her my jacket. I'm not giving her my jacket. If I do, I'll never get it back, and it will give the impression something more is going on here than just humoring Quinn. Because I don't want to let Quinn know I really don't want to date anyone else. I don't want to fuck anyone else, and I can't imagine Quinn's lips on anyone else. In fact, it makes me so angry that I think about punching any guy who lays a hand on her. And I'm not a violent person. I may play football, but that's usually where I let all my rage out. On the field.

"Let's go in here," Camille says, tugging me in the direction of a club I've been in countless times. A club that is well-known by every one of my college buddies. A club I've taken Quinn to before.

"Nah, that place is overrated. Let's try somewhere more low key," I say.

Camille doesn't stop; instead, she pulls harder. "Oh, come on. I know you go in here all the time, and I really want to dance."

I groan but let her pull me into the club anyway. I can dance with her for a few hours, get her good and drunk, and then drop her off at her place, and she won't question why I didn't kiss her at the end of the night or why I didn't try to sleep with her when I have the reputation of sleeping with women after the first date.

Once inside, Camille heads straight to the bar. As soon as the bartender spots me, she comes over despite the fact that the bar is completely full and it's clear that everyone else standing here has been waiting for a long time to get a drink. But that's the benefit of being the best player on the football team. Everybody knows who I am. And everybody wants to impress me.

"It's been a while since I've seen you in here, Hunter," the bartender says while she flutters her eyelashes at me and leans over the bar to get as close to me as possible.

"Yeah, been a bit busy," I say.

"That's what I've heard," she says, winking at me. "What can I get you and Qui..." She stops when she sees I'm with Camille instead and raises an eyebrow, looking at me curiously.

"I'll have a beer. Camille will have an old fashioned."

Camille nods.

I hate that I know her drink order, but I do. That's what happens when I've been good friends with her since high school.

The bartender frowns and then walks away to begin making our drink order. That's when I realize I should know this girl's name. I'm pretty sure I've made out with her before, maybe even fucked her before. I don't know. The women in my life all blend. Only a handful of women have made any sort of impression on my life. Four, to be exact. Four women have changed my life, each in powerful ways. Three of them are still in my life. Camille, Quinn, and Ava.

I really need to get that number down to two.

She comes back with our drinks. I hand her a couple of twenty dollar bills to cover the drinks and a nice tip to make up for the fact I can't remember her name.

"Thanks," I say, raising my beer, and then lead Camille over to the crowded dance floor to enjoy our drinks and "dance." Although with this crowd, I wouldn't really consider it dancing since there isn't room to move.

Camille says something—at least, I assume she says something because her mouth is moving, but I don't hear a word of it.

I just smile and nod, realizing a benefit of coming here. I can't hear Camille, which will leave me to think about Quinn and where Chaz is taking her on their "date." Probably someplace cheesy and boring. A romantic movie, the park, maybe ice skating, or something like that. He didn't take her to a club. He didn't take her dancing. He didn't take her anyplace that would require him to look cool or get close to Quinn. I doubt he gets further than a chaste kiss when he drops her off at a reasonable hour of the evening around midnight or something. No, I have nothing to worry about Chaz taking Quinn out on a date.

I look back at Camille and watch as her hips sway to the beat of the music. She finishes her drink, and I flag down one of the bar girls carrying shots. I buy one for Camille, who takes it without even noticing that I don't take one. The bartender takes our empty glasses, and then Camille leans in closer this time to say, "Dance with me."

I begin moving to the music, but I keep a respectable distance between us. Our bodies aren't really touching so much as moving to the beat in the same general area. She tries to move closer, but I maintain distance between us. It feels awkward; I've never danced this far away from a woman before. I know that dancing close to a woman is the best way to get her to come home with me that night. But I've never not wanted to take a woman home before. So I keep dancing, keeping my space, but then I stop altogether when I see Quinn.

Quinn's across the dance floor laughing. I expect that she lost Chaz and instead found Mandy or one of her other friends to hang out with after work. That it was Mandy who made her laugh. But then Chaz comes into view, and I cock my head to the side completely confused as to what is happening. Chaz isn't cool. He would never take her here.

Yet here they are, but they are just drinking at the edge of the crowd. They aren't dancing and not even really a part of the group. I relax a little when I see they are just drinking.

"It would help if you would move. I know you can dance better than that," Camille says into my ear. She had taken the opportunity to move into my arms when I was paying attention to Quinn and Chaz.

I start dancing with her automatically like I would with any other girl who I was taking on a date. Camille flashes me a smile when I do. "That's the Hunter I know."

I grin although it's not at her; it's because Quinn looks gorgeous standing in a dress I bought her to go out with me last weekend when she said she only owned one dress. She looks hot as hell. The blue dress brings out the hint of blue in her gray eyes, it cuts off around mid-thigh, making her legs look long and her ass look amazing. Her hair is braided like it often is when she doesn't want to fuss with it. And she has the tiniest hint of makeup on, which is a rarity since she doesn't spend her money on frivolous things and ensures any makeup she does own lasts all year. I'm a bit surprised that she took the time to change after she got off work.

"Beautiful," I say.

Camille kisses me on the cheek. "You don't look too bad yourself."

I frown when I realize that Camille thinks I just called her beautiful.

I spin her around, so she is no longer looking at me and feel her ass back up against me; my hands grab her hips, and her ass rubs against the crotch of my jeans as she does her best to turn me on.

I glance over at Quinn, and Chaz is holding her hand, leading her to the dance floor. I hate and love it at the same time. I hate his hands on her, but love that she is coming closer to me.

They stop a little bit away, but it isn't before Quinn spots me. She flashes me a sweet smile but immediately turns her attention back to Chaz, who starts dancing with her. Quinn isn't a dancer, but she goes along with Chaz. Chaz, on the other hand, is an excellent dancer.

He makes Quinn look like a dancer. He makes her laugh. He makes her smile. I've done the same thing dancing with her, but I thought it was because what we had was special, but now, I'm not so sure.

I keep dancing with Camille, but then I catch Quinn sneaking glances in our direction, and I realize who she is really smiling for. Me. Because she is mine. Not his. She will never be his.

I pick up my dancing and pretend I'm dancing with Quinn. Which only makes her watch me closer. I kiss Camille's neck, and Quinn bites her lip. I smile when I see her react to what I'm doing to Camille, so I take it one step further, tugging on Camille's ear. Quinn runs her tongue across her lip.

I grin. Until I see Chaz's lips touch Quinn's. Then my body fills with rage. Instant horrible rage. I'm sure my face is red with my blood pumping fast throughout my body ready to attack if need be.

When Chaz stops kissing her, though, and I see her look at me, it stops me from killing him. Because I see the shock in her eyes from his kiss, and I see the love in her eyes when she looks at me.

I watch as Chaz whispers something in Quinn's ear. She nods, and then they are walking out of the club. She glances over her shoulder just before they leave to look at me, but I can't read her face. I don't know what she is thinking.

I try to keep dancing with Camille. I try, but I can't. My heart is racing as I think about Quinn kissing Chaz again.

I'm sweating as I think about Quinn inviting him into her place.

"I'm sorry. I need to go," I say, stopping dancing with Camille suddenly.

I start walking out of the club, but Camille runs in front of me.

"Why?" she asks.

"Sorry, something came up."

She smiles. "Like your dick?"

I clear my throat. "No. I'm sorry, Camille. I'll talk to you later; I really need to go."

"I think you should consult your dick first because I'm pretty sure he would disagree with you and think you should fuck me instead."

I shake my head. "Camille, you and I are never going to be anything other than friends. I was just trying to prove a point to Quinn. I was turned on back there because of Quinn, not you. I'm sorry, but I really have to go."

Camille stands in front of me frozen. Her eyes are wide, and her lips are parted like she has no idea how to react or what to say. I hate that I just hurt her, but I really can't waste any time here with her.

I dig into my pocket to pull out my phone to get an Uber for her. "I'll get you an Uber home."

"Fuck you, Hunter! Don't bother, I'll find someone else to take me home," Camille says, heading back into the crowd, and I have no doubt that's the truth. She will find a guy to go home with tonight if she wants, but I don't have time to ensure that she goes home with a good guy instead of the douchebag she is likely to end up with. Instead, I run outside and pull the one card that I can to get Quinn to do whatever I want.

I begin texting.

Me: I need you. Right the fuck now. Ditch that asshole and tell me where to meet you. Where you want me to pick you up.

I'm just about to press send when I get a text message. I open the message and grin.

Quinn: I need you to meet me around the corner at the park in five minutes.

Thank fucking God. She didn't go home with that asshole. And she can't stand this any more than I can. But now I don't have to worry about admitting how much it drove me crazy to see her with another man.

I text her back.

Me: Be there soon.

I don't want her to think I already got rid of Camille before she texted me, so I take my time walking to the park. When I get there, I see her sitting on one of the old park benches looking worried. She looks up at me with her sad eyes, and I can't act cool any longer. I rush toward her, and she stands up from the bench, which makes it all the easier to pick her up and twirl her around while kissing her.

She grins against my lips as I kiss her over and over. Chicken pecks. Long kisses. And everything in between. I kiss her over and over, claiming her and letting her know she is mine. Not anyone else's.

When I put her feet back on the ground, she wears a gorgeous smile on her lips as she says, "Good. I was afraid you didn't feel the same way."

I kiss her again. "And what way is that?"

"That you love me and can't stand to watch me out with anyone else. That you want me to be yours."

I nod. "You're mine. Don't go on a date with anyone else ever again."

"Deal. As long as you don't go on a date with anyone else ever again."

"I won't go on a date with anyone else." I kiss her neck. "I won't kiss anyone else's neck like this." I kiss her lips. "I won't kiss anyone else, just you."

She smiles. "And why is that?" She raises an eyebrow, taunting me a little, but I see her chest rising and falling quickly. She's eager to hear my words because I still haven't said what she wants to hear.

I could be cruel and mean like I have been before, but I want to mark my claim to my girl because she is mine and needs to hear the truth.

"Because you are mine …"

Her face falls just the slightest.

I kiss her again.

"And because I love you, Quinn Ashby. How could I not?"

1 week earlier

quinn

HUNTER: Get your ass to my apartment as fast as you can.

I read the text message from Hunter and giggle a little to myself because he makes it quite obvious what he *needs* from me at this moment.

I text back.

Me: I'm in class. And I don't think a booty call qualifies as a reason to text me.

I put the phone back on my desk and try to pay attention to what the teacher is saying, but I don't hear one word he is saying. My phone buzzes again, and I open the message.

Hunter: This is the most important reason to text you. I'm dying here.

I smile and respond.

Me: I was over there last night. We literally fucked less than three hours ago.

I press send and wait.

Hunter: My dick doesn't care. I need you like every hour. Three hours is the max I can go without you.

I glance up at my teacher, who is dismissing class a few minutes early. I text back while I walk.

Me: Well, your dick is in luck because I got out of class early and don't have another class for an hour.

He responds.

Hunter: Good. Then we have time to do it at least twice.

I giggle and then head to my bike to ride over to his apartment.

Hunter doesn't say anything when I appear at his front door. Instead, he grabs me and flips me over his shoulder.

I giggle at his caveman tendencies.

"You can't just grab me without saying hello properly after summoning me here to have sex with you. I'm not your girlfriend, and I do have a life outside of fucking you. You can't just expect me to show up whenever you want."

"Yes, I can. I want you, and I know how to convince you to get your ass over here because you want this as much as I do. Don't deny it."

I bite my lip. He's right. I hadn't thought of anything since last night when we fucked.

"See you want this too."

I continue to bite my lip and stay silent. He carries me past Marshall's room, who is sitting on his bed with his laptop. He smiles when he sees me.

"Hey, Quinn. How's it going?" he shouts as Hunter carries me by.

"Good. If Hunter would stop being an asshole," I shout back.

I think I hear Marshall laugh, but I'm not sure as Hunter carries me into his room. I expect to be thrown down on the bed, but he doesn't; he keeps walking into his bathroom, which I'm almost more jealous of than his oversized bedroom with a huge king-size bed in it.

His bathroom is a million times better. It has a double sink even though it's just his own private bathroom. It has a jacuzzi and a huge rock shower that at least five people could fit in at the same time. I haven't showered in it yet, but I've had my eye on it.

Hunter walks to the shower and throws the handle up. The water shoots out of the showerhead while Hunter stands just outside it still holding me over his shoulder.

"Do you need to go somewhere soon?" I ask, assuming he is planning to fuck me fast and then need to shower quickly before he goes.

"Not that soon, but I thought we'd kill two birds with one stone."

"What do you mean?" I ask.

He steps into the water with me still over his shoulder.

I scream when the still cool water hits my ass. Hunter lowers me until I'm standing and kisses me hard, moving me back out of the water pressure until I'm pressed between his body and the wall. His kiss warms me up quickly, and then he pulls me back under the water with him when the water warms up.

"I've never done it in a shower before," I say excitedly as he kisses me.

He tugs on my bottom lip with his mouth. "It sucks, to be honest, usually, but with you, I think I'm going to like shower sex again."

I frown. *Why would he bring me in here if it usually sucks?*

He tugs at my shirt, peeling it off my wet skin. And then my bra is off. His shirt is already off, and I try to keep my eyes open under the water so I can watch the water roll off his hard body, but I can barely open them at all with the water pouring down on top of us. I expect him to take my breasts in his mouth.

Instead, he spins me around while flipping on more showerheads that come out of the walls. One hits right against my breasts, beating my sensitive skin over and over.

I close my eyes, not caring that I can't see Hunter's body or that his hands aren't the ones touching my breasts because the feeling would be enough for me to come on my own.

Hunter pulls down my jeans, though, and then he's pressed against my back; his cock pushes against my ass.

"You're beautiful soaking wet."

I take a deep breath so I can respond, but I don't. I can't get words out. Hunter moves me so that the showerheads are no longer hitting my breasts. I pout.

"Don't pout. Bend over and hold the bench for support."

I do.

And then his cock slides into me, and I no longer care that my breasts aren't feeling the pleasure of the water. He takes his time, moving in and out slowly. Not what I was expecting at all after his text message saying how badly he needed me. But if we moved any faster, I don't think I would be able to stay standing.

"God, I love looking at your ass when I fuck you."

I bite my lip to keep from coming too quickly. But he hits another button, and more water shoots on me, and this time, it hits me perfectly against my clit, and I come. Instantly, hard, and fast. And I know that Marshall heard me.

I think Hunter comes soon after, but I don't know. I'm too wrapped up in my own body to know what he did. But he stops and slides out and kisses me on the lips.

"I don't know how you could ever not love shower sex. I think it became my new favorite."

He grins. "I think it became my new favorite too."

He turns off the shower and hands me a towel but doesn't help me dry off as much as I want him to. Instead, he wraps a towel around his waist and heads to his bedroom. I take my time drying off and then follow him to his bedroom. He is getting dressed when I enter the bedroom, and it's then that I realize I have nothing to wear.

"I don't have clothes to wear to my next class."

Hunter looks up at me like he forgot I was even there, and then walks over to his closet and pulls a pair of sweatpants and a sweatshirt out and hands them to me. "You can wear these."

I take them and slowly dress while he finishes without speaking to me or even looking at me.

"You weren't kidding when you said you were in a hurry," I say, laughing even though there is nothing to laugh at. I'm just nervous I did something wrong.

Hunter freezes and looks at me this time. "I think we need to start seeing other people."

"Oh."

He takes a step forward. "No, I said that wrong."

I run my hand through my wet hair and sit on the edge of the bed because this seems like a conversation I need to sit for. "What do you mean then? You don't want to sleep with me anymore?"

"No. I mean yes. I mean I absolutely want to keep fucking you, but we also need to fuck other people between fucking each other."

"Why?"

He sits down next to me and tucks a loose strand of hair behind my ear. "Because if we don't, I'm going to fall fucking in love with you, and that can't happen."

TEXT MESSAGE #4

1 month earlier

quinn

LAST NIGHT WAS AMAZING. And all we did was talk. I thought it was about sex. It was the first time we had spent any real time together in over a year. We just spent time together on the roof of a club snuggling. Nothing happened yet everything happened.

He dropped me off at my apartment a little over an hour ago without the promise of anything more. We might never see each other again. Or we might see each other every day.

I'm supposed to go to class in an hour. Instead, all I can do is stare at my phone, contemplating my next move. I've never texted him before. I've never told him that I needed him. I don't even know if I do need him. But I want him. I want to share something that changed my life.

So I take a chance. I open my flip phone and text him.

Me: I need you. Now. Can you meet me at my apartment as soon as you can?

And then I wait.

I don't get a response for over thirty minutes. He's not coming. Evidently, the text messaging for help thing only works on one day a year. I sigh; I guess I'll have to wait until next year. I walk to the bathroom and strip off my shirt and start unzipping my skirt when I hear the doorbell.

It's probably a package or something getting dropped off. I ignore it and turn the water on to the shower. My phone buzzes, and I look down. It's Faith, my roommate. I open the message.

Faith: Let me in! Left my keys!

I sigh and walk out of the bathroom without bothering to put my shirt back on to let Faith in. I open the door, and Faith slumps by me, but I blush bright red when I see Hunter standing behind where she stood with the goofiest grin on his face.

"So you need me, huh?" he asks, stepping inside my apartment; his eyes drop to my exposed breasts only covered by an old nude bra and then looks back at my face.

"Yep," I say, backing up into my apartment as he walks forward, seemingly ready to pounce on me if I just say the word.

He keeps walking, pushing me back, and I keep walking backward until I'm in my bedroom. Until I'm lying back on my bed and his body is over mine. I'm breathing hard and fast as Hunter's body hovers over me.

"What did you need me so badly for?" he asks. Not making the first move even though he got us into this position.

"I ... uh ..." I can't form words. At this moment, I can't think about why I wanted him to come here; all I can think about is his lips touching mine. His body pressed against me.

He grins. "You need to say the words, Quinn. Tell me what you want."

"Um ... I want ..."

He grins brighter and then kisses me ever so softly on the lips. We both keep our eyes open as we kiss, and it's like seeing into his soul.

"I need you to fuck me, Hunter."

That's all it takes, and then he's kissing me again. I grab at his T-shirt but can't get it off him, which just frustrates me. He laughs as he pins my hands above my head and then takes off his shirt, revealing his hard body that has gotten so much harder since the last time we did this.

"Like what you see?"

I nod while biting my lip.

He lowers his mouth and pulls his lip into my mouth.

"I've thought about you every night since that night a year ago." He undoes my bra and then gives me an appreciative look. "Somehow, I think tonight is going to be better than my memory of that night was."

I kiss him. "Not possible."

He flips me over and grabs my ass. "We'll see, beautiful."

He grabs my mane of hair and pulls tightly as he enters me from behind. I forgot how big he was. How he completely fills me. How protected I feel in his arms.

"God, I missed this more than you know. I was stupid for letting it go this long without you."

I moan as he moves, somehow hitting me in all the right places.

"I was stupid for ever thinking I could go without this."

He moves again, and then neither of us can speak. We can only moan.

"Hunter!" I scream into the pillow as I come, and then he collapses on top of me.

He kisses my neck as his body recovers. "If you are going to text me when you need sex, I hope you text me every day because I'll be happy to come over whenever you want."

I laugh, and he gets off me, helping me up. He kisses me again, and I have to stop him from speaking before we end up doing it all over again. "As much as you may think this is why I needed you to come over, it wasn't."

He frowns. "But you …"

I smile and kiss him again. "Yes, I wanted that. Trust me," I say, winking. "I think I even told you to fuck me. But get dressed." I get up and throw my shirt on and pants while Hunter gets dressed too.

When we are both dressed, I say, "You drove over, right?"

He nods.

"Good. I need you to drive me somewhere."

I walk out of my apartment, and Hunter follows quietly toward his Jeep. We climb in. "So that's all you needed. A ride?"

I laugh and shake my head. "No. I wanted to share something I haven't shared with anyone. Start driving."

"You have more secrets you haven't shared with me?"

"Of course, just like you haven't shared things with me, I'm sure. Turn left here."

He does, and then I get nervous because I'm not sure what he is going to say.

"And turn in the parking lot here."

He does and then parks the car. "Where are we?" He looks at the building. "Why are we at a Chuck E. Cheese's?"

I take a deep breath. "Because I want to introduce you to my daughter."

His eyes widen just enough that I know he's surprised but not enough that I could accuse him of being judgmental. But he doesn't say anything; he just waits for me to say what I need to say.

"Well, she's not really my daughter. Not biologically anyway. And she's not mine yet. But she will be; the day I turn twenty-one and legally can adopt, she's mine."

He still doesn't speak. He just stares at me, and I can't tell what he is thinking.

"She's three. Her name is Ava, and she lives with foster parents. Actually, they have a series of babysitters who watch the kids; they don't ever really watch the kids. I'm one of the babysitters. I watch her as often as I can ever since they started fostering her, and I fell in love almost three years ago."

"Why are you telling me this?" he asks.

"Because you told me when we first met why we can never date. Your reason we can never be together. She's my reason we can never be together. I know you don't want to be a father at twenty-one. I know you have a whole life ahead of you that doesn't involve settling down." I take a deep breath and then say, "Want to meet her?"

hunter

"WHY DO YOU WANT me to meet her if you don't want me a part of her life?"

She shakes her head. "I didn't say that. I said that's my reason for us not getting serious because if you want to date me, she is part of the package. I think meeting her will help you realize that the sex isn't worth it."

I laugh. "The sex is always worth it. But you're right. I should meet her. It might make me behave."

She laughs. "I doubt that, but come on."

I exit my car and follow her in.

And before I have time to think, a tiny little girl runs over to Quinn and jumps into her arms. Quinn picks her up and squeezes her tight and kisses her pink little cheeks. Quinn smiles as she looks at the girl. She really smiles, brighter than I think I've ever seen her smile. It's incredible to see.

An older woman walks over to Quinn and says, "You're late."

"I'm sorry."

The woman glares at Quinn and then leaves without telling the little girl goodbye.

Quinn doesn't seem bothered; she just turns toward me still holding the girl. "Ava, I want you to meet a friend of mine. This is Hunter."

Ava smiles at me and then reaches her arms out to me. I stand frozen, looking at her.

"Hold her," Quinn says.

I extend my arms, and Quinn puts Ava into my arms.

"Hello, Hunter," she says so politely she seems like a grown-up.

"Hi, Ava," I put my fist out, and to my surprise, she gives me a fist bump and then laughs like that was the coolest thing ever.

"What do you do?" she asks.

"I play football."

Her eyes light up, and then she starts wiggling in my arms, and I assume she wants me to put her down. So I do. Her tiny hand grabs mine and then she starts pulling me toward a machine. She points with her other hand. "Can we play?"

I smile. "Hell yeah, we can." I pull out some quarters to put in the machine to play football and then hand a football to Ava who does her best to throw the ball at the target, but her tiny arms aren't strong enough. She pouts when the ball hits the ground instead of the target.

I smile and grab another ball and hand it to her. "Try again."

She begins to throw it, but this time, I lift her up so that she is close to the target and she hits it right it the middle. She laughs, and it's the most beautiful laugh I've ever heard.

"You're a natural."

"Again!" she screams.

I smile and grab another ball to hand to her.

"Be careful," Quinn says from behind us. I turn and see her smiling with her arms crossed, but there is concern in her eyes.

"It's just a football. I don't think she can get too hurt."

She shakes her head. "That's not what I'm talking about. Don't fall ..." She doesn't finish her sentence because Ava is looking at her. But it doesn't take me long to realize what she means. Don't fall in love with Ava. She's not mine. But I can see why Quinn fell so quickly for her because I know if I spend much more time with Ava, I will be hers. I put Ava down and pat her on the head. "Sorry, squirt, I have to go." And then I leave before I fall any harder.

1 week earlier

quinn

I STARE AT MY computer screen while I hold my head in my hands. I can't turn my eyes away from the single message that fills my email inbox. Yet I can't bring myself to click the message and open it either. Instead, I've been in this same position just staring at the screen in disbelief. I've stared at the screen like this for the entire hour and a half since I've been in the tutoring center. I'm supposed to be working, but instead, I'm sulking in terror at what the email might contain. No, what I know in my heart it contains.

I have turned away all my usual students who I'm supposed to tutor; not that I have many students to tutor on my usual list anyway. I'm not the best teacher. I really only took this job so I would have two hours a day to make a little extra income that I desperately need while using the time to study myself. Because of that, no one on this campus chooses me to be their tutor; most of the students have learned I'm just a heartless grump who doesn't have time to worry about anyone else's needs. I have to put myself first. If not, I won't survive.

"Hey, Quinn," Meredith, the other woman who works at the student center the same hours that I do, says, I think, although I can barely make out her voice in the background. Her voice is not enough for me to force my eyes from the email in front of me.

"Quinn!" she shouts, loud enough that the other students in the tutoring center turn their attention to us. Loud enough that I don't have a choice but to look at her. "What?" I say even grumpier than my usual voice.

"There is a new student here who needs your help."

"Can't you take him?" I ask.

"No," she says firmly through clenched teeth, and I know she's had enough. Meredith loves teaching; in fact, she loves it so much that her degree will be in teaching. And unlike me, she has a scholarship and parents who can afford to pay for her college. This is her only job outside of attending classes, and she's just doing it because she actually enjoys it and it might look good on her resume.

"Why not?" I ask.

"For one, I'm already tutoring three students at once. For two, you are sitting there doing absolutely nothing. And for three, he is a computer science major, which is not an area that I can help with."

That has been our arrangement since we started working this shift together. She would take all the students that she could, but I would take the computer science students—an area that Meredith, unfortunately, has no experience in. I sigh. I get up from the hard plastic chair and round tabletop. I close the laptop reluctantly. I guess it really doesn't matter that I have to close the computer without reading the email. It wasn't like I was going to find the courage in my last half-hour here to open it anyway.

I walk from my table in the far back corner of the room, past Meredith with her army of students who sit behind the only other three tables in the small tutoring center, around to the entrance where a man stands next to the entrance. A rolling cabinet contains laptops that can be checked out for use in the tutoring center, and on top, a sign-in log where students can use to request specific tutors and their time slots sits on top of the cabinet to his right. I hardly look at the man; I just look long enough to see he's wearing the usual nerd outfit of a T-shirt, jeans, and sneakers. I glance at the sign-in book and find his name. Chaz. He didn't even bother to write his last name in the book. I continue reading under the area of help needed: computer class.

I let the slow smile grow on my face; the first genuine smile I have probably given anyone in days.

"I'm Quinn. I see here that you need help with a junior level computer science class. And while I'm a computer science major, I'm only a freshman. So I really can't help you out, especially not in the half-hour or less I have left in my shift. I suggest you try to find time in your schedule to meet with one of the computer science tutors." I flip the sign-in calendar open to reveal the other times and tutors who might be able to help him.

"This is really the only time I have in my schedule. I really need some help with this class, or I'm going to fail," Chaz says.

I look at this man—no, boy—who stands in front of me. He looks so sad and desperate for help. His eyes are red, swollen like he has been crying and might cry again if I turn him down. But I don't believe his story about this being the only time in his schedule that he has free time to get help. Although, if I needed help, this will be the only time in my schedule I would have to get help. I tuck a strand of my long moppy brown hair that fell out of the braid I did earlier behind my ear.

I could probably help him if I really wanted to. If I had some time to read the textbook for the class, I know I could. Despite only being a freshman and it being October of my freshman year, I have plenty of experience in coding, website, and app development from messing around with it on my own for the few years that I tried working my ass off between high school and college. I knew I couldn't afford college, and I thought I could get a good job without it. Boy, was I wrong. I couldn't get any decent job without being able to check the box that said I have a college degree. And despite having no time in my schedule to even get my own homework done, I could help him if I really wanted to without much effort at all. School comes easy; it's life that's hard.

"Try to talk with the other tutors to see if they can arrange to meet you during this time. If not, I'll see what I can do to help you next week. But I'm not promising I can help you."

I watch as Chaz's face lights up, no longer any signs of the tears that would have so quickly fallen earlier.

Dammit. Because I know I'm going to end up helping this guy graduate when I'm not even sure I'm going to make it another semester.

I shake my head as I turn back around. I begin walking back to my table in the corner of the small room. I undo the braid and then redo it. I can't stand my long hair on my neck, not when I'm anxious. And the braid will help give my hair a nice wavy sexy look later tonight without actually doing anything before my waitressing job. I need to look as sexy as possible to ensure I get the best tips I so desperately need. I don't care about my hair, though; not now that my whole world is over anyway. I need to stop thinking this way. My whole world isn't going to end because of this. I've been through much worse, and both times have turned out to be the best things that ever happened to me.

By the time I walk back to my desk and flip the laptop checked out from the tutoring center open, my anger turns back into terror as I take a seat. Because I genuinely don't know what I'm going to do after I open this email and realize that my college days are numbered. I stare at the email that has been teasing me all afternoon a second longer, and then I finally click it open. My eyes close for just a split second, no longer than a blink hiding what the email says from me. But then my eyes open, and I begin to quickly scan the email.

To Ms. Quinn Ashby,

I am writing to inform you that your tuition for the summer semester is now three months late as well as your tuition for this fall semester. You are currently enrolled in a monthly payment plan but have missed the last three payments. We are removing you from the monthly payment plan and informing you that if you don't pay your last semester and this semester's tuition in full by December 1st of this year, the credits you are taking will not be earned nor will you have the ability to enroll in classes next semester. If you have any questions or concerns regarding your payment, please email or call me at 555-3987.

Sincerely,

Heidi Hunt, Financial Department, University of Boulder

I read the email with no emotion. I already knew what the email was going to say. I already knew I was behind on my payments, but it was the only thing I could do in order to pay my rent and afford food these first three months. The amount I owe for tuition is astronomical. It's more money than I currently make at my three jobs combined over the remaining two and a half months of the semester. So even if all I did was pay my tuition, it still wouldn't be enough to cover my costs.

I should cry, looking at my situation. And although it's tragic, it's by far not the worst thing that has happened to me. It's by far not the worst predicament I've ever been in.

I brought this on myself. My grades in high school were terrible, despite actually being pretty smart, which meant I couldn't get a scholarship despite scoring high on my ACT. I could've taken out loans to pay for college, but I was too stupid to realize that I needed them. I thought if I worked hard, if I worked any job I could the entire time I wasn't in class, then I could afford to live, to survive. I thought I had enough saved these past two years when all I did was work between classes. But after only a few months into my college career, I've already failed. Because I was wrong. I can't do this on my own.

I could make excuses for why I am in a situation. I grew up in foster care; I was neglected. I had no shot at a future. But they would all just be excuses. I'm better than excuses. So instead of making excuses, I hit the reply button on the email and begin typing my quick response.

To Miss Hunt,

I need to set up an appointment to discuss what financial arrangements need to be made and what options I have left. The best times to meet with you would be Tuesday or Thursday afternoon. Please let me know your availability during those times.

Thank you for your time,

Quinn Ashby

I press send and then slam the laptop shut without even bothering to log out. It doesn't matter that I didn't log out; I'm the only person who uses this computer. It might as well be mine. Everyone else has their own computers. Most have expensive Apple products and those less fortunate have some version of the hundred dollar Google product. I take the computer off the table and walk to the cabinet that is on wheels near the front of the room that has the sign-in sheet on top of it. I kneel to open the cabinet and place the computer back inside. I close the cabinet and take the key out of my pocket to lock it up for the day. Even though I still have a good fifteen to twenty minutes left on my tutor schedule for today, I can't stay here any longer. And if a student arrived now, it's not like I would have time to really help them anyway. I put the key into the lock and begin to lock the cabinet when I hear a voice say, "Have you seen Camille?"

I sigh as I turn the key and assure the cabinet is locked. I wouldn't want anyone to steal one of the laptops. I'm the only one who uses them, so I'm sure I would be blamed for any theft. And I definitely can't deal with having to pay the university back for a laptop right now. So I make sure it is locked before I stand to look at the man standing at the entrance of the tutoring center.

"I'm looking for Camille. She usually has an appointment in a tutoring center at this time. Have you seen her?"

I glance up at him and feel my mouth drop open at the sight of him. Because standing before me isn't a boy; he's one of the most goddamn beautiful species of man I've ever seen. A man I honestly never thought I would see again after one incredible night almost a year ago. And for some reason that I need to thank later, he's not wearing a shirt, just exercise shorts. His body glistens with sweat, showing off every single one of his hard muscles. My eyes dance over his body, counting every single one of his abs. I've seen some men who have a nice six-pack, but I've never seen a man this up close and personal who has an eight pack so clearly defined. Somehow, his body looks even more perfect than the last time I saw him. His muscles even more defined.

It's strange how we both look the same but different; my hair has grown back out, and his hair is shorter. I have lost some weight while he packed on more muscles. I have more determination than ever while he seems to have gained more confidence, more arrogance—that's clear in the way he stands. The only difference that matters though is that we have both gotten rid of our pain. Or at the very least found a way to hide it.

My eyes drop lower to the muscle that forms a v and then disappears beneath his shorts. I gulp as I think about what lies on the other side of those shorts. It only happened one time, but I will never forget that night. I will never forget what lies beneath those shorts.

I hear a small chuckle escape his lips, and it forces my eyes up to meet his. My cheeks flush a bright red as my eyes meet his dark brown all-consuming eyes. The room is silent except for my beating heart, and I'm afraid everyone in the room can hear it. And I can feel everyone's eyes on us without looking in their direction.

But a smell distracts me from all that. A strong, delicious smell of warm bread and a meat I can't quite make out. I glance at his large hands, and that's when I see him grasping the largest sandwich I think I've ever seen. I sniff the air again, and this time, I pick up a little of his sweat smell mixed with the sandwich, which somehow makes the sandwich seem even more appetizing. And I realize what kind of sandwich it is. "Pastrami," I say, something I haven't tasted in years.

He chuckles at me again. "Yes. It's pastrami."

I shake off my embarrassment at just blurting out the name of a sandwich he is holding. It's just because I'm starving and haven't eaten all day. "Sorry, but I don't think there is a Camille here," I say, acting like I don't remember him. *But how could I forget a man who saved me from untold darkness even when I didn't want to be saved?* I can tell in his eyes that he remembers exactly who I am. Of course, he does. Two nights—one in which he saved me, and another in which he gave me the best fuck of my life—

why wouldn't he remember me? It's just been a long time since either of us spoke or texted, and I never thought we would again. Somehow, he found me even if it was accidental. But it doesn't mean just because we are here together that we are going to pick up where we left off.

I glance back at Meredith, who nods in agreement with me.

"You sure she's not here?" he asks, popping a piece of gum into his mouth. It's just regular mint gum, which relaxes my heart a little to see that he is finally over the smoking habit I started him on.

"Have a look around yourself, but I don't know any Camilles. Just check the calendar with the tutor schedule on it. You might have your day and time mixed up." I point toward the schedule and then walk back to my table to begin packing up my backpack to leave. This doesn't change our agreement. We don't see each other unless we text each other that we need each other. And since neither of us has texted, our relationship ends here.

I begin putting my notebook and pen into the backpack. I keep my eyes on him the whole time as he scans the rest of the room. He begins flipping through the book, and I get distracted for a second when he puts his sandwich down on the table. I could grab his sandwich and make a run for it without him knowing. But I know he could easily outrun me, and then he would think we could become more than just strangers who shared two nights together.

He glances over in my direction, and the intensity in his eyes makes me freeze. Not that I was moving very fast to begin with, but then a woman pops her head in and must say something to him because he turns in her direction. I watch as his body lights up when he sees her, and I get the sinking suspicion she's his girlfriend. I watch as he follows her. I watch as he leaves without so much as a second glance in my direction. Not that he has any reason to look at me. He's doing exactly what I wanted. Pretending I don't exist. He moved on while I have barely had time for a date this past year.

I get up from the table and sling the backpack over my shoulder. I quickly sign my name out on the sign-out sheet even though it's ten minutes before I should leave. As I'm signing out, I notice his sandwich still sitting right next to me. It smells so good, so tempting. *How could he just leave it? How could he forget about something so delicious?* It's impossible for me to understand as my own stomach growls.

It takes me less than a second to decide. I reach out and snatch the sandwich and then watch as something black falls to the floor. I bend down to pick it up and realize it's his wallet. *Dammit.*

I was hoping to grab the sandwich and disappear and never have to see that man again. I don't even know his name because we never shared it with each other. I spent the entire time we were together calling him Asshole. But now that he left his wallet, I might see him again. I need to find some way to return it without having to see him in person. And finding out who he is could help me. Knowing his real name could help me avoid him in the future. I snatch the wallet and the sandwich and toss both quickly into my backpack, and then I leave. I will worry about what to do about the wallet later. Right now, I need to find a place to enjoy the delicious sandwich I just acquired. And enjoy eating it because eating it will be the only escape I get. After that, I have to be an adult. I have to find a way to pay for college; it's not just me who depends on it.

quinn

"CAN I GET YOU anything to drink other than water?" I ask the two women who just sat down at the booth in my section.

"I'll have a beer," the blonde says.

"Same," says the woman with shorter spiky dark hair.

I smile at them and jot down their beer choices.

"Are you ready to order or do you want me to get your beers first?"

"We are ready. We are going to share a Margherita pizza."

"What size?" I ask even though I know I shouldn't. I should just put in a medium, which is the perfect size for them to share. Instead, I ask and have to wait while the women decide if they can share a small. They can't. They will starve if they do. I've seen it happen before.

"Does a medium sound good? That is what is recommended for two people."

"Yes, that will be fine," the blonde finally says.

I write it down even though I won't have a problem remembering their order and then walk away from their table to enter the order into our computers. I begin typing in the women's order when Mandy, who still works here mainly to flirt with the male customers, comes over and rests her head on the desk where the computer is.

"God, it's going to be another long night, isn't it?" Mandy asks.

"Yes, I think it's going to be a slow night. I only have one table at the moment."

"I guess I shouldn't complain. I'm doing slightly better with two tables."

I finish typing in the order, and I step to the side as Mandy types in her own order. As I watch her, his wallet burns a hole in the pocket of my apron. Asshole's wallet. Except now I know his real name. The second I left the tutoring center and as soon as I finished his glorious sandwich that's going to keep me full for the rest of the day, I sneaked a peek inside his wallet. And found out plenty about the hot stranger who made his way into my life two years ago.

The asshole is Hunter Metcalf. Age twenty-one. Eyes brown, hair color blond although I already knew both of those without having to look at his ID. Height six-foot-six. But I also find out much more than just what his driver's license said. I found a picture of a beautiful woman who looks to be more than just his friend from the way he is holding her in the picture. When I found her picture, I was immediately jealous. She is beautiful with long brown hair with curls that look natural, not fake. She looks beautiful even though all I can see is the back of her head. Hunter's arm is wrapped around her as they stare off into the distant sunset. It's clear she is striking in the most beautiful way while I'm boring. Not that I've ever given much attention to how I look before. It's never mattered before, and I wouldn't have the time or the money to do much about my looks anyway.

I also learned while rummaging through his wallet that Hunter Metcalf has money. Lots of money. Although, I guessed that last time I was with him too. I counted half a dozen credit cards, the nice kind of credit cards with outrageous spending limits, and I also found over five hundred in cash in his wallet. My first thought when I saw the money was this guy is asking to be robbed. He obviously had no worry about losing the money since he placed his wallet so casually in the tutoring center and then left it there without thought. If I had five hundred dollars in cash, no way would I let that money out of my sight for even a second. I would be an anxious wreck until I got the money somewhere safe. It's extremely tempting to take the money out and shove it into my own pocket. Because while five hundred dollars might not mean much to him, five hundred dollars would change my whole world.

The last thing I learned is that Hunter carries a condom in his wallet. And from the XXL on the label, he either thinks highly of himself or he really does have a large member. A member I have imagined way too many times since we fucked last year, only to let reality strike when I think of the picture of the woman in his wallet who he's reserving that condom for. Not me. I gave up my chance at ever getting more.

"Do you know a man named Hunter Metcalf?" I ask Mandy as she finishes typing in her order. Curious to see if she recognizes that he is who she set me up with last year.

Although she drank so much that night, I doubt she remembers. She doesn't even know we hung out. I told her I went home alone.

Mandy sighs and puts her hands on her hips as she stares at me in disbelief. "Of course, I know him. Everybody knows Hunter." She tilts her head to the side. "Why do you want to talk about Hunter?"

"Because he left his wallet in the tutoring center earlier today," I say, leaving out the part of how I know him.

Mandy raises her eyebrows. "You have Hunter's wallet on you?"

"Yes."

Before I can stop her, Mandy's hands go to my apron, searching for the wallet. I struggle to pull her off me but finally do. She reaches for the wallet I'm holding high above my head thankful I'm tall and lanky for once in my life. "Why do you want the wallet so badly?"

"Because it belongs to Hunter Metcalf. *The Hunter Metcalf*. It could contain the secret to getting him to ask me out."

"I hate to break it to you, but he has a girlfriend. There's a picture of her in his wallet."

"He doesn't have a girlfriend. He's the star tight end for our football team. He is the only reason we ever win games. Hunter doesn't do girlfriends. He's a fuck 'em and leave 'em kinda guy. There is no reason for him to date just one woman when he can have all the women he wants."

Behind Mandy, I see that our manager, Tina, is looking in our direction. "We'd better get back to work. Tina is coming toward us and doesn't look happy."

Mandy glances behind her and sighs. "This isn't over."

I turn in the direction of the bar to pick up the women's two beers and then head back to the table to give it to them. Neither looks up when I set the beers on the table. Neither says thank you or even gives me an appreciative smile. *I'm going to get squat for tips*, I think.

I notice that Mandy somehow picked up a table while I still just have the one. I'm going to have to have another talk with the hostesses about how to make things fair around here. I know I'm not the best waitress. I don't flirt or come off as overly friendly, and I hardly even make small talk. I just get down to business. While Mandy flirts with everybody, including the women, and knows how to small talk with the best of them. Somehow, she always manages to bring in at least double or triple the tip money that I do. I should learn from her, but I'm just not sure I can.

Since I only have one table right now, it gives me way too much time to think about the five hundred dollars in his wallet and how I could spend that money. On rent. Food. Tuition. The choices are endless. The money could be the difference between surviving or not.

I make up my mind, and I pull the cash out of the wallet, more cash than I've ever seen in one place in my lifetime and shove it in my back pocket, and then I take the wallet and go in search of Mandy. I find her by the bar and hold it out to her. "You can have it to give back to him." If Mandy gives it back to him, he will think she took the money, not me. He will probably never even miss the money anyway. And more importantly, I don't have to see him again.

"You don't want to give it him yourself?"

"No."

She studies me. "I don't believe you for a second. But I'm glad you gave me the honor to try to make him mine first."

I shake my head as I walk away. I decide to head back and check on my table one more time first to make sure they don't need anything else and tell them their pizza should be out shortly. I begin to look in the direction of their table, but they are both giggling with each other as their eyes focus on something across the restaurant. I follow their gaze to a man sitting in a booth down from them. A booth in my section. And I know the man sitting in that booth.

I walk over to the girls, needing a second to regain my composure and to figure out what I'm going to do. My hands clench into tight fists. "You guys need anything else?"

Both women shake their head slowly without looking at me; instead, they're staring in Hunter's direction, looking like horny teenagers. The butterflies form in my stomach, but I refuse to turn in Hunter's direction. I refuse to succumb to his charms just like these women did.

"Your pizza should be out shortly, ladies."

I don't wait for them to respond; I just begin walking toward Hunter's booth. He's not looking at me or the ladies in the booth; instead, he's looking down at his menu. I shake off my now clammy clenched hands as I walk, but with each step that I take closer to him, my hands are shaking a little. *Dammit.* I'm not going to let this man know he affects me. Just because he's sexy and confident and arrogant doesn't mean I'm going to fawn all over him just yet. I have a lot more to worry about than this silly man. I can get him to leave me alone just like last time.

I walk the final steps to his booth as confidently as I can and say, "Can I get you anything to drink?"

Hunter looks up from his menu slowly. "Yes. I'll take a beer."

I nod and write his order. My eyes glance up at him from beneath the notepad I just scribbled on, and I watch his cocky grin creep up on his face as he says, "Do you want to see an ID?"

"Um, I ..." Crap. He knows I stole his wallet. Although, technically, I didn't steal his wallet; I just took it, but now, it's no longer in my possession. "No, I know you're twenty-one."

His cocky smirk widens, and a gleam in his eye has me speechless. I couldn't speak even if I wanted to. He waits as I struggle to form words to fix this, but I can't. He finally decides to be kind and break me from my spell. "You have something else to ask me?"

"Yes. Are you ready to order food or do you want me to wait until your beer comes up?"

He cocks his head to the side as his eyes travel over my attire. My tight fitting black shirt with the restaurant's name on it and tight black boy shorts that barely cover my ass. The uniform does nothing to flatter me; it just makes my legs look long, lanky, and pale.

"I would normally say wait until my beer comes out, but I'm starving. See somebody stole my sandwich today that was meant to be my lunch. A sandwich that I was very much looking forward to, but now, I guess I'll have to settle for a double cheeseburger with everything."

My mouth drops open. He knows I ate his sandwich too. I don't have an answer for him. Not one single answer. Not some smartass comeback that I'm used to doling out.

Nothing. This man has caught me in his web, and I'm oogling him just like the rest of the women in the restaurant are. He's turned me into any other woman. A woman who only cares about how good looking a man is instead of being concerned with how he treats her.

I turn and walk away without saying anything back. I'm afraid if I do that, I will turn into a puddle in front of this man who I've let fuck me, who I've shared all my secrets with but still feels like a stranger on one hand and like I've known him my entire life on the other. I head back to the computer and quickly enter his order and then search for Mandy. I'm hoping she will give me the wallet back so I can stuff the money back into it and return it to him before he realizes I stole his money too. I find Mandy picking up her own drinks up from the bar.

"I need the wallet back."

"Why?"

"Because Hunter is sitting at one of my tables, and he knows that I took the wallet."

"No way."

I panic and grab her arm. "Please, Mandy. I know we have not always gotten along the best but please just do this for me just this once."

Mandy smiles. "You gave the wallet to me; it's mine now."

"You're going to give it back to him, though, right?"

"Yes, in good time."

I watch as Mandy walks away, and I resist the urge to follow her and tackle her to get the wallet back. Instead, I pick up his beer and carry it to his table, walking confidently until I place the beer on the table in front of him just like I do every other client in the restaurant.

"Your food should be out shortly."

"Good because I'm starving."

I turn around to go check on the ladies' food when he says, "Thank you, Quinn."

I freeze. Then glance back at him just a second with a tight smile on my face before gathering my composure and finally walking away. I have no idea how he knows my name, but I can't give him them the satisfaction of asking. I never remember to wear my name tag, so he didn't find it there. I didn't introduce myself at the tutoring center. But he broke his promise and came looking for me.

That means he looked me up after he left the tutoring center. I walk back to the kitchen and pick up the pizza from the kitchen for my first table. I place the pizza on their table while they continue to flirt across the room with Hunter. Hunter sips his beer, ignoring them. His eyes are on me every time I move, and I don't understand why. He's supposed to stay away. He said he hated me and would stay away. *So why is he so interested? Is it because he's interested in me or is he really that upset with me that I stole his wallet and sandwich?*

I walk back to the kitchen and find his burger ready. I grab every condiment we have—mustard, mayo, and ketchup—to bring along with me. I don't want any reason to have to revisit his table. I just want to drop off his food, do my job, and then leave him alone. I carry the food out on the tray confident as ever and then put it down in front of Hunter along with all the condiments. "Can I get you anything else?"

"Yeah—"

"I'm not sorry or ashamed that I ate your sandwich. You left it, and I was starving. I didn't have lunch, so I ate it.

I'm not going to apologize for eating a sandwich. And as for your wallet, I don't have it. My friend Mandy said she knew you, so she was going to give it back to you."

I point at Mandy from across the room, but his eyes don't leave mine. "And just so you know, she wants you. So if you're looking for an easy lay, she's the one, not me."

He grins. "I was just going to ask for another beer." He holds up his empty cup. "And I already knew you were a thief. You stole the pizza remember? Or did you just pretend to steal it and pay this place back later?"

My cheeks flush in embarrassment. I walk away to go put his beer order in but will have someone else bring him his beer. I don't think I can face him again so soon. But it doesn't stop me from glancing over at him every chance I get. I watch him eat, watch him drink. I watch him talk and laugh with some of his football buddies who walk through the restaurant. I watch him flirt with other girls.

But nothing is as painful as watching Mandy go over to him to return his wallet. They both smile at each other, and I watch him enter her number into his phone.

I'm really nothing to him other than the girl who stole his wallet and sandwich. I don't know why he tried to find me. But it's obvious it doesn't mean anything. I just don't want to be around when he realizes the cash is gone. I have to find a different way to get him the cash back. While he's talking with Mandy, I slip the bill on his table. He doesn't glance up at me just keeps his focus on Mandy.

I hurry away and find myself in the bathroom upset for taking the money and not having the strength to just give it back to him. But I know it's what I have to do. I'm not a thief.

When I come back out of the bathroom, he's gone. I head over to his table, and I grab the cash he left which is over a hundred dollars even though his meal cost less than thirty. I sigh; he must have left the tip for Mandy. The fact he was so taken with Mandy just makes me want to give his money back even more. I don't want any reason to run into him again. I just want to give his money back, and then return to my normal life that doesn't involve men.

quinn

MY EYES POP OPEN as the smell overwhelms my nostrils. Not again. I'm not going to survive the semester living with my roommate if she keeps this up. I throw the covers off me and then slowly crawl out of bed. I've never been a morning person, but there's nothing like anger to motivate me out of bed in the morning.

The air is cold as I climb out of bed, so I grab a ratty old sweatshirt and throw it on over my T-shirt and shorts. I don't own pajamas or a robe or slippers or anything that would make getting out of bed more comfortable in the morning. I don't spend my money on frivolous things.

As soon as I get the sweatshirt over my head, I feel warmer but not even a tiny bit more relaxed as I walk to my bedroom door. I throw it open, and that's when the smell really hits me. Our whole apartment reeks. Like really reeks. I follow the smell across our apartment, past the room next to mine that Mandy used to occupy, and through the small connected living and kitchen area. I walk past the patio that connects to the living area, if you can call it a patio. It's more like a slab of concrete that one person can stand on at a time. I walk down the hallway opposite of mine until I come face to face with the third bedroom door. I pound on the door, my eyes no longer carrying an ounce of sleep in them. I'm now fully awake from the fumes. I pound on the door hard as I yell, "Faith!"

No answer.

I pound again harder this time, using both of my fists. I don't stop; I just continually pound over and over again as I yell, "Faith! Faith Welling, get your ass out here right now."

I keep pounding, and eventually, the door creaks open, and my roommate, Faith, stands in the doorway holding a joint in her hand. She blows the smoke in my direction, making me cough. I've had enough of this, and I'm not going to deal with her crap any longer. I grab the joint out of her hand and push into her bedroom and find her pot-loving boyfriend on her bed smoking a joint as well. I grab his joint out of his fingers. He's so high I don't think he even notices that I took it.

I storm over to the ashtray and immediately put them out with Faith on my heels. "What the hell are you doing, Quinn? You can't just come in here and take my things."

"You can't be smoking these in my apartment. You agreed when we became roommates that you wouldn't do drugs. I can't have drugs in my apartment."

She reaches for the joint, but I raise them both higher out of reach.

"Those aren't drugs; it's just a little pot. It's legal."

"I don't care if it's legal. It's not happening in my apartment."

"It's my apartment too, and I can do whatever I want."

"No, you can't. The apartment is in my name. I can't have anybody who's doing drugs live in my apartment. What do you need to do drugs for anyway? It's seven thirty in the morning."

"It's none of your damn business what I do or when."

"It's my business when the apartment is in my name," I say again, getting frustrated.

"It doesn't matter whose name is on it. It's legal. We are not going to get kicked out of the apartment when it is legal. Everyone on our campus does it, so why can't you just lighten up and smoke a joint as well. Trust me; it will make you feel a lot better." She reaches into her pocket and pulls out another joint and holds it out to me.

I stare at it. I'm sure it would make me feel better. It's not that I haven't smoked a joint or two in my life because I have. But I no longer have that option. I have to be responsible now.

I push it away. "Just smoke at your boyfriend's place from now on. I can't have that here anymore."

I expect her to say that's fine, that she will just do that from now on. I expect her to just start spending a lot more time at his place than ours. I'm sure wherever he lives it's a lot nicer and larger than this place is.

I see the fire in her eyes, though, and I'm afraid I've made a huge mistake. "Fine. I'll have my things moved out by the end of the day. Good luck paying rent on your own."

I freeze in terror. I can't afford this small apartment on my own. I'm not sure I'm going to be able to find another roommate quickly this late in the semester. I wasn't planning to have to come up with more money to pay rent.

But I can't have somebody who smokes and does drugs living here.

I glance over at Faith who has a rotten smile on her face. She crosses her arms and tosses her jet black hair over her shoulder. "Now, get out of my bedroom. You'll have plenty of time to spend in this room when I'm gone."

She shoves me in the shoulder to get me moving. I turn and walk out as her door slams shut behind me.

Fuck.

I stand outside her door for far too long, wondering if I should go back and apologize or even offer to lower her rent a little bit. It would be much easier and more doable than figuring out how to pay for this apartment by myself. I shake my head. I know what I'm going to do. I'm going to let her leave, and then I'm going to talk to my financial advisor at school and get this figured out. I'm going to find a better job that allows me to move forward and pay for this. Because I can do this.

I walk back down the hallway to the bathroom we both share. It's tiny with a pedestal sink, a toilet, and a shower that anyone larger than myself would have a hard time fitting in. I flip on the hot water and then begin undressing, hoping that a shower will get the stench aroma off me enough that people at school don't think I've been smoking pot all morning.

After I strip, I quickly step under the hot water in the shower. I shampoo and condition my long brown locks and quickly rinse off my body and then get out and dry off with a towel. I wrap it around my body and head to my closet in my bedroom. I pull out my one nice pair of jeans and the only sweater that makes me look somewhat feminine. I quickly dress and run a brush through my hair before I grab my backpack from the makeshift desk in the corner of my room made of boxes and pillows. I reach into the front pocket and pull out the wad of cash that I took from Hunter's wallet. No, stole. Because that's what I am—a thief.

I could use this money now more than ever. But that's not who I am. I'm not a thief; I don't even take handouts. This is my life, and I'm going to figure it out on my own.

I shove the money back into my backpack and zip it closed before swinging it over my shoulder and heading to the kitchen. I scour the empty fridge and find a couple of hot sauce and ketchup packets. That's it. I throw open the pantry, and I find a box of granola bars. They don't belong to me; they belong to Faith, but right now, I don't care. I pull the box off the shelf and pull out one of the bars; I doubt she will miss it anyway.

I sigh; even returning the money won't remedy the fact I'm still a thief. I may not steal anything of any real value, but I do steal food when I need it to survive. This isn't the first time I've stolen food from Faith. And yesterday wasn't the first time I stole someone else's sandwich. I'm a thief.

I head out of the apartment without a goodbye to Faith. I jog down the stairs and throw open the door to exit the building. I turn the corner and head to the bike rack that thankfully still has my bike attached. Although, nobody would want to steal my crappy bike when hundreds of others attached to the bike rack are way more expensive.

I bend down and begin moving the numbers around to enter the code and unlock my bike from the bike rack and then toss the bike lock into my backpack. I climb onto my bike; it's the nicest possession I own, but even it has seen better days. I bought it used from a college student, spending only about a hundred dollars for a used bike that would cost me well over a thousand if it were new. But despite being at least seven or eight years old, it still gets me where I need to be even though the pretty purple stripes that used to cover it are faded, the gears could use a little extra oil, and the tires need changing. The bike still works, and that's all that matters.

I begin pedaling toward campus even though I don't have a class for another hour. I only got four, maybe five hours of sleep last night, but I need to spend the time to find Hunter and return the money. As I pedal a couple of miles to campus, I try to think of where I'll start to look for Hunter. Before yesterday, I'd never seen him, and I have no idea where to start looking now. I try to remember the address on his driver's license, but as the numbers start forming in my head, I remember the address isn't in Boulder; it's Aspen. Most likely where his parents live, not the house or apartment he is living in while he attends school. Driving a couple of hours to Aspen wouldn't be of help.

I don't know what classes he takes or even what his major is. The only real clue I have about him is that he's a football player. Most college kids would be able to pull out their cell phone and Google him to get more information, but I don't even have that. I have a pay-as-you-go flip phone that doesn't do anything except call and text. I could text him, but I'd prefer to just sneak him the money instead of having to talk to him. So the only way I can get more info on him is if I head to the library and spend some time on the computers there searching. I'm not even sure if that would be helpful, so instead, I head toward my only clue— the football practice fields.

I can tell as I ride up that few people are on the field and definitely not enough to be a full football team. But a few people wearing football uniforms are there, so I don't give up hope yet. I pedal faster until I reach the top of the hill that leads down to the field. I reluctantly jump off the bike, leaving the bike outside the fence that surrounds the field. I don't bother to lock it up as I run inside the fence to the few remaining players walking toward the locker rooms.

"Hey!" I shout, out of breath from pedaling so hard and running down onto the field.

Neither of the two men closest to me looks up or even turns in my direction; they just keep talking to each other, holding their helmets as they walk closer to the building.

I run faster, cutting them off from going into the building. I hold out my hand in a stop motion since I'm unable to say anything until I catch my breath. It takes a couple of seconds until I do finally catch my breath. "I need to talk with Hunter Metcalf." I say one word at a time, stopping to catch my breath after each word.

The players look at each other and then back at me. And then one of them says, smiling, "Sorry, sweetie, but I think Hunter already has a date to the party this weekend. But I'd be more than willing to take you."

I roll my eyes at their assumption that the only reason I would want Hunter is for him to take me to one of the football team's parties. Or that I'd be happy to let this stranger take me as a replacement.

"I'm not looking for a date. I just have something of his that I need to return."

"Darling, if Hunter left something of his at your place, it's because he wanted you to have it, not because he wanted you to return it. Don't worry about it, just enjoy it."

He winks at me, and the two begin walking again. I run my hand through my hair, frustrated that these two men don't understand.

But I've never been one to let a guy or anyone else tell me what to do. They obviously just got done with practice, so I know Hunter's most likely inside. And if I can't convince these two bozos to get Hunter to come out for me, I doubt I'm going to be able to convince anyone else. I don't have time to wait for Hunter to come out, so I head toward the door the men just disappeared inside. I open the door and then follow them down the hallway to the locker room. I don't hesitate at the door; I just push the door open and step inside without thinking about what I'm doing.

I begin going up and down every aisle filled with half-naked stinky men looking for him. I get several raised eyebrows as I walk, but no one tries to stop me or throw me out. I get the impression this isn't the first time an angry woman has stormed the men's locker room. Around the corner, I see a man dressed in khakis and a polo with the university's logo printed on it; a man who's much too old to still be in college and whose arms are folded across his chest as he looks at me. "Can I help you?"

"Yes. I need to see Hunter Metcalf. Now."

I say every word firmly, not at all embarrassed or ashamed to be in here. I expect the man to throw me out or threaten me with whatever form of punishment he can give. Not that I'm sure what punishment he can give me. It's not like high school where he could throw me in detention.

The man smiles, and now, I know he's going to throw me out. "Hunter! Get your ass over here," he says instead.

My eyebrows rise in surprise. I glance past the man and am rewarded with a half-naked Hunter with just a towel wrapped around his waist as he makes his way from around the corner of the last row of lockers. I watch as he runs a hand through his slick wet hair. I watch as the water drips down onto his firm chest and then rolls down over each of his abs. I bite down on my lip hard to keep it from gaping open.

"Yes, Coach," Hunter says. His eyes travel from his coach to me, and I see the tiniest hint of shock before his lips curl up into a grin when he sees me.

"This young lady is here to see you. And if I hear that you mistreated her in any way, your ass is going to be doing laps the entire next practice. You hear me, boy?"

Hunter continues to look at me with the same grin on his face. "I would never dream of mistreating Quinn. Not when I plan on making her mine."

My jaw drops; I can't help it. I don't know why he said he wants me to be his. He has a girlfriend and has told me in the past that we can never happen.

"Good," Coach says. He turns to me. "If he does anything wrong or if you need to reach him again, you just call me, Miss Quinn, and I'll take care of it. I'm sick and tired of my boys mistreating the women on this campus. And I cannot tolerate it any further. Too many women have had to come through this locker room to deal with some issue or another. From now on, just talk to me."

I smile at the man and put the business card he held up in my pocket, thankful to have some ally even though I don't deserve it. If he knew what I was really here to do, he wouldn't be so kind to me.

"You two can discuss your business in my office." He points at the door to his office behind Hunter and then walks away.

Hunter raises an eyebrow at me and then holds his hand out to the side. "After you."

I hesitantly walk past him. I can't help it; I keep an eye on the towel wrapped around his waist that has inched lower, secreting hoping it has dropped low enough that I will be able to sneak a peek at his goods. But I have no such luck as I walk into the small office. I slowly turn around as Hunter steps inside and closes the door behind him.

"I'm sorry if I got you in trouble with your coach. I didn't mean for him to give you a lecture; I just needed to find you and—"

Hunter holds up his hand. "No need to apologize; if you knew Coach at all, you would know that's not really a lecture, not even a stern talking-to. He's much worse every day on the field."

I nod. "I'm still sorry, and I'm sorry for ... " I just can't seem to get the words to leave my mouth.

"Stealing my wallet and not having the balls to return it yourself and instead having your friend do it?"

"No, I'm not sorry for that." I take my backpack off my shoulders, reach into the pocket, and pull out the money. I reluctantly hold it out to him. "I'm sorry for stealing your money from the wallet."

Hunter stares at me; his eyes narrow, he still has the smug grin plastered on his face. His arms fold across his bare chest, and I see out of the corner of my eye his towel slip just an inch farther on his hips until I swear I can see the top of ... I gulp and keep my eyes locked firmly on his. "I'm sorry," I say again.

He still doesn't say anything; he just studies me as I can practically see the wheels turning in his head as he thinks. What about, I haven't a clue, but it must be something important because he takes his time and the smile slips off his face.

Is he thinking about ratting me out to the police? He couldn't really do that, though, now that I returned the money, could be? He could rat me out to the school, though, and I would probably get expelled for sure if he did that. I have no idea what he's thinking. His grin returns quickly, though, as he says, "Keep it."

I look at him in confusion. I thrust the money at him again. "I can't. It's not mine."

"Keep it. It's not a gift or charity. It's not stolen money either. It's payment."

My eyes widened because I have no idea what he's talking about. "Payment for what? You also way over tipped for your dinner last night, but I'm not giving you back that money. Was that money meant to be a payment for something as well?"

"Payment to go out with me this year on the same day as last year—October 23rd."

I feel like he just slapped me. "You disgust me." I thrust the money toward him again, begging him to take it so I can leave and never see him again.

He doesn't take it. Instead, he looks at me seriously as his eyes narrow.

"Go out with me for one night again."

"No. You can't just pay me to go out with you. I'm not a whore."

"I never said that."

"Well, you implied it when you offered me money in exchange for sleeping with you."

His damn grin returns, and I can't help it; my stomach does a little loop at the sight.

"I never said anything about sex."

"Whatever. I know that's what you want. You couldn't get enough after last time."

"I didn't get enough last time, but I just want to take you out and help you out. You obviously need the money if you're desperate enough to steal it."

I throw my hands up in the air. "Great. Now, I'm a charity case." I thrust the money against his naked chest. "Take it."

My heart flutters at the touch of my hand against his strong muscular chest.

"Go out with me then and forget about the money."

I can't believe him. I was right when I called him an asshole. And I'm afraid if I stay here any longer, I'll do something stupid like say yes I want to go out with him on a real date. I want him to take me home and fuck me. I want him to date me, to save me again. He can't, and he wouldn't if he knew the whole truth. I won't give in to the temptation or my curiosity that surrounds Hunter Metcalf.

I put the money on Coach's desk. I know Hunter won't leave the money for his coach to see. And then I move to slip past him and out the door. I miscalculate, though, just a step, and our bodies brush against each other. He tries to grab my arm to keep me in the room, but I slip out of his grasp.

"Quinn," Hunter says.

I turn for just a second, just long enough to see that when I brushed past him, the towel fell to the floor. He didn't notice partly because I don't think he cares. I stare at his nakedness in all its glory for just a split second. But that second will be ingrained in my head forever because his body is perfection. Every large bit of him is. And I definitely want him inside me again even if I won't really be his afterward.

I run out of the office to get away as fast as possible because the sight of his naked body would make any woman say yes to anything he wants. To make any women do exactly what he wants. And despite how fun it would be to pretend to be his girlfriend for just one night, I can't. I don't get to have fun, even for one night. I can't fuck up again as I have in the past because I might lose the only thing I really care about if I do.

hunter

I'M LEFT ALONE standing in my coach's office. I glance over at the money she tossed down on his desk and smile as I picked it up. She's desperate, which means she'll be back. She's desperate, and I understand desperate. She'll come back for me because she's intrigued and for the money because she has no other choice. I don't know why she needs the money, and I don't care, but she could have all it, whatever she needs, if she comes back and lets me take her on one date when I need it the most. Because I'm desperate too. And money is nothing to me.

I pick up the money and then pick up the towel that fell to the floor. The look on her face will forever be ingrained in my mind. A look that said fuck me. And I would have if she hadn't had the advantage and run out before I could kiss her again. The lip that she has a habit of biting without even being aware of would taste delicious, I'm sure of it. And I would have, dammit, if I could've only gotten close enough to kiss her. But she slipped through my grasp before I even realized what she was doing.

It's not something I'm used to. I'm used to women throwing themselves at me. At least, the women who I usually choose do. They're easy. They know what I'm about. One night, maybe two, but definitely not more than that. Definitely not a girlfriend or a future wife. She's different. She pretends she doesn't want me, yet she forgets I've already had her and know how much she still wants me.

With the towel wrapped around my waist and the money in my grasp, I leave Coach's office to head back to my locker. As soon as I step foot out of the office, I'm greeted with high-fives and hoots and hollers from the men in the room excited to see me with another woman. Most likely all assuming we just hooked up or at the very least made out. I get a high-five from Heinz as I round the corner to my locker. "You tap that? She was a hot mess, bro. She looked easy."

I ignore him and open my locker, trying to not let his locker room talk get to me.

"If you're done with her, mind if I take a ride?" Heinz asks.

I frown. My face tightens, and I glare at him. I tighten my hand into a fist, ready to attack if necessary. "Leave her alone. She's mine."

Heinz looks at me like it's the most ridiculous thing he's ever heard. "That woman was a lot of things, but she is definitely not yours. She wouldn't run out of here like that if she was."

I open my locker, trying to distract myself. I throw the money that I plan on giving back to Quinn in my bag.

"She's mine, or at least, she will be soon enough."

"You haven't fucked her yet?"

"Don't talk about Quinn like that."

Heinz laughs again. "So she has a name."

"Stop teasing Hunter, Heinz; you know Coach will kick your ass if you get our star player all flustered this week and he sucks at practice," Marshall, my teammate and roommate, says.

"Coach doesn't care. Not this week anyway since we don't have a game this weekend. He doesn't give a shit what we do."

Heinz doesn't see him, but Marshall and I do. Coach is standing behind Heinz listening. He doesn't say anything; he just watches. He knows I can fight my own battles, but still, he is always there watching over me. Not that I need him to. I can take care myself. He just worries about me, especially this time of year. This month sucks for me, and he just wants to protect me. He doesn't realize, though, that I'm fine. I already have a way to cope this week.

"Just drop it and worry about your own date to the party this weekend," I say.

"Don't worry about my date; she already said yes. I think you need to worry about your own because, from what I just saw, you need the help."

I grab my clothes and bag out of my locker then slam it shut. I'm tired of listening to this bullshit. And I know I'm losing control of my temper, and I hate losing control. My life is all about control. Instead of dealing with this idiot like I want to, I storm off to dress somewhere else, anywhere else but here.

My classes today have been a breeze. Nothing but turning in papers and taking tests. It's midterm week, one of the weeks most people dread; not me, though. It's one of the easiest weeks for me. By the time midterms come around, I've already done the work, and now it's about reaping those rewards and knowing that you won't have to do any homework at least on the few days over fall break.

And every time I leave class, I know I won't have to think about it again until the class meets next week. School comes easy for me; since I'm part of the football team, I have full access to as many tutors and helpers as I want, but it's not only that. I have people who can attend class for me if I can't. I have people who'll take notes, people who will do all the homework. I have a great memory, though, which means I read it once and remember it forever. It makes taking tests easy, and writing papers even isn't a struggle for me. School is easy. It's an escape just like football is. But despite how easy and uneventful my classes have been compared to this morning with Quinn, I still look forward to my lunch with Camille.

Despite having dozens of teammates to hang out with on a daily basis and classmates from high school who attend the same college, Camille is still my best friend and always will be. I've known her for years. We have a connection no one else will understand.

I head over to our usual spot on the grass in the middle of campus where I meet Camille for lunch. I make myself comfortable on the grass before pulling out my foot-long sandwich from a nearby sandwich shop along with some fruit and water. Just as I begin to eat my sandwich, I hear her say, "Hey bud, sorry I'm late."

A smile instantly warms my face. I glance up and watch as Camille plops down next to me in her long dress complete with dark tights. I'll never understand why she dresses up so much and looks so good just to go to class. All it results in is me having to fight off every man on campus who looks at her wrong.

"You're not late," I say, starting our usual banter.

She smiles, flashing me her perfectly white straight teeth. "Yes, I am. We are supposed to meet at 1:00. It's 1:07."

I laugh. I can't help it; I always do when I'm around her. I think that's why she makes sure to have lunch with me every day even though her schedule hardly allows it. Camille can always make me smile, laugh. It's something that doesn't genuinely happen often in my life anymore.

She pulls out her bag, and we both dig into our lunches just enjoying sitting next to each other.

With a mouthful of her tuna sandwich, she asks, "Anything new with you?"

I take another bite, buying myself some time while I try to decide if I should tell her, but I decide not to. Although I have talked to Camille plenty about women who I have dated, I'm not ready to tell her about Quinn yet. I never told her about our time together last year or the year before. I still have a lot of work to do to convince Quinn to go out with me next weekend, and I'm running out of time quickly. I could always text her that I need her and force her to go out with me, but I would prefer to convince her without forcing her.

"Just preparing for the game this weekend and trying to stay focused."

Camille laughs. "Like you don't make time to enjoy yourself at parties even when you have a game."

I grin and shrug my shoulders. Because, of course, she's right. It doesn't matter if I have a game or not. I will go out and party either way. Life's too short not to.

"So who's the girl?" Camille asks, looking up at me with her big gorgeous green eyes before she takes the bite of her sandwich.

"What girl?" I ask, playing dumb even though there is no reason to. She knows me too well.

"Don't play dumb. You can't survive next weekend without a girl by your side. So who's the lucky girl? Or did you decide for once that you just want to spend it with your best friend?"

I frown.

"That's not fair, and you know it. I love spending time with you. This month, next week, I just ..."

She smiles weakly. "Can't."

I nod.

I watch as she takes a bit of her sandwich, and we both ignore each other for a minute as we eat. Camille finishes her sandwich, and I know our time is almost up. She has a class to get to, but instead, she tries again "Who's the girl?"

"I'm not sure yet, but I'm working on it."

"Promise you'll just hang out with me if you don't convince her by the twenty-third?"

"I promise." I promise, but not because I'm afraid I won't find someone to go out on a date with me next Saturday. I've already found her; I just need to convince her. I promise because I know Quinn won't say no to me again. That despite how much Camille wishes I would spend the day with her, she knows that's never going to happen. She reminds me too much of the worst day of my life for anything more to ever happen.

quinn

I HAVE ONE MORE class until I'm supposed to meet with my financial advisor. I'm skipping my last class to meet with her because this was the only time she had open this week, and I can't wait until next week to meet with her. I just can't wait that long to figure out my financial situation. So I agreed to meet with her today.

And even though this class is my favorite and this teacher is my favorite, I don't think it will be enough to distract me from worrying about the fact I can't afford college. I walk into his class and take a seat in the back even though I usually sit in the front. I just can't handle it today. Honestly, I'm not sure why I even showed up. The test for this class isn't until Friday. Today is just a review day, and I'm more than prepared to take the test on Friday. I just came because it gave me something to do. And because I'm sure my professor would ask me Friday why I didn't show up on Wednesday. He would corner me and question me and assume something was wrong, and I don't need anyone else to worry about me. I can take care of myself.

My professor walks in right on time and begins going over the basic outline again to help us prepare for the test. I barely hear what he is saying; instead, I focus on the panic churning inside my chest. Panic, terror, fear. I wish I could be like any other college student. Then I could have been delighted Hunter Metcalf asked me out instead of focusing on how I'm going to pay for this class. Despite the panic that has eaten away at my stomach all day, my mind has still flickered to him and imagined what it would be like to say yes and go out on that day.

Hunter's out of my life now, though, and I need to stop daydreaming about him because I have more important things to worry about. One thing I need to come up with is a plan on how to deal with my roommate bailing on me ASAP. I could try to find a new apartment although I doubt I could find anything cheaper than the apartment where I'm now living. It was the cheapest thing I could find when I was looking two years ago. I'll have to find a new roommate. I take a pen and paper out of the backpack and begin writing down any ideas I have about finding a new roommate:

- Create flyers to put around campus
- See how expensive ads with the campus newsletter are
- Talk with friends and classmates to see if they know of anyone looking for an apartment
- Find another job or take on more hours to be able to pay for the apartment myself
- ???

I run out of ideas quickly, which leaves me frustrated. I have to be able to afford this apartment.

"Quinn," I hear someone say, but it doesn't really register.

"Quinn," I hear again.

I look up to see Mr. Dawes, my professor, standing over my desk with a raised eyebrow. "Class is over, Quinn."

I nod and smile before packing my things into my backpack and stand ready to get out of his way.

He doesn't move, though. "Is everything okay?"

"Yes."

"You sure?"

"Yes."

I see the worry on his face as he looks at me. I know he cares about me, but he can't help. This is not like math class where we can work out the problem together. Life, unfortunately, isn't like that. "I should get to my next class."

I brush past him and head toward the exit, but I can still hear his voice. "I'm here if you need help. Just say the word."

I'm thankful for his offer to help, but it doesn't make me hesitate, not even for a second. I just walk out of his classroom and keep walking until I get to the business offices. I'm early to the meeting even though I left class a little late. The closed door to her office indicates another student is in there, so I take a seat outside the office and wait. The waiting brings back the panic, which quickly turns to terror. My whole body shakes nervously while sitting outside her office until the door finally opens.

I see a young man step out with a smile on his face; whatever she had to say, it's obvious that it is good news.

Maybe I can be so lucky. Maybe there's some hidden way I can get money for the school. Heidi, the financial advisor, smiles at me and says, "Come in."

I nod.

I follow her into her office. She shuts the door behind us and takes a seat behind her large desk. I hesitate for a second before I take a seat in the chair in front of her. Like if I don't sit in the chair, I can't hear the bad news.

"Thank you for meeting with me. I know these meetings are hard, but it is best to discuss your financial situation now before you do the work and don't get the credit for it."

I nod and watch as she clicks on her computer screen and then types some things in. "I pulled up your financial history, and it looks like you owe for summer and fall semester tuition and that you are behind on the monthly payments we set up at the beginning of the year."

I nod.

"Unfortunately, it looks like you are on our lowest payment plan option, so there's really nothing else we can do there. You can apply for student loans, but you already missed the deadlines for this semester. The best we could do for you is get loans for next semester. In the meantime, I suggest dropping classes down to a load that you are able to pay for."

Again, I nod.

"Does this all seem reasonable to you?"

"I don't want to drop any classes. Give me whatever information you can on the student loans and exactly how much I owe for the summer and fall semesters and I'll figure it out."

She frowns. She doesn't think I can do this, which is all it takes for the panic to disappear. She doesn't know me at all. I can do this. I've survived a lot worse. Coming up with some money is nothing. I just needed to remind myself from deep inside my gut that I can.

I watch as she presses print on the computer and the printer comes to life. When it's done, she hands me the stack of papers.

"Thank you," I say, getting up and walking out of her office. It isn't until I look at the tuition number that I owe that I realize I'm in deep trouble. It's even more than I thought it was.

I shake off the feeling, though. Along with the feeling that I should text Hunter for help. I can do this ... I can do this ... I can do this ...

hunter

"WE WON! We fucking won. I still can't believe that really just happened," an already drunk Marshall, our quarterback and my roommate, says, stumbling up to the table I'm sitting at with a couple of other teammates. He pulls a chair up to the table and takes a seat.

"Damn right, we are still undefeated, man, and knocked down a number three seat in the process. We are unstoppable," Charlie, our defensive tackle, says.

"No thanks to either of you. You let them score over fifty points. Do you know how hard it is to score that many points?" I say.

Charlie laughs. "Aw, come on. You love the challenge of scoring that many points. It makes you look that much better."

"Well, it wouldn't hurt if you would stop worrying about flirting with the cheerleaders on the sidelines and worry more about tackling someone, preferably the guy with the ball," I say.

"Give Charlie a break; you know he doesn't know how to tackle. He bruises too easily. He can't tackle someone when he could get bruised," Marshall says.

I raise an eyebrow at Marshall. "You are one to talk. You could have at least thrown a couple of catchable balls tonight."

"Everything I threw was catchable; obviously, you caught them," Marshall says.

"Yeah, because I'm awesome, not because they were catchable," I say.

"Oh, here we go again. The great Hunter Metcalf saved the day again. Come on, let's hear it. Get it out of your system so we can actually enjoy the rest of the night and spend time finding some hot girls to take home tonight instead of having to hear this bullshit," Marshall says.

"I am awesome. I carried your asses out there. If it wasn't for me, we would have lost the game, and with it, our chances of going to the playoffs or championship game. Who scored five touchdowns?"

"You," the table responds in unison, used to my stupid banter, but it doesn't make me stop. I need this tonight more than ever.

"Who intercepted the ball at the bottom of the fourth with time running out?"

"You," they all say again, sounding annoyed, but I don't stop.

"Who caught the game-winning pass despite a terrible throw and in double coverage?" I glance over at Marshall as I say it, and he knows it's true. His passes were horrible tonight. Worse than usual.

"You," comes everyone's response.

"That's what I thought. So when one of you does all that, then you can brag about how awesome you are and how we wouldn't have won the game without you. Until then, I get to do all the bragging."

Charlie smiles. "And do all the buying. The next round is on you, our fearless captain who we couldn't win a game without."

The sassy looking bartender comes over to our table. "Another round, guys?"

"Hell, yeah. This dude is buying, so we want a round of the best whiskey you got," Charlie says, pointing at me.

I pull out my wallet and grab a credit card to start a tab. The guys all think making me pay for shit is their way of getting back at me, but it isn't. I have endless amounts of money. And I'm about to make millions more when I get drafted after the end of this season.

I hold out my credit card while I take a moment to look at our bartender. She's wearing a black top with spaghetti straps that reveals the top of her cleavage along with tiny black shorts. She has a full face of makeup and long blond hair that she obviously spent time styling before coming in to work. She's beautiful, probably one of the most beautiful girls in this bar, and if I play my cards right, I know I can have her in my bed tonight or at least in the bathroom later.

But this is the first time in a long time that I don't. Instead of appreciating her beauty, all I can do is compare her to Quinn. This woman's beauty is obvious. It's clear as day that she's beautiful. Quinn, on the other hand, hides her beauty or at least doesn't flaunt it like this woman. This girl is easy while Quinn is hard. She's lived a much harder life, and that has made her into a stronger woman; one who doesn't bother with silly things like doing her makeup or styling her hair. Quinn worries about important things like her job. Her grades. She worries about surviving. While this woman in front of me has never had to worry about surviving a day in her life.

Most of my life, I've been like this woman. I didn't have worry or care in the world. Now, every day is a struggle to survive, to just keep living, especially this time of the year. I need to get out of this town before it kills me. And I plan to just as soon as I'm called up to the NFL.

I must have been quiet for too long because Marshall grabs the credit card from me and hands it to our bartender who is smiling at me. "You can put everything on Mr. Bigshot's credit card. Sorry he's got such a dumb expression on his face. He's just our dumb captain who can catch a ball but not much else."

The woman isn't listening to Marshall, though. She is staring intently at me as she runs her tongue across her lower lip. "You're Hunter Metcalf, right?"

I shake out of the daydream I was having. "That's me. You can call me Oh God, though."

I get snickers from around the table. They have heard this line too many times to count. It works, though, so why bother changing up my game? It doesn't really matter what I say anyway. I just need to get her thinking about us together in bed; after that, she'll do anything to make that possibility come true.

"What?" She cocks her head to the side.

I glance at her name tag. "It's Alison, right?"

She nods and smiles, thinking I must know her from somewhere else instead of just glancing at her name tag. Women lose their minds around me.

"Well, Alison, you can call me Oh God, Fuck Yeah, or Jesus Christ. The choice is yours. Although, my guess is you'll call me Oh God." I wink at her and watch her cheeks blush a deep pink color as the vision of the two of us together seeps into her head. She loves the idea. She's desperate for the idea.

"I don't know why you would want a dick like him when you could have me or any other of these fine gentlemen at the table, but if you really want Mr. Bigshot over there, we will make sure he finds you by the end of the night. Right now, we could really do with another round of drinks," Charlie says.

That snaps Alison back to reality from dreaming about all the naughty things I could do to her. She smiles at the table. "I'll take Mr. Bigshot, I think. I'll be right back with your drinks, though, first."

She scurries away.

"I can't believe you get away with that shit, Hunter. I'm the quarterback, for Christ's sake, and I can't get away with dumb lines like that," Marshall says.

"Yeah, if I said something like that, I would get slapped," Heinz says.

"That's because you're a lineman. Nobody wants to date a lineman, Heinz," Charlie says.

Heinz throws something at Charlie from across the table.

"Well, now that Mr. Bigshot has chosen his victim for tonight, it leaves less competition for the rest of us tonight at least," Marshall says.

I nod although Alison wasn't who I was hoping to choose. I was hoping Quinn would have come crawling back to me by now. I figured she would be curious enough to see what I'm like in bed or at the very least be smart enough to know that I'm made of money, and she can get plenty from me.

Quinn hasn't, though. I haven't heard one word from her. I haven't seen any sign of her although that doesn't mean she didn't seek me out. She could have come to the game today to watch me, and I wouldn't have a clue. She has me at an advantage there. I can't easily stalk her without being seen all over campus doing so.

I just don't think women like Alison are going to be enough of a distraction especially next week with no game. There is nothing to distract me. Nothing to keep my pain away. Alison might be enough for tonight, but she's not enough for next week. She's not enough to get me focused for the game after next week, but Quinn just might be.

I just need a better plan to get Quinn to agree to be my distraction.

Alison returns with a round of whiskey for everyone. She's also brought a couple of pitchers of beer. She sets all the alcohol on the table as everyone scrambles to grab a drink for themselves. When she's done, she looks at me.

"I'm off in an hour." She winks at me and then returns to the bar.

"Dammit, we only have an hour to drink free, boys. Better make the most of it and find our own dates for tonight," Marshall says, lifting his glass to his lips and downing the whiskey.

I begin to drink my own whiskey, but it does nothing to make the pain sneaking back into my life each day go away. It's a pain, a darkness that puts a haze on the whole day. And I know only two ways to dampen that darkness, at least temporarily. Football and a hot woman in my bed. I just have to wait an hour for the second one to help get me through the rest of the night. But I know as soon as I wake up tomorrow morning, the pain is going to be worse, and I'm going to need a bigger fix. A fix only Quinn may be able to give me.

***

"Hey God, now's your chance. I'm done with my shift," Alison says, standing at the end of our table.

I grin. I throw down the last of my whiskey and then stand. "It's Oh God, Alison."

She smiles as I tuck a strand of her hair behind her ear. I make the same moves every time to hook a woman. The same line, followed by the sexy grin, and then the tucking of the hair. I've done them so many times that I can hit on a girl on autopilot and still get a girl to say yes. I only really come alive when it comes to the fucking. That's something I'm more creative with.

"We are headed to the bar next door. You coming, bigshot?" Marshall asks.

"Give me a few to pay off our tab and then I'll be right there," I say. Keeping my eyes on Alison, I let her know with the lust in my eyes that her tip will be paid in orgasms.

I grab Alison's hand, and we make a beeline for the bathrooms. Alison is steady on her feet as she walks behind me. It's been a long time since I've had sex with a woman who hasn't been drunk or at least tipsy. I'm honestly surprised she hasn't taken a couple of drinks herself behind the bar. She must be a 'good girl,' which surprises me even more that she is going to let me do what I'm about to do to her. Because after I'm done, she won't think of herself as a 'good girl' anymore.

I reach the bathroom and turn toward the men's room until I finally feel resistance from her, but then I expected that from a 'good girl.'

"We can't go in there," she whispers.

I turn flashing her another grin. "Of course, we can."

"But ... men are probably in there, and it's disgusting in there," Alison says.

I grab her chin and pull her lips to mine so I can kiss her. I push my tongue into her mouth and swirl it around, making sure she knows how I feel. That I want her. Here. Now. And that it isn't going to happen anywhere else but here. I kiss her until I hear the moan letting me know that she wants this, and then I stop the kiss, denying her what she really wants.

She bites her lip. "Okay," she says.

I grin and pull her into the bathroom where a drunk guy is using one of the urinals. He smiles when he sees us. I don't. I frown.

"Get out," I say.

"Why?" the guy responds before he looks at me. When he sees the fury that I will do to him if he doesn't leave on his own accord, he quickly starts stumbling out despite not zipping up his zipper.

I don't give Alison time to scan the bathroom. I don't give her time to see the pee on the floor or the toilet paper stuck to the walls or the intense smell that will make her wish she was anywhere but here. I don't give her time to think.

I devour her lips as I push her against one of the walls. It startles her, and I watch her eyes grow wide but then close as I run my hand over her tiny hips. She moans softly against my lips.

I kiss down her bare neck. I feel her swallow hard in her throat as I kiss her neck. She's nervous. I chose poorly; I thought she was more confident than this. I like strong, confident woman who know what they want and aren't afraid to ask me for it. I don't have the time or patience to deal with someone nervous or insecure. Someone who is... shit.

I stop kissing her. "Are you a virgin, Alison?"

She doesn't answer me, but the bright red covering her cheeks tells me that she is. Dammit. I don't want to be someone's first time. Or someone's last time. I just want something that can be enjoyable for a couple of nights until I push her off onto another guy who will be happy to show her a good time. I don't do this.

I sigh. "I'm not going to fuck you, Alison."

Her eyes grow big, and I swear I see tears there. Goddammit. Fuck, fuck, fuck. If I was better on my game tonight, I would have seen that she was a virgin earlier and never gone after her. Instead, I was more worried about Quinn.

Now, I'm stuck between doing what I want to do, which is getting the hell out of here but knowing that I made her cry, or doing something nice for her.

"I'm going to give you the best damn orgasm you've ever had, though," I say. I kiss her again as I lift her off the ground by grabbing her hips. I carry her over to the counter next to the sinks as I kiss her harder, deeper until she is moaning loudly again and has hopefully forgotten about the fact I'm not going to fuck her—at least, not with my dick.

I stop kissing her when I set her on the counter and then grab her shorts and underwear and pull them down, revealing her pussy. But not a bare pussy like I'm used to. A hair covered one. It's not that I'm opposed to the idea, but if I had my way, all pussies would be bare, and if a woman isn't going to bother shaving, then don't expect a lot of tongue action down there. Right now, though, I'm too far into this to back out. I can't just forget about the licking and go straight to the fucking when the licking is all I was planning to do in the first place.

So I suck it up and lower my lips to her pussy and begin licking her, hair and all. She moans loudly as I do. God, I deserve a medal for how nice I'm being to this stranger. If the guys ever found out about what I'm doing, they would never let it go.

I push my tongue inside her, and she screams, "Oh, God."

I bring my tongue back out and replace it with two fingers as my tongue flicks over her clit, and her 'oh gods' get louder and more intense. Just a couple of more flicks, I think.

It only takes one to make her come undone. She pulses around my fingers and screams another, "Oh, God."

I smile and remove my fingers from inside her before pulling her shorts back up over her hips as she looks at me in shock. That is the gentlemanly thing to do, and I guess that's who I am today. A fucking gentleman.

"I told you that your name for me was Oh God." I suck my fingers, cleaning myself of her juices. "I'll see you around, Alison."

I walk out of the bathroom, and despite how nice I was to that girl, I feel like complete shit. I need help. I need a fuck and soon, or I'm going to lose it. Quinn pops back into my head. I need a plan. There are only two ways I know to run into Quinn again. One is at the restaurant where she works at. The other is the tutoring center. Eating that crappy bar food every night is going to make me sick and piss off Coach. I make straight As and have more than enough tutors provided through the athletic department to help me if I was struggling. But Quinn doesn't need to know that. I can pretend to be dumb.

quinn

I'VE WORKED MY butt off these past few days and have only managed to make an extra hundred dollars. That's it. One hundred dollars. I tried picking up more shifts at the coffee shop and pizza place where I work, but I'm already working as many shifts as they will allow. I've tried being nicer to my customers to get more tips, but that hardly made a difference. Only a hundred dollars' difference. That's not enough to cover my tuition costs or the extra rent. None of it is enough.

I have to find a new job that pays a lot more. That's just hard to do when I have no skills and only minimal schooling.

I open the door and walk into the building that contains the tutoring center, feeling the warm heat from the building as I step inside from the cold fall day outside. So cold there is a chance of snow this afternoon. Everyone else on campus has been fretting about how cold it is, but I love winter. I love how pretty the snow looks covering the mountains.

I walk down the busy hallway to the tutoring center, trying to bring a smile to my face before I open the door. Meredith texted me when she got in that I have two students on my list today so not to be late. I was really hoping I would have none so I could spend the time applying for jobs. My tutor job is by far my least paying job, so I could easily fill the four hours a week I work here with another job. And hopefully, I can find a better paying job to replace my jobs as a barista and waitress.

Tomorrow is going to be a better day. The best day. I just have to get through today, and then I'll get the best reminder of why everything I've been putting myself through these past few days is worth it. Tomorrow, all the stress I have experienced will be worth it.

I pull the door open and step inside, trying to keep a smile on my face. I manage a weak smile for a couple of seconds until I see Chaz sitting at my table. My smile instantly disappears.

I was hoping I would just be working with some freshmen who are struggling in their calculus class or something easy that I could do in my sleep. I don't want to have to think and figure out complex computer science problems.

I begin to walk over to the table as Meredith gives me a dirty look before pointing at her watch. I roll my eyes. I'm two minutes late; that's not late.

"Hi, Chaz," I say, taking a seat opposite him. "So you couldn't find any other tutors to help you, huh?" I study him, waiting for his answer.

"Nope," he says, smiling brightly like it's an accomplishment.

I sigh.

"Did you bring your textbook then?"

He nods and begins digging in his backpack.

I shrug off the jacket I'm wearing over my thin long-sleeved shirt. I braid my hair quickly to keep it out of my face and then pull a notebook and pen out of my backpack to take notes on. A flyer I made looking for a roommate slides out of the notebook and onto the floor next to my chair, but I'm too lazy to bend down and pick it up.

Chaz flips open the textbook to the chapter he's on. I begin scanning to see what section he is on.

"What are you struggling with?" I ask.

"Everything." Chaz chuckles.

I don't. I glance up at him. "I'll need a few minutes to read the chapters you are on to see if I can comprehend it myself." I flip to the back of the chapter where there are practice exam questions. I stand and head over to the printer next to where the laptops for checking out are. I scan the page and then print it out before walking back to the table and taking a seat.

"Work on these questions while I'm reading this chapter, and then when we are both finished, we can go over them together," I say, sliding the paper over to Chaz.

He smiles. His fingers brush against mine as he takes the paper out of my hand. I pull my hand away quickly, trying my best not to let him think anything is going on between us because nothing other than me trying to explain this chapter to him as quickly as possible and then getting him out of here is going to happen.

My hands grasp the textbook in front of me as I begin to read the chapter. It's boring. Easy. I flip through the ten pages quickly, checking Chaz's progress on his exam sheet as I go.

Chaz takes his time answering each question, but I'm not sure if it is because he is struggling to answer or because he just can't keep his eyes off me. It makes me nervous every time he looks at me. I'm not interested in dating. I don't have time for men. If he had known I turned down Hunter Metcalf, for Christ's sake, he wouldn't be undressing me with his eyes. He would be treating me like most guys do, like I'm invisible.

"All finished?" I ask when Chaz looks up at me again.

"Almost." He smiles again, and I shiver, silently begging him to stop.

"Well, let's see how you did so far." I grab the paper from him and begin scanning his answers.

Every single answer is wrong. Every single one. And as much as I don't like his creepy smile, Chaz doesn't come off as an unintelligent guy. So it seems improbable that he would get every single answer wrong if he was trying at all. What's weirder is that the answers aren't that far off from the correct answers. Just one step wrong in each that creates the wrong answer. And each time, he did something different wrong instead of making the same mistake over and over again.

I glance up from the paper to Chaz. "Great job. You got them all correct. I don't think you need my help after all."

Chaz wrinkles his nose as his eyes narrow in confusion. "What? That's not possible ... I ..."

I cock my head to the side with a smile on my face. "Why isn't it possible?"

Chaz thinks for a moment. "Because I know I didn't know the answers to those questions."

"And how would you know that unless you purposely answered them incorrectly?"

Chaz looks at me, stunned.

"You didn't come to me to get help in your computer science class, did you?"

Chaz smiles innocently. "No."

"Then why did you?"

"Because I like you, Quinn. And I want to ask you out."

I take a deep breath, trying to calm myself and to keep myself from yelling like I really want to do. "I don't have time for this, Chaz. Please leave," I say, proud of myself for not raising my voice or saying the things I really want to say.

"Come on, Quinn, just go out with me on one date," Chaz says.

"No, get out," I say, my voice getting louder, angrier.

Chaz touches my arm, and I jump up, not okay with any of this. "Why the hell do you think it is okay to touch me? Get out, now. You don't need a tutor, and I'm not going on a date with you," I say loudly. I'm shaking a little from my anger, and everyone's eyes are on me.

I take a deep breath, and then I gather my stuff and begin to walk out. "I'm done," I say to Meredith as I walk by her.

She stands up from her desk stopping me before I get to the door. "You can't. You have another student coming in for your help. I can't take him. Today, I have issues of my own to work through, Quinn," she says with a worried look on her face.

I frown. I feel bad that I never ask Meredith how she is doing. I'm always too stressed with my own issues to think about anyone else. I'm sure she is dealing with crap I don't know about. But that doesn't mean I can help her.

"I need to go. I'm sorry."

I turn to head out the door when the door is pulled open, and I find out who I'm supposed to tutor next. Hunter.

hunter

I SMILE WHEN I SEE HER, but she isn't smiling. She's angry. Her face is red, and she has been yelling. I look past her, searching for the cause of her anger. I'll do whatever's necessary to stop her pain caused by any asshole in this tutoring center.

But when I look back at her, I realize I might be the arrogant asshole.

Quinn throws up her hands. "I'm so done with men." She glances at the guy in the corner and then back at me. "You can't just come in here and pretend you need a tutor when you don't just to try to get me to go out with you! It doesn't work that way!"

She stops just in front of me. "And you. You don't get to have me one day every year. That's not how this works. You said it was a one-time thing. That we couldn't be together again. So stick to your promise and leave me alone!"

Quinn walks out of the tutoring center and effectively out of my life. I don't know how to convince her that I need her tomorrow night. I need her desperately. And I think she needs me too. I just don't know how to convince her.

I glance around the tutoring center and see everyone's eyes on me.

"What are you looking at?" I say to the crowd. Everyone immediately looks down at their computers and the papers scattered on their desks. And I feel like an idiot for yelling.

I turn and walk out of the tutoring center, trying to think of another plan to get Quinn to go out with me. But all I can think about are her words. *Stick to your promise.* I smile. I plan to.

quinn

MY PHONE BUZZES in my pocket as I ride my bike back to my apartment. I don't check it because I never get messages from anyone important anyway. Instead, I try to think about what the hell I'm going to do for money. But Hunter keeps sneaking into every thought. His grin, his chest, how good his lips feel when he kisses me. How nice it would be to fuck him and forget about all my troubles for a couple of days.

I keep pedaling hard to get back to my apartment. If I get back quickly, then I can take at least a twenty-minute nap before I have to get ready to go to work.

I get back to my apartment and collapse on my bed before my phone buzzes again, reminding me that I need to check my phone. I pull my phone out of my back pocket and read from the number that is my contacts as *Text in case of an emergency.*

I haven't seen a message from this number in a year. I change the contact listing to Hunter now that I know his real name and then read the message.

Hunter: I need you. Tomorrow night. I'll pick you up at your apartment.

I shouldn't have opened the message. I text back.

Me: I already told you no.

I wait and my phone buzzes again. I read his message.

Hunter: We both promised if we ever needed each other we were just a text message away. You wouldn't break a promise, would you?

I sigh. He's not going to back down, and honestly, I don't want him to. I could use the break from reality tomorrow as well. So I text …

Me: What time are you coming to pick me up?

"You look so frumpy in that. You sure you don't want to borrow something of mine?" Mandy says.

"Nope. I want to wear my own clothing," I say, running my hand through my hair again to loosen the curls that I may have overdone.

"But you aren't going to get him to sleep with you if you wear that. Your skirt is far too long and don't even get me started on that ugly ass sweater. Hunter Metcalf is a one-date kind of guy. You only get one shot with him, you know," Mandy says, tugging on my skirt that is plenty short since it hits me mid-thigh.

I hear a knock on the door and go over and open it to Hunter standing in the doorway. He looks handsome as hell and a million times better than I do right now in his dark jeans and button-down shirt. But his eyes scanning all over my body tell me differently. They tell me exactly what I already knew.

I grab my purse off the counter and then turn to look at Mandy before I leave. "Don't worry. He'll sleep with me before the night is over."

I walk out of my apartment, winking at Hunter who is standing there frozen. He quickly regains his consciousness and begins walking with me.

"You know that isn't what tonight is about, right?" he asks.

I shrug. "You forget we've already done this once before, and you told me the same thing then. I don't believe you."

We walk out of the apartment building. "So where are we going?" I ask.

"To a club."

I smirk.

"You can wipe that smirk right off your face, Quinn. It's not what you think."

I laugh. "I think it's exactly what I think."

Hunter holds the door open, and I climb into his Jeep. Hunter climbs in the driver's seat and begins driving toward this club.

Hunter is silent as he drives. Too silent. So silent that I can't handle the silence because I know when he's silent what he is thinking about. I know how hard today is for him; I just don't know why I make it any better for him.

"Why me? I know today is hard for you, but don't you have friends or family who would be better to spend time with today? Who could help you get through today," I say.

Hunter looks over at me; his eyes narrow, and his grip on the wheel tightens. But he doesn't answer me.

"Hunter?"

"Because we share a connection to that night that no one else will ever understand. And when I'm with you, you help me. I don't understand it, but you help me. And I know that even though you won't ever admit you need help, you do."

I sigh. "Fine. So what do you need tonight? Fun? Someone to reminisce with? Sex? What?"

He frowns. "I just need you."

Hunter parks his car in front of a hotel in downtown Denver.

"I thought you were taking me to a club?"

Hunter climbs out of the car and opens my door. "I am." He holds his hand out to me, and I hesitantly take it, but my hand is shaking.

"You don't need to be nervous. I just want to be with you. That's it."

I nod as he leads me into an elevator. He doesn't get it. I have everything to be nervous about. Because being around him makes me realize what I've been missing in my life. Someone who cares about me.

The elevator doors open, and my mouth drops when I get a good look at the view.

"It's pretty impressive, right?" Hunter says into my ear.

"Yeah ..." is all I get out as I look at the expansive view of the city and the sunset.

Hunter guides me in, and although the crowd is small at the moment, this isn't a typical college crowd; this crowd is well dressed and a bit older than we are.

I glance down at my attire. "Is it okay that I'm wearing this?"

Hunter grins. "No one here cares what you're wearing. Only I care what you look like."

"And?"

"And I think you look hot. You already knew that, though."

I smile. "It's still nice to hear it again. It has been what? A year since the last time I heard that."

"Come on, let's dance."

"No drink first?"

"Are you twenty-one?" he asks, raising an eyebrow.

"No," I say blushing.

"Then you aren't drinking. And I'm not drinking because I want to remember every second of tonight."

I pause. "Why would you want to remember every moment of tonight? I thought you would want to forget. That's what I want."

He shakes his head. "I don't want to forget. I just want to live, and you help me do that."

"Then why did you bring me to a club if you don't want to drink?"

"Because I want to dance and talk and show you the best view in Denver."

"I don't dance."

He frowns.

I sigh and let him lead me onto the empty dance floor, which just makes it worse because it means I can't hide in the crowd; everyone can see me.

But Hunter puts his arms around me, and I no longer care that people are watching me. That I'm horrible at dancing. That the man whose arms are around me isn't my man. He's not mine, I repeat over and over. But God, do I want him to be.

Another song starts and I ...

"I'm sorry; I can't dance with you. It's too hard for me," I say.

I start walking out, just needing some air, but Hunter grabs my hand. "Go out on the balcony with me."

I stop and nod because I think I can handle that. I can go outside.

Hunter leads me outside, and we take a seat on a bench next to the edge of the balcony that overlooks the city. He drapes his arm around me, and it feels so normal, so natural.

"It's beautiful," I say, looking out at the sky that is quickly turning from shades of orange to darkness and stars.

He nods, and then we sit in silence. I snuggle into his chest as we both just breathe.

"I don't feel like I'm helping you," I say as I snuggle deeper into his chest.

His chest rises and falls, and then he laughs. "This is helping me, Quinn. And it's helping you too."

Silence again as we just sit and hold each other. I thought this night was about sex. I thought it was about forgetting. But it isn't; it's about living.

"I don't regret what happened two years ago. It sucked. It was the worst darkest day of both of our lives, but we wouldn't be here experiencing this if it wasn't for that night."

He smiles and then kisses me. It's a sweet, perfect kiss. But it still isn't about sex; it's about living. Something that has been hard for both of us for the past two years, but tonight, that's going to change. Tonight, living is going to get a bit easier.

TEXT MESSAGE #2

1 year earlier

quinn

TODAY IS THE WORST DAY. Ever. I don't want to think about what is going to happen today. I won't be there when it happens, so it's better if I don't think about it. It's better if I don't see with my own eyes. It's better that I don't know the exact moment when my life is over.

I thought I had experienced the worst day of my life a year ago. But that wasn't the worst day; in fact, that day turned out to be one of the best days of my life now when I look back on it. That won't happen when I look back a year from now on today. When I look back a year from now, I know that today was the day my life ended.

Because today a family in West Virginia is adopting Ava. And I won't ever be able to see her again. Ava, who I have thought of as my own daughter and have basically been her mother, is not mine. She's leaving, and I can't do anything to stop it.

Today is also my nineteenth birthday. It should be a day to celebrate, but it's not. And I haven't even been able to get myself out of this bed.

I roll over and feel the bed creak as it always does. I need a new bed, but working as a waitress in the evenings and a barista in the mornings doesn't allow for much extra income to buy luxury items like a new bed.

I roll and hear the creak of the bed again. And even if I had the money, I'm not sure I would replace the mattress or bed. I like the creak. I like how the twinmattress dips in the middle where I sleep, forming a cocoon around me. I don't want a new bed.

I don't want new clothes despite all mine being used items I bought at Goodwill.

I don't want a new apartment despite sharing my tiny apartment with two to four other people, depending on whose boyfriend is staying over.

I don't want a new bike despite the worn gears and the bald tires.

And I don't want a car to replace my bike.

All I want is for today not to happen. I can handle all the old things that would depress most people. I can handle the stress of living paycheck to paycheck. I can handle not being able to afford much other than rent and food. I can handle all that if I'm happy.

But when the happiness is taken from me, it all becomes too much. Life becomes too much. And I don't know how to deal anymore.

I open my eyes wide. I can't keep thinking like this. This was the exact kind of thinking that got me into trouble the last time almost a year ago. Today can't be too much, no matter how bad it is. I have to find a way to get through today. And then tomorrow. And then the day after that.

I just don't want to. I want to sleep.

I hear the door to our apartment open and then slam shut outside my bedroom door. Mandy is home from her morning classes. I don't know if her boyfriend, Frank, is with her, and I doubt my other roommate, Faith, has even left her bedroom. And if she has, she's probably smoking a joint somewhere. She sure as hell didn't leave to attend a class.

I slowly get out of bed and throw an old sweatshirt on over the T-shirt and shorts that I wore to bed. I don't bother with my tangled brown mess of hair on top of my head. I cut it off to shoulder length this past week, which I now realize was a mistake. I'm used to being able to braid my hair to get it out of my way, and now, I can barely pull it up into a ponytail let alone braid it.

I walk out to the kitchen to see if I can find any food and to see what Mandy is up to. *Maybe she can keep me company today?*

I walk to the pantry and find a banana. I grab it and take a seat in the living room next to where Mandy studies her phone.

"Are you just now getting out of bed? It's after noon," Mandy says, staring at me with wide eyes.

I yawn as I peel my banana. "I don't have anywhere to be. I don't work today. What else am I supposed to do with my time?"

"I don't know. Get a boyfriend or something is what most girls would do with their time off. Or go wherever you sneak off to every other night."

I take a bite of the banana and then answer with my mouth full. "I don't care about guys. And I can't."

Mandy scrunches her nose at me like I'm the most disgusting thing she has ever seen. "Don't you have manners? Stop being so gross."

I roll my eyes. I don't know how she can stand to live here with me and Faith and Faith's boyfriend of the week and Frank, Mandy's boyfriend. I suspect she won't make it much longer. Her family can afford a much nicer apartment than this, but Mandy wanted to try to live like a "normal" student and get a "normal" experience. Although, living with us is anything but "normal," if you ask me.

I finish eating my banana before I ask. "What are you and Frank doing tonight?"

Mandy sighs. "Nothing. Frank has to work. Can you believe it? It's Friday night. Why would he work on Friday night?"

I want to laugh; the same reason I almost always work Friday nights. Money. You make more money on the weekends when you work at a restaurant or bar. I took today off to celebrate my birthday, and now, I wish I hadn't. Now, I wish I had the distraction.

I take a deep breath, contemplating my options. If I really want to ask Mandy what I'm thinking or if I would rather just head back to bed and sleep the rest of the day away with only my tears to keep me comfort.

I glance back at my bedroom. I already know what will happen if I go back to bed. I've lived that life before, and it doesn't turn out good; I have the scars to prove it.

"Do you want to go out with me tonight?"

Mandy stops scrolling through the pictures on her phone. "What? I'm sorry, Quinn, but I'm not a lesbian ..."

I laugh. "I didn't mean on a date, Mandy. I just meant go out with me as friends. I don't really have any friends, and I could use some company tonight."

Mandy frowns. "Why? We aren't friends, though. We just tolerate each other here and at work. And that is just until I find a place I like better to move to."

Anger boils up inside me, ready to explode. I knew this morning was going to be too much for me to handle. I should have chosen to stay in bed. "Because today is my birthday! And I want to go out and celebrate like any other teenager would and pretend for one day I have friends."

Mandy looks at me a bit taken aback. She sits thinking for a moment as I breathe heavily. I need another plan. Mandy is going to say no. I could ask Faith, but if I ask her, we will just end up smoking in her room all day. I'm not sure that spending my day smoking a joint is any better for me than spending my time under my covers.

I frown when I see a slow smile spread over Mandy's face.

"Okay, let's do this. You just have to agree to one thing," Mandy says.

"What?" I ask hesitantly.

"That I get to decide everything we do today. Everything that you do today. Agree?"

My frown deepens. "What do you mean you decide everything that I do today?"

Mandy smiles, pleased with herself as she leans back on the leather couch that she brought when she moved in. I'm going to miss this couch when she leaves.

"I decide everything. What you wear, where we go, what you do."

I swallow. "I don't have much money to spend tonight, though, so we can't go to a bunch of expensive places or to buy new clothes."

Mandy shakes her head still smiling. "Don't worry about that. I have money, and tonight, we are going to have some fun. Do you agree?"

I suck in one last breath. It may be my last breath if I let my crazy roommate decide everything I do the rest of the night. But I don't really have a choice. The alternative is much worse.

"I agree."

What the hell did I get myself into? is all I keep thinking as I let Mandy drag me to a strip club in a black backless dress and heels that I can barely walk in. I take a seat in the booth across from Mandy, thankful that my feet are finally getting a break. The last bar we went to was standing room only. Thankfully, this strip club has plenty of seats. But it also has lots of naked women on stage. And mostly naked women taking orders.

"If you are going to bring me to a strip club, you could as least bring me to one with male strippers," I say.

Mandy shakes her head. "Nah, females have nicer bodies, and women stripping get the men in the room hot and ready to go, so you just find a hot one and they are already ready to fuck."

"I doubt they are hot. More like gross, ugly men."

Mandy rolls her eyes.

A barely clothed waitress in what looks like a bra and panties comes up to our booth. "What can I get you?"

I don't answer. I have realized after I made a mistake at the first bar of answering that Mandy isn't letting me make any decisions tonight, not even what poison I want to pour into my body.

"Two shots of tequila and two margaritas," Mandy says to the waitress.

I moan. I don't think I can handle much more sugar in my stomach. The tequila is fine, but not the margaritas.

"Can I see your IDs?" the waitress asks.

I pull out the fake ID that Mandy got me that says I'm twenty-one, even though I'm just turning nineteen. The waitress barely glances at either of our IDs before she heads off to get us our drinks.

"I don't think I'm going to make it to any other bars after this one. I really appreciate you taking me out, though. It's been a lot of fun," I lie. It's not been much fun listening to Mandy ramble on about her love life, what new designer clothes she can't wait to get, or how silly college is. But it has been distracting, which is what I've needed tonight. At this point, though, I have enough alcohol in me that I could go home and pass out until this god-awful day is over.

Mandy laughs. "You are such a lightweight."

The waitress brings us our shots and margaritas.

I nod to Mandy. I'm not a lightweight. I can drink my way through plenty of alcohol. Just not the sugar.

"Fine," Mandy says before putting salt on her hand and holding up her shot glass.

I do the same, not knowing what we are cheering to.

"If this is the last bar, then it's time to find you a guy to go home with tonight. To finding you the best goddamn guy in this bar." Mandy licks the salt off her hand before she slams her shot glass on the table and then takes the shot followed by the lime.

I do the same nervously. I don't want to go home with whatever guy she chooses for me and decides I should. It's not that I haven't had my fair share of one-night stands. I have. I just don't want Mandy to choose the guy. I'm afraid I'm going to end up with some preppy, rich guy who isn't even good looking. That she is going to say go fuck.

I begin to sip on my margarita, realizing that I may need a lot more alcohol as I scan the crowd in the strip club, trying to avoid looking at the naked woman. I haven't found anyone I would be interested in fucking. I glance over at Mandy who has a frown on her face; obviously, she's not impressed by the crowd in the room either.

I can tell on her face the moment she spots him. Her eyes get big, and her smile grows larger than I've ever seen it.

I don't look in the direction she is looking. I just continue to sip my margarita, hoping that the guy will leave so she won't force me to go over and basically ask him to take me home and fuck me.

"I found him," Mandy says.

I nod.

"The guy sitting at the end of the table to your far right with the dark brown messy hair, the sexy five o'clock shadow, and the muscles that can't be contained by the button-down he's wearing. He's perfect. If I wasn't dating Frank, I would totally ..."

I don't listen to her as she keeps talking. I glance over my right shoulder and find him almost immediately sitting at the end of a table filled with at least a dozen people getting a lap dance. I have to admit he is sexy as hell. She picked the sexiest guy in the strip club. He's fit; I can tell from the muscles popping from beneath his gray T-shirt. His light hair curls over his head in waves.

I can't take my eyes off him even as another woman dances on top of him. It's clear, though, that he is the center of attention at the table as everyone else can't keep their eyes off him either. No way would he go for a girl like me. Not when he could have any of the girls surrounding him at the table or on his lap.

"Go talk to him," I hear Mandy say.

"No. He's not going to want me when he can have any of them. I'm a poor girl who has never had her hair properly cut or colored. I don't have fancy clothes or nice makeup. I'm not smart. I didn't even get into college. I'm a waitress; what would he want with me?"

Mandy laughs. "He's not marrying you. He doesn't care if you go to college or not or that you are just a waitress. He cares that you look hot as hell and that you want to sleep with him."

I don't argue with her. Because I do. I want to sleep with him. I want him to take me home and fuck me against the wall because he can't wait a second longer to make it to bed. I want to feel his stubble against my cheek, between my legs. I want ...

He glances over at me. I swallow but don't look away. He looked so happy a few seconds ago, laughing with the other women, but when he looks at me, he looks sad. In pain. He looks at me, and I can see the reflection of my own pain in his eyes.

My stomach does a little flip, and I'm not sure if it is the good kind of flip. The kind you get when you are excited to do something. Or the bad kind when you know you are about to do something you don't want to do. Either way, it makes me nervous.

He looks back at the woman on his lap who gets off and begins to work on another man. He then turns his attention to the woman on his left who touches him seductively on his hand. I take another sip of my margarita.

"Go," Mandy says.

I finish my margarita and stand prepared to go when I see him stand, holding the woman's hand. I then watch in horror as he leads her toward the back of the restaurant and into the bathroom.

I slump back into the booth. "You're going to have to pick a new guy for me. He's already taken."

Mandy laughs. "No. He's perfect."

"What? He clearly already has a date for tonight."

Mandy laughs again. "No, he doesn't. He's hooking up. No guy who is on a date with a woman takes her to the bathroom. As soon as they leave the bathroom, he's going to be through with her. And then you can have him."

"Pick a new guy and order me another drink."

Mandy motions to our waitress, and as much as I appreciate her help tonight and the money she has spent, I can't suck down one more margarita. When the waitress approaches our table, I say, "I'll take a tequila."

Mandy smiles but doesn't protest my drink order. "I'll have another margarita," Mandy says.

The waitress leaves, and I begin scanning the bar, looking for another man who can make me forget for one night. A man capable of fucking me and making me come until I forget everything floating around in my head despite Mandy's efforts to give me a great birthday.

But I don't see any other man when I look around the bar. All I see is the man who was sitting at the end of the table with eyes that bared his soul. All I can think about is his lips, his hands covering that woman's body right now, and how it would feel to have his hands on me. I imagine her screaming as he thrusts inside her and wishes she was me. When he comes back out, I could get him to fuck me too. Just like her.

The thought is ridiculous. I'm not going to let a man who I don't even know fuck me right after he had sex with another woman. I'm better than this. I have more self-respect than this. I can find another man.

Mandy laughs.

"What?"

"You're seriously considering it. Aren't you?"

I shake my head. "I'm not considering anything."

The waitress places our drinks in front of us, and I take a drink of the tequila.

"There is nothing wrong with you. Who cares that he was just with another girl and who knows how many before you. You aren't going to date him. You just want him to show you a good time, and trust me, that man knows how to do that. So use a condom and let him."

I glance at the door to the bathroom as I sip my tequila. It hasn't been more than a couple of minutes since he took her in there and started doing dirty, filthy things. Things I need.

My mind flips between taking a chance with him or another man, or just going home and hoping the alcohol keeps me from thinking. But if I'm okay with letting another man fuck me, then why am I not okay with him?

The door to the bathroom suddenly opens, and the man leads her back out, still holding her hand. I watch as she stumbles a little bit, and he catches her, keeping her from falling to the floor. He leads her back toward the table and then whispers into one of the guy's ears who is sitting at the table. The man immediately stands up and wraps one of the woman's arms around his shoulder while the man who has bared his soul to me does the same.

I frown when I see them begin to walk out of the bar with the girl.

"Well, I guess that's that," I say, finishing my drink.

Mandy sighs. She pulls some cash out of her purse and throws it on the table. "Let's get out of here. I know one final place where we can at least ogle some hot male strippers."

I smile; not because I want to do that but because Mandy is nicer than I thought. And I should at least repay everything she has done for me tonight by going with her to one last place.

Mandy gets up from the booth and begins walking out of the bar. I follow her. We walk out into the cool night air.

"How far away is the bar?" I ask, wondering if we are walking or if we are going to need to get an Uber.

"It's just a couple ... oh, my God!" Mandy squeals as she runs over to her boyfriend, Frank. "What are you doing? I thought you were working tonight?"

They kiss, and I know our night is ending. Frank has been working a lot this week, so the two of them have barely spent any time together. I wait a minute, thinking that they will stop long enough that I can talk to them, but they don't stop kissing.

"I'm going to walk home. You guys have fun," I say, but they still don't stop kissing.

I begin walking the five or so blocks back to our apartment but stumble after a couple of steps in my high heels. I stop and lean against the side of the restaurant as I remove the shoes Mandy lent to me. My feet feel free now that the shoes are off. I hate to admit it, but I enjoyed being Cinderella for a night. Even though I didn't find a prince to dance with or take me home, I got more attention wearing the shoes and this red dress than I have in a long time.

I begin walking again.

"You having a rough night?"

I stop and turn to see who asked me the question.

Him.

"You?" I ask, and I realize he isn't a stranger. At least, not a complete stranger. I've met this man one time before. Although, we never exchanged names. And ever since, I've just called him asshole in my head. I can't believe I didn't recognize him earlier from across the bar.

The corner of his lip curls up just a little in what I think is a smile, but I'm not sure.

"Me too," he says.

I stare at him, still not believing he's standing here talking to me.

"I thought you went home with ..."

His lips curl up higher, and now, he's smiling at me. "No, just got her an Uber to take her home. My roommate went along to make sure she made it safely inside."

I cock my head to one side. "You really are a fuck 'em and leave 'em kind of guy. You didn't even make sure she made it home safely yourself."

He laughs. "You think I fucked her in the bathroom?"

I raise my eyebrows. "Didn't you?"

"No. She threw up the second we made it inside the bathroom. She was drunk. I helped her out."

"And would you have fucked her if she wasn't drunk?"

A slow grin creeps over his face. "Yes."

My own face drops. I don't why, but it makes me sad to hear that because looking at his sad face, I don't think fucking her would have made him feel any better. Just like fucking him won't make me feel any better. But I can't just leave him alone; he looks too sad. And I can't go home because I'm too sad.

I watch as he pulls a pack of gum out of his pocket and pops one into his mouth. I study the box closely as he slips it back intothe pocket of his jeans because I used the same gum for about a week before going cold turkey when I stopped smoking.

"Is that nicotine gum?"

He nods.

"Shit. I'm sorry you started smoking because of me, didn't you?"

He doesn't answer me; he just stares into my eyes so intensely that I can't move. He's so broken today. It's the anniversary of that day a year ago. Of course, he's sad and broken.

"Want to grab some food? I'm starving," I say, not sure why I'm asking this asshole to do anything with me. But despite him acting like a jerk to me the last time we were together, I still want to have a good ending to my night.

He studies me for a second. "Sure."

I glance around to see if any place is open. I don't see anything immediately, but I know of a place about two blocks from here that is always open.

"Pizza okay?" I ask.

"Sure."

I begin walking, and he falls in line next to me, matching my pace. He looks down at my bare feet as I walk but doesn't offer to do anything about my feet. He doesn't offer to give me a piggyback ride even though I know he's plenty strong enough. He doesn't offer to give me his shoes. Nothing. I kind of like it that way. I like that he isn't the kind of person who always tries to take care of me even though he knows my past and probably feels he should.

"So I never got around to asking last time, but what's your name?" he asks.

I open my mouth to tell him and then stop. "I don't think we should tell each other our names."

"Why not?"

I look into his sad eyes that are doing nothing to hide the pain. "Because we are both sad and running from pain, and as much as we both want to save each other, we can't. We have to save ourselves."

He stops, looking at me, instead looks forward as a rowdy crowd passes us. The girls stopping for a second to eye the man I'm walking with.

"What does that have to do with telling each other our names?" he asks.

"If we tell each other our names, it will be easier to find each other after tonight. If we distract each other from our pain tonight, then we will want that again and again and use each other as a crutch. We will rely on each other. That's not good for me."

He frowns, and I realize we are standing outside the pizza parlor. I walk toward the door, and he follows.

"A table for two please," I say.

The hostess leads us to a booth in the busy restaurant. Probably the only one left. Despite being after midnight, this place has the greasiest pizza, and you can get it all night long.

I take a seat, and he slides in across from me. I stare at him, waiting for him to answer. He watches me for a long time. Long enough that I have to order us both a beer and pizza without getting any input from him.

"I think you're wrong. I think you are going to want to come find me after tonight. Good thing you have my number in case you decide to. But I'll play along with your game in the meantime. So what should I call you?" he asks.

"Whatever you want to call me."

He studies me a second. "Pretty girl. And what are you going to call me?"

I think for a second. I want to call him sad eyes, but that's not constructive in helping us both forget about our pain and sadness, so instead, I say, "Asshole."

He cocks his head to his side and then laughs. "Really, that's what you are going to call me all night? Even when my cock is thrusting inside you, making you come, you're going to call me an asshole?"

I smile. "First, I doubt that's going to happen. And second, yes because that's what you are."

He leans back. "Fair enough."

We both smile at each other as our beer and pizza arrive. We both scarf down a couple of slices of pizza and our beer. When we started eating, we were both smiling, but by the time we finished eating, he's sad again. Not smiling. He was thinking about everything but me. We need to get out of here and do something fun. Something adventurous to take our minds off tonight. Because I know that tonight is going to suck for both of us if we just go home now. Tonight is the anniversary of his worst day too, unless he's had a worse day in the past year, but I doubt the universe could throw anything worse at him.

The waitress drops our bill off on the table, but I don't have money to pay for my half, and I'm not going to let him pay for me. I'm not going to let him owe me. I'll make sure to have the waitress take the money out of my paycheck tomorrow when I arrive to work here.

I stand and hold out my hand. "Let's go, asshole."

"One second, pretty girl," he begins to reach into his wallet to pull out money.

I grab his hand. "No, now."

"We aren't dining and ditching."

I smile widely, "Yes, we are."

I yank his arm up and am surprised when he comes with me. I begin running. I don't know why I do, but that's what they do in the movies. We aren't the first ones who have dined and ditched in this restaurant. It's happened to me on several occasions, but it doesn't affect the restaurant's bottom line at all. In fact, most waitresses just delete the order and act like we were never here. But I'll make sure to pay back the restaurant tomorrow.

Right now, we are running like the silly teenagers we are; at least, I think he is a teenager. I glance back at Asshole running right after me and see his smile returning to his face as we make our way out of the restaurant and onto the street. We keep running because it's fun. I don't think about where we are going, we just run.

We stop when I'm out of breath and can't run any farther. He isn't even breathing hard when we stop. He just looks up in awe. "We going to climb it?"

I glance up at the hill of a trail. A trail you can climb to the top in ten to fifteen minutes but get rewarded with an awesome view of the city for such a quick climb. It's my go-to short climb when I just need to get away from life. Today seems like the perfect day to climb it.

"Yes."

I walk past him and begin heading up the trail. He follows, both of us still not talking, but this time as we climb, there is no reason to climb. The climb is enough of a distraction that we forget about everything else. The climb is hard in my dress and without shoes on and because I've had quite a bit more of alcohol. But I keep moving forward. I trip once on my way up, and he puts a hand on the small of my back to keep me from falling, but otherwise, he doesn't help me.

We reach the top, and I'm panting. I'm out of shape, and the alcohol makes it worse, but when I look out over the city in the dark, it doesn't matter. It's beautiful. The world is beautiful.

Several other people up here are doing the same thing as we are. He takes my hand and leads me over to spot near the edge, and we take a seat, carefully placing our feet over the edge as we sit. He doesn't let go of my hand after we sit, and I don't want him to. It feels magical here. Perfect.

"I've lived in Boulder for two years now, and I've never hiked here. I've done plenty back home but none here. I've been too busy. I forgot how beautiful it is when you climb to the top, no matter how big or small of a climb."

I nod.

"I've climbed this trail several times, but it has never looked so beautiful as it does right now."

I turn from the view of the city to look at him, and he does the same. We don't speak, but as we look, we trade our souls. I don't know why he is in pain, but I understand it is a lot like mine and vice versa.

"Why are you so sad, pretty girl? Why did you try to hurt ..." He stops when he realizes he shouldn't bring up the past again.

I suck in a breath as his head leans forward until our foreheads are touching and he closes his eyes. I do the same, realizing he wasn't expecting an answer to his question but just wanted me to know he was wondering.

"I wish I could take your sadness and pain away, pretty girl. You don't deserve to be in such pain. No one does."

I swallow. "Maybe I deserve it."

His eyes fly open as do mine. "You don't."

I don't argue with him. I don't try to reason who is right. It doesn't matter.

His finger touches my chin, lifting my lips up without hesitation. He doesn't ask if he can kiss me, he just does. We kiss. It's long and unreserved. And I swear he sucks some of my pain away when he kisses me.

We both pull back slowly and look at each other. I don't know what happened when he kissed me, but I both want and don't want it to happen again. I want more than just another kiss. But if that kiss was any indication—if I let him kiss me again, he'll save me from the pain, and then I'll be lost forever. Because no one can really save me. I've learned my lesson. I thought Ava saved me, and she did. But now that she is leaving, I need a new savior.

The wind picks up, and I shiver a little. He doesn't have a jacket to offer me, and even if he did, I wouldn't take it. I pick up my shoes that I set down beside me and stand.

"Time to go," I say and begin heading back down the trail with him following me.

We make it about halfway down when the sleet and rain mix starts pouring down on us. My feet are a frozen muddy mess as we climb down. I trip again, and this time, I know for sure I'm going down and am going to ruin the only nice dress I have. A dress that Mandy bought for me, but I vowed to treasure forever because it was so pretty.

Hands catch me again, somehow knowing that was about to happen. He scoops me up in his arms, and as much as I didn't want him to protect me before, I'm losing any will to protest because his arms are so nice. So warm and strong and comforting. I could get used to feeling like this. It's something I have never really felt before in my life.

When we make it down the trail, he doesn't put me down. And I don't ask him to.

"I'm not ready to take you home yet. So where do you want me to take you, pretty girl?"

I think for a second as the cold rain and sleet continue to soak us, making me shiver again. He holds me tighter against his body. We need somewhere to warm up. "The St. Julien."

He doesn't question me. He just begins walking in that direction while I rub my head against his soaked shirt, making it even easier to feel every muscle underneath it. His muscles are hard, strong, but also clearly used and not just to lift weights. The way he carries me with such ease makes me more and more suspicious of what he does when he's not trying to rescue someone.

My mind immediately starts guessing—he's a personal trainer, he does construction, he's a football or basketball player. The last two seem most plausible for his age and pedigree. It's clear from the designer jeans he is wearing that he has money. He probably attends college on a full scholarship despite not needing the money to pay for college.

I stop trying to guess what he does or who he is. It doesn't matter.

He carries me into the hotel and begins to walk toward the check-in desk.

"Stop," I say.

He does.

"Put me down."

He doesn't.

I look at him, and I know he won't put me down until he has to. I shiver again, proving his silent point that I need protection.

"Go to the swimming pool on the left side of the hotel."

He begins carrying me.

"How are we going to get in? Are you staying here or something?"

"Not exactly," I say while laughing silently to myself. This is one of the nicest hotels in the city. One night's stay here costs more than my entire month's rent. I couldn't afford something this nice, but it's clear he has stayed in hotels like this. He fits in this world. I don't.

"Don't worry; just keep walking like you live here." Not that I have to tell him how to do that. He already fits in wherever he goes.

We pass a hotel staffer.

"Sir, my and my fiancé's key doesn't seem to be working for the pool door. Would you mind letting us in?" I ask.

The man looks at me and then the man whose arms I'm still in.

"I'm sorry, ma'am, but we usually close the pool at midnight."

"Do you mind opening it for us? We felt like taking a warm swim since we got caught in the rain and snow," he says.

The man nods and pulls out his key. "Certainly, sir."

He leads us to the pool door and unlocks it for us.

"You will find plenty of towels to your left," the staffer says before leaving.

"You can put me down now," I say.

He finally does.

"Fiancé, huh?"

"I didn't think saying we were boyfriend and girlfriend explained why we were staying at this nice of a hotel, and I wasn't going to tell him we just met."

"You've gotten me to break the law twice tonight. You know we could be arrested for this."

I laugh. "I doubt it. We stole a ten-dollar pizza and snuck into a hotel pool when we aren't staying here. That's not exactly crimes we can be arrested for."

He gives me a stern look.

"Okay, we could get arrested. Live a little. I'm sure you would make bail," I say, winking at him.

I drop my heels on the ground and reach for the hem of my red dress and pull it over my head without thinking. Despite how nice my dress is, what's underneath isn't that nice. I don't own lingerie. The bra that I'm wearing is a boring tan color. No lace, nothing pretty about it. The straps are worn, frayed, and need replacing. And my pink underwear is even worse. What was once bright pink is now a faded shade with a couple of small holes on the side.

I immediately regret not just swimming in my dress. I glance up at him, though, and how he is staring at me makes me realize how stupid I was to worry about what my underwear looked like. It's clear he isn't looking at that anyway. Instead, he is looking at every inch of skin he can find on my body.

He removes his dark gray shirt while he kicks off his shoes. He unbuttons his jeans and pulls them down, and I gasp. I freaking gasp when I see him standing before me in his underwear.

He's wearing boxer briefs, but I've never seen them fit a man so nicely before. They fit snugly just below the v of muscle that disappears inside. They fit so tightly that I can see everything, including his cock straining against them. I look away from it quickly but only find myself staring at his abs, his pecs, his arms, legs, everything.

When I meet his eyes again, he's grinning. It's a cocky grin that tells me he plans on seeing me again after tonight. He thinks he's won. He hasn't. He won't win no matter how hard he tries. He doesn't understand what I've been through.

He runs toward me, and then he's grabbing me as we both fall into the water, making a huge splash. We both go under the warm water together, and I know in any other circumstances this would have been it. I would have given in and said I'm his forever.

I should swim away, stay away from him. Instead, I relish the feeling of being in his arms.

We both come up for air at the same time, still holding each other. He kisses me again as my arms go around his neck. This kiss is deeper, more familiar than the first kiss. It's a kiss I could never get enough of.

We pull away as he kisses me gently in small pecks on my lips and cheeks.

"I wish I could have met you before ..." he says and then stops talking.

I nod in understanding. If we had both just met each other before last year, he might have asked me out, and I might have said yes. We could have had a real relationship instead of this. We could have actually fallen in love instead of us both being too scared and him hating me, making it impossible to fall in love with me anyway.

He shakes his head and releases me.

I run my hand through my wet hair as I watch him swim toward the deep end of the pool. I wait for a second, giving him his space to get the memory out of his head before I swim over to the edge of the pool near where he stopped.

"What do you want in life, pretty girl? What do you live for?"

His question surprises me. I didn't think he would ask me anything deep. That was our unspoken rule governing our night together. "I don't know."

His eyes turn darker, deeper as he looks at me.

"What do you want from life?" he asks again.

I take a deep breath. He isn't going to let this go. This question is important to him, and I don't think he is going to stop questioning me until I answer him.

"I want to save myself. To love myself ... and in turn be able to love someone else."

He nods. "And you haven't saved yourself yet?"

"No. I haven't."

"What's stopping you?"

I exhale deeply. "Letting others save me because it's easier."

He dips under the water and then pops back up, I think, to try to stop himself from trying to save me.

"What about you? What do you want?"

He looks sad. His eyes carry the weight of the world as he says, "To save you."

I put my clothes back on and dry my hair as best as I can with the towel.

"I need to get back," I say, placing the towel in the container for used towels and then I walk out of the pool room. I walk out of the hotel and don't look back. I didn't even tell him goodbye or thank you for a nice night. I just left.

I don't understand him. He's a complete contradiction. Last time we were together, he told me why we could never be anything but friends who occasionally text each other for help. And the only reason he wanted me to text him was if I tried to do something stupid again like last time. But now, he said he wants to save me. *Maybe that was what the text message thing was about?* That he wanted to save me if I got into trouble again.

I don't want him to save me, though. I want to date him. I want to kiss him. I want to be able to call him mine.

The rain has stopped, but it's still cold outside and late. I want to call an Uber or, at the very least, take a short bus ride. But I don't have money to waste on things like my comfort. So I start walking the dozen or more blocks back to my apartment.

My phone buzzes, to my surprise. Hopefully, it's Mandy, and I can see if she and Frank will come pick me up. But when I pull out my phone, it's from the number he put in almost a year ago.

Him: I need you to stay with me tonight. I need to have you, but I'll settle for you just staying with me. Meet me by the elevators.

I bite my lip as I look at the message. He wants me. He wants to fuck me. He needs me.

I take a deep breath. I need him too.

I turn around, my mind already made up that I'm going to take this thing with him as far as it can go tonight, and tomorrow ... it will be painful to say goodbye. But tonight is going to be amazing.

The rain starts as I run back, completely soaking me again before I enter the hotel. I don't see him initially or the elevators. I don't see anyone but the man behind the desk in the lobby. I smile at the man and then walk past him like I know where I'm going, glancing down each hallway that leads from the lobby as I look for him.

I stop breathing when I see him standing outside the elevators just like he said he was. He grins when he sees me, but I can't manage to make my feet move toward him. I'm frozen. I'm scared because if I let this man kiss me again, that is all it's going to take to make me crazy for him. Much less if I do anything more.

He runs over to me, and this time, he wraps his arms around me, trying to warm me up. He doesn't realize I don't need him to warm me up. I'm already warm just thinking about what he wants to do with me. To me. How his rough, strong hands will feel touching my body in places no man has touched in a very long time. My whole body warms thinking about our last kiss. There is no point in trying to dry me off because I know I'm dripping wet just thinking about him inside me.

He releases me and grabs my hand. "We don't have to go up. We can just hang out in the lobby or somewhere else more public for a while. I just need you, pretty girl."

I look up at him with what I know are sad eyes, which makes him think I'm going to say no. I grab the back of his neck, feeling how strong his muscles are even there, and then I tentatively kiss him. His kiss is just as tentative.

"Why are you so sad, pretty girl?"

"I know tomorrow will never be as good as tonight is going to be. But I want to really live tonight. I want you, you asshole."

He grins and takes my hand and leads me to the elevator as my heart races faster. When the doors to the elevator close with us inside, he presses the top floor and then even though no one else is the elevator with us, he whispers in my ear, "I can't wait to hear you scream asshole when I make you come. Are you sure you don't want to know what my name is?"

I giggle nervously. "No. I think asshole fits you perfectly. And we will see about the screaming part. I doubt you're capable of making me scream."

He pushes me up against the wall and kisses me like I know he's wanted to since he kissed me on our hike. He slips his tongue into my mouth as his hands find their way under my shirt, pushing it up to expose my stomach and bra.

The elevator doors open, and he stops and grabs my hand again. "Oh, you'll scream, pretty girl. I've been told I'm the best."

I laugh. "You probably are, but that doesn't mean you will do anything for me."

He shakes his head and yanks on my hand until he finds our hotel room and pulls me inside.

"Oh, wow. You must have spent a fortune on this room. We could have gone to a different hotel."

He doesn't say anything about how nice or expensive the room was. His eyes say he doesn't care. Instead, he is looking at me like I'm the biggest challenge of his life, and he plans on winning.

He walks over to me and grabs my soaking wet dress. He pulls it over my head and then yanks my panties down.

I bite my lip to keep from blushing now that I'm naked and he is still fully dressed.

"So we are just going to do this?" I ask nervously.

"Yes. You want me to make you scream. I'll make you scream."

That's all the warning he gives me before he picks me up and lifts me high above his head. He lifts me so that my legs are lying on his shoulders and my pussy is covering his face. He walks me backward until my back is against the wall. I hold his head.

"How the hell did you do that?" I ask, seriously afraid of how strong he is.

He licks my pussy, though, and I forget words. I forget why I'm here. I forget that I barely know this man, and right now, he has his face buried in my pussy. All I can do is hold his head and moan.

I squirm when his tongue laps over my clit, making me so close to coming.

"Hold still, pretty girl."

He grins now as he licks again; my toes curl, my legs start tightening around his head, and I grab his head, both holding it there and pulling it away at the same time. I don't know what the hell he does with his tongue, but I come as I scream, "Fuck, asshole!"

When I'm done screaming and coming, he slowly lowers me to the ground. "So you want me to fuck you in the asshole next time? I can handle that."

I hit him, and then I tug on his jeans, pulling them down so that he is as naked as I am.

"No, I want you to fuck me and make me scream again."

He grins. "My pleasure."

hunter

IT'S MORNING. I can tell because the light is barely peeking in covering the room. It was the first night in a long time I haven't woken up because of a nightmare.

She's lying against my bare chest. The pretty girl who I should have called strong girl because in the few moments since I've met her, that's what she most embodies. She's pretty, for sure, but her strength is where her true beauty lies. She wants to take on the world alone. *Why?* I don't understand. But I think of all the people I have met, she is the only person strong enough to do it.

I just wish she didn't want to face the world alone. Last night, I don't know why I told her the truth. That I wanted to save her. But it was the absolute truth. Sure, I want other things in life. I want to sleep without nightmares. I want to graduate from college. I want to make it to the NFL. I want to make a difference in the world. I want to stop being in pain every goddamn day of my life. I want her

...

And after I had her three times last night, I want her more than all the things I thought I wanted in my life right now.

I don't know how, but I convinced her to actually stay in a room with me in this hotel after our dip in the pool. She let me fuck her. She let me make her mine. She let me form a memory I will never be able to erase. And now, I don't think I can ever give her up.

She stirs in my arms.

"Morning, pretty girl."

She smiles and stretches as the covers creep lower to reveal her bare breast. She immediately grabs the covers and pulls them up to her chin in embarrassment and begins going through last night in her head.

"Really? You know I saw you naked a lot last night." I pull on the covers, revealing her perfect full breasts.

She frowns, but it's a cute smiley frown that shows me she isn't really mad.

I watch the memory coming back in her head. "It was a good night. Wasn't it?"

I tilt her chin up and kiss her softly on the lips. "I haven't had a better night in a long time."

She looks a little sad when I add in the long time tag. But I have to tell her the truth. It was a great night, but I've had better. I want to tell her that if we spent more time together, we would eventually have the best night possible together. But that's not the truth. I don't know if anything in my future could beat my past.

"I should go," she says.

"Tell me your name," I demand even though I already know it. I just don't want her to know that I know it. I want her to tell me on her own. I want to hear how it sounds falling from her lips.

"It's pretty girl."

"No, it's not. I won, and you know it."

"How did you win? I still haven't told you my real name unless I did in my sleep, which doesn't count. And I'm still leaving and not looking back when I do."

"I got more than a night with you. I got a morning too. And this morning could turn into another day and then another and another. It doesn't have to stop here."

"Yes, it does."

"But ..."

She gets out of bed now, and this time, she doesn't care that she is naked in the slightest bit. I watch her round bare ass sway back and forth as she walks over to the pile of clothes strewn over the chair. She picks up the dress and tugs it over her body. And then picks up her shoes and bra and underwear.

I climb out of bed and throw on my jeans and T-shirt.

"Share an Uber home with me," I say, hoping she will forget about the fact that then I would know where she lives and could find her again.

She smiles and kisses me on the lips. "Thank you."

"For what?"

"For giving me one of the best nights of my life."

I feel it. The same stab of pain she must have felt when I said it wasn't my best night either. But I know it's her truth just as much as it was my truth when I said it. That's why we both are in such pain. We have both loved before. Both loved so deeply that whenever they left us, they left us in such deep pain that we can't bear to let them go. And now, we can't bear to move on and have another night that might allow us to fall in love again.

She kisses me again.

"Goodbye, asshole. I hope you find someone else to save. It can't be me, though."

I kiss her.

"Goodbye, pretty girl. I hope you change your mind and try to find me. Or at least text me the next time you need me."

She shakes her head. "It's not going to happen."

"I can still hope."

"Please don't hope. Just move on and do all those other things you had wanted with your life before you met me. I was just a distraction to keep the pain away for one night when we both needed it most."

I nod.

"I'm still going to hope. Because what I still want most is to save you."

We both kiss again, and I know that this time, it will be the last. Last kiss. Last goodbye.

The pain returns in droves as we kiss. But this time, unlike any other time, I get to say goodbye to someone who I have fallen for. To someone I could love. I get closure.

We pull away.

"Goodbye, asshole. Don't come find me."

"Goodbye, pretty girl. Come find me when you finish saving yourself. I would be honored to be the person you eventually love and in turn save."

She smiles a little, and then she leaves, walking out the door of the hotel room without looking back. I think of all the ways I could find her. I could leave now and follow her. Find out where she lives. I could have someone take her fingerprints and learn who she is. I could spend the next week searching for her.

I won't, though. As much as I want to, I won't. I'll respect her decision. I won't go after her unless she comes looking for me. Unless she texts me. And I won't text her again. It's her turn to need me. It's for the best, really. Because as much as I want to be around her, I can't. I can't put myself through the pain of loving someone again, and she, although strong, is not strong enough to fight when she needs to.

Either way, it was one of the best nights of my life. Because whether or not she thinks it's really possible to save someone else, she saved me.

TEXT MESSAGE #1

1 year earlier

quinn

THE NURSES AREN'T watching me for the first time since I've been here, and I really need a break. I need a break from their fussing. I need a break from their sad stares. I need a break from all the pitiful looks. They shouldn't feel sorry for me. I made a decision. I chose this life. It's not their fault I failed.

They think I'm sedated enough that I won't bother to leave or do anything to hurt myself. They are wrong to leave me alone, though. Because I took the IV out a long time ago. I hate not being in control. I hate being sedated. I just pretend I am any time they come in the room. I pretend I'm asleep. I pretend I'm not here.

I get out of bed and find my pack of cigarettes in the pocket of my jeans they cut off me earlier. I'm surprised they thought I would want my jeans back after they did that. *Don't they understand I can't afford to buy jeans? Don't they understand those were my only ones?* They should have been more careful when they were saving my life. If they were going to save me, they should have at least

301

made sure I would have something to wear after they saved me.

I go over to the monitor I'm hooked up to that lets the nurses know I'm still alive, still breathing, and my heart is still beating. I press the power button to turn it off just like I watched the nurse do earlier when the machine was malfunctioning. I pull off the patches stuck to my chest, and then I grab the blanket off my bed and wrap it around myself. I make sure to hide the cigarettes inside the blanket in case anyone stops me, and then I leave my hospital room.

I don't have to worry about my parents stopping me because they aren't here. I don't have to worry about any family members finding me because no one cares enough to be here. All I have to worry about are the nurses. But as I walk down the hallway, I don't see any of my usual nurses. And the ones I do see smile at me, like they are happy to see a patient walking around out of their bed. It must mean I'm going home soon and that their workload may decrease.

I walk until I get to the stairwell at the end of the hallway, and then I climb up the stairs until I get to the roof. I know the emergency door doesn't set off the alarm because I've been in this hospital before when I lost the only person who ever mattered to me.

I push the door open, and no alarm sounds, so I walk out onto the roof and take a seat in the same spot I did last time. A spot that overlooks nothing but blackness. It's exactly how I feel at this moment.

I take out my pack of cigarettes and light one. Taking a puff, I feel my lungs fill with the cancerous smoke. I don't care, though. I wish cancer would take me. Then life would be easier.

The emergency door opens, and my heart rate rises. I need more time out here by myself. I need to at least smoke one cigarette, but if a nurse saw me right now, they might assume I was getting ready to jump. But it's not a nurse. Just a boy. The saddest looking boy in the whole world.

He doesn't see me, and I don't say anything as he walks out to the roof's edge and looks over into the dark nothingness. I just smoke my cigarette and watch him. I can't tell because it's dark outside and there is very little lighting on the roof, but I think he's crying. He's not in a hospital gown like me, so he must be here visiting someone else. He must have gotten some bad news. Someone he loves is dying or is already dead. I feel bad that I'm just sitting here watching him cry when he doesn't know I'm here. He probably came up here to get some time to himself away from his family and friends.

"Do you smoke?" I ask so that he knows I'm here. Although I would have thought the smoke smell would have given me away.

He turns and looks at me, and I can see the tears on his face. I should go; it's clear he needs to be alone out here a lot more than I do. But I'm selfish, so I don't move.

He doesn't say anything; he just walks over to me and takes a seat next to me. I pull another cigarette out and hand it to him. He puts it in his mouth, and I light it for him, but almost immediately, he starts coughing.

I laugh. It's the first time I've laughed this week. "You're not a smoker, are you?"

He shakes his head but brings the cigarette back to his lips.

"Don't inhale as much smoke this time; only a little bit until you get used to it." I look at how awkwardly he is holding the cigarette. "And here, hold it like this." I reposition his fingers, so his grasp on the cigarette is more relaxed.

He inhales again, and this time doesn't end up coughing.

"Sorry, I'm such a bad influence on you. You really shouldn't smoke." I bring the cigarette to my lips again.

"Don't worry; I'm not going to become a smoker. I just need something to take the pain away for a moment. I would never do something that would cause my life to end early like become a smoker."

I let out a puff of air.

"You should really stop smoking."

I laugh. "Smoking is the least worrisome of my bad habits."

He frowns. "What else do you do?"

"Smoke joints, drink alcohol, have sex with men I don't even know." I leave off the worst of my habits that I recently picked up. *But is it a habit if you only did it once?* No, I decide.

"You should stop."

I shake my head. "You don't get to tell me what I should or shouldn't do. You don't even know me."

He grabs my cigarette and stomps it out on the ground along with his. "You're wrong. I know you better than you think. You're broken just like me. You're in pain, and while yours might be physical and mine is tied to someone else, it's still pain. And while I have only been dealing with the pain for a couple of days and it looks like you might have been dealing with it your whole life, it doesn't mean that you can just do whatever the hell you want. You have to fight."

"You think something is physically wrong with me?" I ask, tightening the blanket around my body so he can't see what is really wrong with me.

"Yeah, I do. That's why people are in the hospital. They are sick." He stops for a second. "You aren't sick because of the smoking and alcohol, are you?"

"No."

"Cancer?"

"No."

He thinks for a second, trying to come up with some other issue that might cause a teenager to end up in the hospital.

"Dehydration?"

"No."

"Bad cramps?"

I sigh. "It's none of your damn business why I'm here!" I pull out my case of cigarettes and pull out another one to light. He grabs my wrist to stop me and then stares into my eyes as he realizes why I'm here.

He looks until he finds my other wrist. Both bandaged. "You tried to kill yourself?"

"Yeah, so? I tried to kill myself. Lots of people try to kill themselves." I light another cigarette.

He stands up. "You're a coward."

"Well, if I didn't want to kill myself before, I do now."

"You're a weak coward who deserves to die if you aren't going to fight harder to live than that!"

"You don't know anything about what I've gone through."

He frowns and then grabs the cigarette out of my hands again and puts it out. I stand, and it's only then that I realize how much taller he is than I am. How much stronger. He's definitely fit for a teenager. He's looking strong compared to any man I know, in fact.

"Those are mine. You now owe me three cigarettes."

He shakes his head. "You are unbelievable; you know that? I don't owe you anything. You are nothing to me. You are just a weak coward who should have died. Whatever you have been through isn't so bad you have to kill yourself. You should fucking fight to live." He runs his hand through his hair, trying to calm himself down, but it doesn't work. "I lost someone. I lost my girlfriend. She died fighting. She was my whole life, and now, she's gone. You don't get to be a weak coward. You are supposed to fight."

A tear rolls down my cheek. "I'm sorry you lost your girlfriend. But that doesn't mean what I did was wrong."

"You're messed up. Something is wrong with you. And I can't stay up here and hang out with someone who won't fight to live when I just lost someone who would do anything to live. To have one more day."

He goes to the door but pauses to look at me. "The universe is fucked up. You should have died instead of her."

He slams the door and leaves me outside on the roof alone. He's an asshole. I don't care how much pain he's in; he was an asshole to me. But he was right about everything; I wish I had died instead of her. Something is wrong with me.

hunter

I'M AN ASSHOLE. That's all I've thought all night as I was tossing and turning in my bed. I promised I would never go back to the hospital after yesterday, but here I am again.

Thankfully, one of the nurses who took care of Sabrina before she died is working the check-in desk. "Hunter?" she asks.

"Hi, Meg. I need your help."

"Of course. What can I help you with?"

"I need you to help me find a girl who was here yesterday."

Meg frowns. "There wasn't anyone here yesterday but family."

I shake my head. "A patient. I need to learn her name and what room she is staying in."

"I'm sorry, but you know I'm not supposed to do that."

I like that she says not supposed to instead of I can't. It means with a little persuasion she will do what I need her to do.

"She's my age. She snuck out on the roof yesterday to smoke, and that's where I met her. She has long brown hair, and I think grayish colored eyes. She's stubborn and has lots of bad habits. She tried to kill herself by slitting her wrists."

"Hunter, I can't."

"I said some awful things to her yesterday that I didn't mean."

"I'm sure whatever you said wasn't that bad."

"I called her weak and a coward." I widen my eyes, begging her to help me. "I just want to apologize to her. I don't want to be the reason she tries to commit suicide again. I wouldn't be able to forgive myself and might commit suicide myself, and then you would have two deaths on your conscience."

"Hunter. Don't say things like that. Are you doing okay? You're going to therapy, right?"

"Yes."

She takes a deep breath. "I know who you are talking about. Her name is Quinn." She writes something down on a piece of paper and then hands it to me. "This is her cell phone number. That's all I'm going to give you. You can text her or call her and apologize, and if I find out you were an ass to her again, I'm going to kick your ass. You don't understand what that girl has been through, Hunter. She isn't as lucky as you are."

I raise my eyebrows. "I'm lucky?"

She looks sad. "Compared to her, yeah."

I frown. "Thanks, Meg."

I take out my cell phone, and I text her.

Me: I need to talk to you. Meet me on the roof in twenty minutes.

I press send and then realize she doesn't know who I am and has no reason to come up to the roof after last night. I shake my head. She knows it's me. No one else would tell her to meet her on the roof. But I do type.

Me: I'm sorry.

And then head up to the roof to wait.

"You came," I say when she opens the door the roof.

"Yeah, but right now I'm not sure why. What do you want?"

"I want to say I'm sorry. I have no idea what you've been through, and I should have never said what I did last night. I was just upset and pissed off."

She nods. She's wearing a robe this time, and the sleeves cover her arms. She's washed her hair since last night. She looks prettier, healthier than she did last night. She looks beautiful. But I just lost the love of my life, and she just tried to kill herself.

"You were an asshole."

I nod. "I was. I'm sorry."

"How did you get my phone number?"

"The nurses."

"Right." She walks over to the edge of the roof and leans on the edge. "So you want to tell me about her?"

I walk over and lean next to her. "Who?"

"The love of your life."

I take a deep breath. "I haven't talked about her to anyone."

"Well, unlike you, I won't be an asshole no matter what you tell me about her."

"Her name was Sabrina." I don't mention that I know her name. Quinn. I don't want to share anything more personal.

She sucks in a breath when I start talking about her but doesn't say anything.

"We dated for two years, and I just knew from the day I met her that I wanted to spend the rest of my life with her. She was special that way. She was just the one. She had long dark brown hair and green eyes. She was beautiful and strong. A real fighter. She fought so hard to live."

"She sounds amazing."

"She was."

I look over at her, and I see the brokenness in her eyes. "I'm glad she had you. Even if you were an asshole to me, it sounds like you treated her right. Like you really loved her."

"I loved her more than anything."

I watch the tiniest tear roll down her cheek. I hate that I made her sad, that I made her cry. "I can't stand to see you cry." I grab her. I kiss her. She kisses me back and then bites me on the lip to get me to stop.

"Why did you kiss me?"

I wipe off the blood I'm sure she caused. "Because it looked like you needed something good, if only for a moment."

How the kiss felt surprised me. It felt good. Too good for being so soon after losing Sabrina. But I would never do that to her. I would never move on so quickly. The kiss was all about apologizing for how I treated her and making her feel better; that's it.

"Give me your phone," I say.

She hands me her phone, and I add my number to her contacts under Text in Case of Emergency.

I hand her phone back to her. "I want you to text me if you ever need me. If you ever feel so bad that you might do something stupid, you text me. If you ever just need to talk, text me. Just like I texted you earlier."

She cocks her head to the side as she looks at me.

"I'm sorry we can't be anything else. We can't be friends even. Which is too bad because I think we could have become good friends. But I'm getting over losing someone who didn't deserve to die and—"

"And I'm not a fighter, just a survivor," she finishes my sentence. She returns the phone to her robe pocket. "I hope life gets easier for you, asshole."

I smile. "You too, pretty girl."

before quinn

hunter

IT'S TWO O'CLOCK IN THE MORNING, and I can't sleep. I haven't been able to sleep at all this entire week. I know why; this week, it's hitting me that my life is about to change forever. I've known it's going to change for months now.

But I guess after seeing my baby on the ultrasound, it all became so much more real. After seeing my girlfriend's stomach popping out, no longer able to hide her secret, makes it more real. The fact I just graduated high school, have no job, and unsupportive parents makes it more real.

I climb out of bed and kiss Sabrina on the forehead, who is thankfully sound asleep. I grab my computer and head to the living room of the apartment we got together last week. The apartment is nice with two bedrooms, a nice balcony, and pool access. I can afford to pay for the apartment for a year on the money I have saved up from family over the years, but I know it won't be enough. I need a job. I have a full scholarship to play football in college, but that won't produce any money for a long time. Not until I graduate or make it to the pros.

I know Sabrina said she was going to try to get a job between taking care of our baby for a year or so before she starts college, but it won't be enough. I need to get a job I can work between classes and practice. It would be easier to just ask my parents for money—I know I could convince them—but they aren't exactly happy that Sabrina and I are keeping the baby. They would have preferred an abortion or, at the very least, adoption. They think we are ruining our lives. We aren't.

I've never been happier than I've been with Sabrina. And I know this baby is going to make things difficult, but it is also going to be a great adventure.

I open my laptop and type in jobs for high school graduates. A string of things pops up. Fast food jobs, janitor jobs, waste management, waiter jobs. All minimum wage. None of them have flexible hours. I'm screwed.

"Hunter," Sabrina says.

I look up from my computer, and I see her hunched over, grabbing her stomach.

"What's wrong?" I ask, running over to her.

"I ... ow. I don't know, my stomach. It hurts a lot. And I'm having trouble breathing," she says.

"Should I call an ambulance or do you want me to drive you?" I ask, trying to remain calm, but my heart feels like it's about to explode out of my chest.

"You drive me."

"Okay," I say, taking a deep breath. I lead her to my Jeep parked just outside our apartment. I hold on as best as I can as we walk. It shouldn't take us long to walk outside and get in the car. But when Sabrina stops after only five steps and holds her stomach as she moans in pain, I'm scared. Scared that we are going to take too long to get there and that something bad is going to happen.

"I should call an ambulance."

"No, just ..." She takes a deep breath. "Just get me to the car."

I don't know what else to do, so I scoop her up and run to the Jeep. Once she's safely inside, I jump in the driver's seat and drive as fast as I can to the hospital not caring about red lights or anything else. I park in front of the emergency doors at the hospital and run to Sabrina's door. She's still in pain and has struggled to breathe properly the whole way here. Something is really wrong. The baby isn't due for another couple of months. She shouldn't be in this much pain.

I walk Sabrina into the hospital, and before I can even say anything, nurses and doctors are swarming us and fussing over Sabrina. She must look bad if we didn't even have to get their attention to come help Sabrina.

A wheelchair is brought over, and Sabrina sits down as she answers the questions the doctors are firing off to her. *How far along are you? When did you first start experiencing pain? What are your symptoms?*

Sabrina answers each question despite the pain while I stand helplessly watching them. The nurses start wheeling her back, and I run along even though no one is paying me any attention. No one even knows I exist.

They wheel her into a room, and they start undressing her and begin hooking her up to monitors and IVs like a well-oiled machine. Everyone is just doing their job. The doctor looks at the machine Sabrina is hooked up to and then to the nurses. "We need to get her into surgery, now."

The nurses begin frantically moving around to get her ready.

"It's too early," Sabrina says.

I run over to her side and grab her hand. "It's going to be okay. Everything is going to be fine. The baby will just be born a little early. The doctors know what they are doing, though, and they'll take good care of both of you."

"I'm scared," she says.

I stroke her hair, trying to calm her, but hating that I can't do anything to calm her. "I'm going to be right here the whole time. I love you." I kiss her forehead.

"Are you the father-to-be?" a nurse asks me.

I nod, still holding Sabrina's hand.

"I'm going to need you to come with me," she says.

"I really need to stay with Sabrina."

She smiles. "If you want to be in surgery with her, you need to come with me and get changed quickly. They are going to wheel her into surgery soon."

I hate her. I hate the nurse for making me leave Sabrina, but I know it's what I have to do. I turn back to Sabrina.

"I have to go change, and then I'll meet you in surgery. Nothing bad is going to happen. I promise. I'll be right back." I kiss her on the forehead again. And then I follow the nurse to go change.

The nurse walks very fast, and I have to run to keep up with her. She stops suddenly and darts into a room and then grabs some scrubs. "Put these on as fast as you can."

I enter the room and put on the scrubs she handed me as fast as I can. I fumble a little bit, as I'm not entirely sure I'm putting them on correctly. As soon as I come back out of the room, the nurse grabs me, and we start running again.

"Sabrina is already in surgery. We have to hurry to make it before the doctor delivers the baby."

My eyes widen, and my legs move faster. I didn't realize how fast they could deliver a baby. The nurse pushes me through a door into the operating room where Sabrina is already lying on a table. I run to her side and grab her hand.

"I'm here, Sabrina. I'm here. You're doing great," I say.

Sabrina smiles at me, but she seems out of it. She seems groggy. She doesn't speak; she just closes her eyes.

I look around to find a nurse who will tell me that Sabrina is okay. But everyone is so focused on her stomach that I know I shouldn't tear any of them away to explain to me why the medications are making Sabrina so sleepy. I'm sure everything is fine.

"I love you, Sabrina. Everything is fine. Everything is going to be okay. Our baby will be born soon, and then you will feel a lot better. Our baby will be perfect. I'm sure of it."

I keep saying the same words over and over, waiting for the procedure to be over.

An alarm goes off, though, and I can see the worry and concern in the doctor's eyes as they look at Sabrina.

"Get the father out of here," one of the doctors says.

"No!" I scream, holding Sabrina's hand.

One of the nurses grabs me. "You need to leave for a couple of minutes so that we can take care of Sabrina and your baby."

"I'm not leaving her!"

"Sir, if you want what's best for her, you'll leave."

"No, I'm not going anywhere."

More alarms go off, and I watch as they pull out paddles to restart her heart. They start shoving a tube down her throat to keep her breathing.

"I can't leave her." I try to reach for Sabrina's hand, but the nurse is blocking me, and another nurse has grabbed my arms from behind me. "Everything is going to be okay, Sabrina. They are going to save you."

"You're going to have to sedate him," someone says from behind me.

I turn, but I feel the needle in my arm.

I open my eyes and look at my father sitting in the chair next to the bed where I'm lying. I'm fully dressed, just lying on top of the covers in a hospital bed.

"Sabrina!"

I jump out of bed ready to go run down the hallways until I find her when I see my father's face. Tears are still streaming down his face. His eyes are bloodshot, and his face is swollen. I sit back down slowly on the edge of the bed because I know my world just ended.

"She's gone, isn't she? She didn't make it."

My father looks at me, but he doesn't seem to be able to speak. But I can tell from the look on his face that it's true. Sabrina's gone.

"And the baby?"

He starts crying harder.

I'm surprised when my tears don't start immediately. Instead, all I feel is pain. Incredible pain.

My father stands up and sits on the edge of the bed. He puts his arms around me. "I'm so sorry, son."

That's when the tears start. Slow at first and then they all explode out of me. "I told her that everything was going to be all right. I promised her."

"It's not your fault. These things happen sometimes," he says.

I shake my head and pull away. "I don't know why you are crying. This is exactly what you wanted. Sabrina and the baby out of my life so that I could become the NFL player you always wanted me to be."

"Hunter, you're wrong. I would do anything to make this better for you."

"Well, you can't."

I get up and leave the room. I promised her everything would be all right, and it wasn't. I will never promise that again. I don't know where to go. I should find someone to let me see Sabrina. I should be with her. I just can't right now. I see her family walking down the hallway, and I can't handle it, so I duck in the stairwell and head up the stairs to the roof.

before hunter

quinn

"HEY, I ORDERED ALREADY. I was starving," Sabrina says as I take a seat in the booth across from her.

I laugh. "It's okay. You're pregnant, and I'm running late."

"When are you going to trade in that bike for a car?"

I laugh again. "When I actually have money to afford it."

"Can I get you anything to eat?" the waitress asks me.

"No, I'm good."

Sabrina frowns at me. "You should eat something."

I shake my head and lie. "I've already eaten. I'm good." I don't want Sabrina to feel sorry for me. I don't want her to know how lucky she is. That she got lucky when her family adopted her. She has all the money and love a kid could ever want. While when I got adopted, I got the worst end of the deal. I got no money and no love.

Sabrina doesn't know about my personal life. We live in different parts of town and go to different schools. The fact we even met was pure luck. I was applying for a job at an ice-cream shop, and she was in getting ice cream. We met and hit it off. She's become my best friend over the past six months. Even though I know I'm not hers. She has plenty of friends, and she has a boyfriend while I have no one but her.

She has a family and adopted sisters and friends while I struggle to eat. I get bullied at school and suffered through losing the only foster parent who ever cared for me. I have nothing, and she has everything.

"I have something I need to tell you," I say with a smile.

"I have something I need to tell you too," she says with a frown.

"You first because whatever your news is sounds bad, and I have good news that will hopefully cheer you up."

"I don't think anything can cheer me up."

I can't wait until after I hear her news. "We're sisters. I talked to my case worker and got my file, and we're biological sisters. How cool is that?"

Sabrina smiles a little and then says, "I'm dying."

"What? That can't be possible. You're healthy; just look at you."

She shakes her head. "No, I'm not healthy." She coughs. "I've never been healthy."

I narrow my eyes, trying to understand.

"I have cystic fibrosis, and it has gotten a lot worse as of late. I am coughing all the time. I have a hard time breathing. I need a lung transplant. I've known that eventually I would need one but I didn't think I would need one sooner rather then later. But I can't get one while I'm pregnant. I'm dying. The doctors haven't told me that yet, but I am. I just want to make it until this baby is healthy enough to be born. But I don't think I'll make it through the birth."

I get up and sit next to her in the booth, leaning my head against her chest as she holds me like I'm the one who needs comfort instead of her. "Don't say that. You are a fighter. You will make it through this."

"I'm not giving up, but I just have this feeling, you know."

I nod. "I can't lose you, sister."

She smiles. "You won't; I'll always be here."

"You weren't surprised to learn I was your sister. You didn't seem shocked at all when I told you."

I sit up and look at her. "It's because I already knew. I was just trying to decide if it was best for you to know we were sisters or not. At least until after."

"I think I always knew too. We just connected." I hold her close to me again. "I can't lose you now that I found you. Your son or daughter is going to need you."

Sabrina looks at me, and I can see the seriousness in her eyes. "I need you to promise me something."

"Anything."

"I need you to promise me you'll take care of my daughter if anything happens to me."

I cock my head to one side. "Of course, I will. But your baby will be so loved by the father, by your family. By everyone. I'll just be one of many who will love her."

She smiles with tears in her eyes. "I know. But I need you to be the strong one. Because if I'm gone, I don't think any of them are strong enough to survive, to function. They are going to need your help. And I want you to be the one to raise her, no one else. Promise me."

"Of course, if that's what you really want. I'll raise her."

"Thank you," she says through tears.

"Wait ... you said daughter. Do you know it's a girl?"

She smiles and wipes her eyes. "No. I just have a feeling."

I frown. "Well, you're wrong. It's probably a boy, and you aren't dying. You are going to be fine."

Sabrina holds me close, and I hold her too. She's my sister. I just found her, and I can't lose her. The world isn't that bad. We're good people. She'll live. She has to.

My phone rings, and I don't know how, but I already know. I've been in pain all night, and I know it has to do with Sabrina. We are sisters. I guess that is what happens when we are so connected.

"Hello?" I answer the phone.

"Is this Quinn Ashby?"

"Yes."

"This is Camille, Sabrina's stepsister. I'm so sorry to call you this late, but I know Sabrina wanted me to call you if anything happened. She passed away tonight."

Pain. Instant pain unlike anything I've ever felt before.

"How is her baby doing?"

There is a pause on the other end of the line. "She didn't make it."

I hang up the phone. There is nothing else to hear, and then I cry. But crying does nothing to numb the pain. I try smoking, but it does nothing for me either. I don't have any alcohol, or I would try that. I go to my bathroom and turn on the water, filling the tiny bathtub. It won't do much to relax me, but I have to try something because I can't deal with this pain.

When the bath fills, I climb in, but as I suspected, it does nothing to fix the pain. I cry, trying to get the pain to stop through my tears. It doesn't work. I hit something and watch my razor blade fall into the water. I hold the blade in my hand and know that it is the only thing that could take away the pain.

"How am I supposed to fulfill my promise if she died too?"

I take the razor blade in my hand, and then I make the pain go away.

5 years after the worst night

hunter

CAMILLE IS CRYING when she finishes telling me the truth about Sabrina. I hold her. "You were just doing what your best friend asked you to do. I don't blame you for anything."

"I'm just so sorry. So sorry I lied to you all these years."

I hold her closer. "I'm sorry too."

"Why are you sorry?"

"For lying to you too. For lying to myself."

Camille narrows her eyes. "What do you mean?"

I let the memories overwhelm me. "I knew, everything. I made a promise to Sabrina before she died that I would live my dream. I would move on and give up our baby if she survived. I would become the best NFL player in the world. I would live even though she died. I pushed that out of my head, though. I pretend that our baby had died along with Sabrina. I let you guys convince me of that. I know that is what Sabrina wanted. She thought it was what was best for me, for our baby. To separate us. To pretend she wasn't even born."

I feel a tear slip out of my eye. "I just wish I had been there for our daughter all this time. That's what I wanted more than playing in the NFL."

Camille shakes her head. "You wouldn't have been able to take care of her back then. You were a complete wreck after losing Sabrina. It took you a year to even be able to function again."

I nod. "I still hate that I lied to myself. That I wasn't there for her."

She sits up, and I let her go. "You should go to her."

"Who?"

She laughs. "Quinn. She's the girl for you, Hunter. She always has been."

"She's married."

"So?"

"She hates me after not going to see her when she texted me."

"So?"

"It's not fair to Ava."

Camille grabs the side of my head and squeezes it. "Hunter, go see Quinn and Ava. Go talk to them. Figure things out."

"What about you?"

She smiles. "I'm happy as long as you are happy. I love you, but I'm not sure I've ever been in love with you. I'll be fine. You need to go talk to her." She hands me my cell phone. "Text her."

My fingers nervously fumble with my phone. But I finally text her.

Me: I need you, Quinn. I know after I didn't show up that I don't deserve anything from you. That's why I'm flying to you. I'll be there later tonight, and I'm not going to stop until I see you.

I wait nervously for a response. She responds with her address which makes me smile. *Maybe I have a chance to make her mine?*

I knock on the door of the house address that Quinn texted me. It's a nice house. Actually, it's the perfect house for Quinn. It is in the heart of Boulder and has a lot of charm and character but still seems updated from what I can tell.

I can't believe she lives here. It's definitely an upgrade from where she was living before. I frown; Callum must make a lot of money.

Quinn opens the door, and my heart is pounding out of my chest.

"You look beautiful," I say unable to help myself. She does. She looks healthy, happy. She's wearing jeans and a fitted shirt. Her hair is curled just a little bit, and she's wearing makeup. She almost never used to wear makeup.

"Thanks," she says, but her eyes aren't happy like the rest of her body; they are sad.

She holds the door open. "Come in."

The inside of her house is just as beautiful as the outside. "I love your house."

"Thank you," she says again. She leads me into the living room and takes a seat. "Can I get you anything to drink?"

"No."

I take a seat on the couch opposite her. I hate being this far away from her.

"Why are you here?"

"I—"

"I mean you have no right to be here. You stood me up. You broke your promise of always being there for me when I needed you. What right do you have to show up here now? I shouldn't have to be here for you when you need it, if you aren't going to do that for me."

"Because I thought I was protecting us, and if I stayed away, everything would be okay."

She has tears in her eyes, and I can't help it. I go over and sit by her, rubbing her leg and trying to comfort her. "We don't believe that everything will be okay, though."

"You're right. It was stupid of me to think that."

She nods.

"I just found out the truth about everything. A truth that others hid from me, but to be fair, I think I also hid from myself."

Quinn holds her breath.

"That Ava is—" God, why is it so hard for me to say.

"She's your daughter," Quinn finishes for me.

I nod. "Ava is mine and Sabrina's."

"Sabrina was my sister. I was in so much pain that I tried to kill myself because of her," Quinn says.

"I know."

We are both silent for a minute.

"Sabrina made everyone promise that if she died but Ava survived, that they would pretend that Ava died too. I knew the truth, but I still lied to myself. It was selfish, but it was also what Sabrina wanted."

Quinn nods.

"I thought Sabrina didn't want me to know about Ava because she wanted me to live the life I always thought I wanted before she got pregnant. Go to college. Then the NFL. Greatness—that's what I always wanted.

"So she had everyone hide the fact that Ava survived from me so that I could live the life that Sabrina wanted for me. To make everything easier for me."

I take a deep breath as tears stream down both of our faces.

"That's what Camille told me when I first realized Ava was my daughter. But it isn't the truth. That's not why Sabrina had everyone try to hide her from me. Ava's sick too."

Quinn nods, her whole face covered in tears, and snot, and pain. Because there is nothing pretty about pain.

"When Ava was in the hospital it wasn't because her foster parents neglected her, it was because she was sick. She's not doing well although the doctors think they can give her a few more years. She's dying. It could be this year, or when she's a teenager, or she could live until her fifties or beyond. They don't know, but right now, she's not doing very well," Quinn says.

"I'm glad you adopted her, Quinn. That's what Sabrina always wanted. She always knew you were the strong one. I was weak. She thought dealing with the fact that Ava might eventually die too would be too much for me. That I wouldn't be able to handle it. That I wouldn't be able to survive getting to know her and then having to watch her die. She knew it would be too hard for me."

Quinn strokes my face. "It's a lot for anyone to handle. It is too much."

I nod.

"Sabrina was wrong, though. Because as much as it is too much for me to handle, I want to be in Ava's life. Even if it is going to cause me unimaginable pain, I want to be her father. I love her. And I love you too, Quinn. I want to be in both of your lives in any way that I can.

"I don't care that you and Callum are married.

"I don't care that you don't need saving.

"It doesn't matter that life isn't fair.

"It doesn't matter if life gets too hard.

"It doesn't matter that nothing is ever going to be okay.

"I want both of you in my life. And I'm not going anywhere. No matter the pain."

quinn

HUNTER GAVE THE most perfect beautiful speech I have ever heard. When he said he was coming here, I thought I would never be able to forgive him for what he did to me. But now that he is here and crying and clearly cares about Ava as much as I do, forgiveness seems to come easy.

Hunter is looking at me with such sadness and pain that all I want to do is take it all away.

So I do the only thing I can do. I kiss him.

His eyes widen.

"What was that for?"

"Because I love you too."

He kisses me again.

"And Callum left me. When he found out about Ava, it was too much for him."

"Oh Quinn, I'm sorry."

I laugh. "Are you really?"

"No. I'm glad he couldn't handle you and Ava; that means I still have a chance."

"I know life is hard, has been hard, and is going to get harder. I know that. I don't want to get married. I don't want the fairy tale. I just want you and Ava for as long as I can have both of you. I want to fight."

Hunter pulls me onto his lap as he kisses me long and hard. His lips devouring mine. His body wrapping around me telling me I'm his. Forever, or as long as forever lasts.

"I want to give you the fairy tale, but I can't promise you that. I won't promise you that because we both know that fairy tales don't exist. At least, not for us. I will just promise to love you and be by your side to fight as long as we can."

"You promise?"

"I promise. I'm not going anywhere. And you aren't going to need to send a text message anymore when you need me. I'll just always be here."

"Mommy, Hunter?" Ava says from the base of the stairs.

I get up and wipe the tears off my face before I go over and pick Ava up and bring her over to the couch where I was sitting next to Hunter.

"Hunter, I missed you," she says, hugging him.

"How you feeling, squirt?" Hunter asks.

"Better now," she says with a smile. "How long are you staying?"

"Forever," Hunter says.

"Really?" She looks from Hunter to me.

"Really," Hunter and I both answer.

"But what about the Cowboys?"

"I'm going to take a break from the Cowboys for a while."

"What will you do for work?" Ava asks.

"Well ..." He looks at me. "I think your mother has been working hard enough that I won't have to work for a little while. I'll live here with both of you if you'll have me."

"Yes," I mouth.

"Yes, yes!" Ava says hugging him again. "You should try to play for the Broncos. They could use a tight end."

"Maybe I'll do that."

"Good. I think you would be great at that, Hunter."

Hunter looks at me, and I nod already knowing what he wants to ask her.

"Ava, I love you and your mom very much. And I have a question to ask you. Is it okay if I'm your father?"

Ava smiles. "You were always my father. I just don't always call you dad because I know it makes you uncomfortable."

Hunter and I both laugh and squeeze Ava tight, and then we start our lives together as a family, for forever.

EPILOGUE

5 years later

quinn

"ARE YOU READY to be my maid of honor?" I ask Ava.

"Yep."

I fuss with her long curly blond hair that she got from Hunter. She swats me away because it's not cool for her mother to be fussing with her hair when she's ten years old. I kiss her cheek and look into her green eyes that she got from Sabrina.

Life is so unfair. It should have been Sabrina and Hunter walking down the aisle today, not me and Hunter. But I'm thankful every day to Sabrina for giving me them. And I hope she is thankful for me for taking care of them when she couldn't.

Music starts playing. I hold out my arm to her. "All right, let's go." She holds my arm, and we walk out of the hotel and onto the beach where Hunter is standing with a preacher along with Mandy and Marshall.

When we get to the where they are standing next to the water, Ava fist bumps Hunter and then stands beside Mandy while I face Hunter.

"I can't believe I am marrying you. You're so beautiful," he says, kissing me on the cheek.

"Thank you, handsome." I can't believe we are getting married either. Neither of us wanted to get married. Hunter didn't think he could after losing Sabrina, and I didn't want to after what happened with Callum. But Ava insisted we get married. She wants to know that we will be together forever. So here we are on the most beautiful beach in Hawaii getting married.

"Quinn, do you to take this man to be your husband for as long as you both shall live?"

"I do," I say, feeling the tears in my eyes. Neither of us knows when our forever is going to end. Ava is doing well right now, but every year or so, she has a bad flare-up and ends up in the hospital. Each time, the doctors say there isn't much they can do and that we should say our goodbyes, but each time, she fights, and she lives.

"Hunter, do you take this woman to be your wife for as long as you both shall live?"

"I do, forever."

Hunter kisses me and then pulls Ava between us, hugging both of us. And then he leans down and whispers into Ava's ear, "I promise to be your father forever, too."

None of us knows how long forever will last. It could be a few more months, a few more weeks, or years from now. Things may never be okay again, but that's okay because we are together now. We love each other now. And our forever will last as long as it lasts. Because forever isn't really forever. But our love is.

free books

Thank you so much for reading! Would you like to receive my free ebooks, receive notifications of sales and new releases, and have a chance to enter my giveaways? Then sign up to my newsletter at the address below:

EllaMiles.com/freebooks

more books by ella

If you enjoyed *Too Much* you should read my *Aligned* series. *Aligned* is a 5-part steamy romance with a bit of suspense.

Looking for a darker read? Try out my *Maybe* and *Definitely* series.

about ella

Ella Miles writes sexy romance with a twist. She's currently living her own happily ever after near the Rocky Mountains with her high school sweetheart husband. Her heart is also taken by her goofy three year old black lab that is scared of everything, including her own shadow.

Ella is the author of the ALIGNED series, MAYBE series, and DEFINITELY series. Get a free book by visiting her website: EllaMiles.com/freebooks.

Stalk me at:

Twitter.com/authorellamiles

Facebook.com/authorellamiles

Instagram.com/authorellamiles

acknowledgements

Too Much is my first standalone. I loved writing this book and hated writing it at the same time. This book took me the longest to write, caused me the most tears, and made me want to rip the whole thing to shreds and just start another book on many occasions. I wrote this book in the middle of the holiday season, while moving. Both would have made any book difficult to write. But this book was especially tough because although I knew exactly what the story was I couldn't determine how to write it. I started the story in so many different places and eventually came up with the idea to write it backwards after I had worked on the book for a couple months and had most of it written. I was already behind schedule at that point since I can usually write a book in a month, but I felt that this book had to be told this way. I hope you agree!

I know not all of you will enjoy the backwardness of this book, but don't worry, I promise most of my books will be written from start to finish. ;)

As for thank yous...

I must thank my editor, Jenny, who went above and beyond on flexibility with her schedule to ensure this book got edited in time to make my release. Thank you Jenny for finding room in your schedule more than two months after I was originally supposed to get it to you. You are amazing!

Thank you Cara, my awesome cover designer, for giving me an amazing artistic cover.

Thank you to my hubby, for not only reading and helping to fix the plot issues with the book, but for listening to me gripe and complain about this book like I haven't ever done with any of my other books before. You kept me sane even when I didn't think it was possible.

Thank you to my street team. You are all so amazing and encouraging no matter what crazy stories I decide to write. Thank you for taking the time to ready my books and review them. I'm so lucky to have found such an amazing group of ladies supporting me in my writing.

And last but not least, I must thank you, my reader! I am so amazed at all the support I have received since I started writing books in late 2015. You are all so amazing! I must thank you for buying and reading my books, for your kind emails, and your support on social media. It's taken a little over a year, but for the first time in my writing career I am actually profitable and will be able to pay myself a livable salary from my writing! And it's all because of you. THANK YOU!